The parlour door opened yet again.

Sarah watched a tall, broad-shouldered man enter the room. He came purposefully, yet gracefully, towards her, and she found herself staring up at a far-from-handsome and unsmiling countenance.

'I understand from the lady of the house that you have been gracious enough to permit me to share your private parlour, ma'am,' he remarked in the most attractive deep masculine voice she had ever heard. 'My name is Ravenhurst.'

Her lovely smile of greeting fading, Sarah sat rigid on the wooden settle, as though turned to stone. Ravenhurst. . .? It couldn't be!

Anne Ashley was born and educated in Leicester. She lived for a time in Scotland, but now lives in the West Country with two cats, her two sons and a husband who has a wonderful and very necessary sense of humour. When not pounding away at the keys of her typewriter, she likes to relax in her garden, which she has opened to the public on more than one occasion in aid of the village church funds.

Recent titles by the same author:

LADY LINFORD'S RETURN
THE EARL OF RAYNE'S WARD

THE NEGLECTFUL
GUARDIAN

Anne Ashley

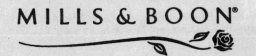

First published in Great Britain 1997
Harlequin Mills & Boon Limited,
Eton House, 18-24 Paradise Road, Richmond, Surrey TW9 1SR

© Anne Ashley 1997

ISBN 0 263 80497 6

Set in Times 10 on 12 pt. by
Rowland Phototypesetting Limited
Bury St Edmunds, Suffolk

04-9712-75009

Printed and bound in Great Britain by
Caledonian International Book Manufacturing Ltd, Glasgow

Chapter One

The perfectly matched greys, admired by many of those august members of Society known as Corinthians, turned under one of the finest examples of an Elizabethan archway to be found anywhere in the County of Wiltshire, and came to a halt in the stableyard.

Marcus Ravenhurst, the much envied owner of the coveted pair, waited only until his trusted head groom had jumped down from the smart racing curricle, and had taken a hold of the spirited pair's heads, before alighting himself with the agility of a healthy, finely tuned athlete.

As Marcus stalked towards the house, the cold February wind caught at his many-caped driving-cloak, sending it billowing about his tall, powerful frame, and dead leaves swirled about the path in front of him before adding to the ever-increasing decaying piles dotted about the grounds.

His dark brows drawing together in one of his famed, heavy scowls, he cast the tall trees shrouding the fine building in a depressingly gloomy blanket a look of staunch disapproval before entering the relative protection of the stone porch.

Reaching out one gloved hand, he raised the highly polished brass door-knocker, and administered several short, sharp raps. It was a minute or two before his summons was answered, and the solid oak door was opened by an ageing, grey-haired retainer.

'Why, Master Marcus!' he exclaimed with genuine warmth, and a familiarity granted to loyal servants of longstanding. He moved to one side, allowing the unexpected visitor to pass into the hall.

'Her ladyship never said she was expecting you, sir.'

'She isn't, Clegg. I'm on my way to Somerset, and on the spur of the moment took it into my head to pay a call. The visit is a very brief one. I shall be staying only one night.'

After placing his curly-brimmed beaver hat and his gloves on the hall table, Marcus removed his cloak to reveal a blue superfine coat of impeccable cut, a snowy-white neckcloth and a pair of tight-fitting buff-coloured pantaloons, which encased his muscular legs without so much as a single crease. His plain double-breasted waistcoat was free from fobs and seals; the only embellishment he ever wore, in fact, was a plain gold signet ring, which emphasised his strong, shapely hands.

As always the elderly retainer was impressed by the sober, yet elegant, attire, and thought there couldn't possibly be a dozen gentlemen in the length and breadth of the land who could carry their clothes so well as his mistress's eldest grandson.

'Her ladyship is in her private sitting-room, sir,' he informed him, relieving him of the cloak and placing it almost reverently over his arm. 'I'll go up and inform her you're here.'

'Save yourself the trouble, Clegg. I'll announce

myself.' Marcus's harsh-featured face was transformed by a rare smile. 'Having no desire whatsoever to see a member of my own sex put out of countenance, I shall spare you the embarrassment of having to stand by while she rings a peal over my head for not having taken the trouble to visit her for some months.'

'As you wish, sir,' the butler responded gravely, but with a betraying twitch to his lips. 'I'll arrange a bed-chamber made ready for you.'

'Thank you, Clegg. And see to it my groom has everything he needs.'

At the head of the stairs Marcus turned to his right, and went along the narrow passageway leading to his grandmother's private apartments. After a perfunctory knock, he entered the room to find the Dowager Countess seated in a chair by the fire, a rug over her legs and a book lying open on her lap.

'Was that a caller I heard, Clegg?' she enquired without bothering to turn her head to see who had entered.

'I cannot tell you how relieved I am to discover there's still naught amiss with your hearing, Grandmama.'

'Ha! Ravenhurst!' She frowned dourly up at her favourite grandchild as he came striding in his usual purposeful way towards her. 'Haven't set eyes on you in a twelvemonth. Was beginning to think you were dead!' she remarked with morbid humour.

'Three months, to be exact, ma'am.' There was a suspicion of a devilish glint in his dark eyes as he placed a chaste salute on one pink cheek. 'And, as you are no doubt overjoyed to discover, I'm still sound in wind and limb.'

A wicked cackle answered this. 'Nothing wrong with your limbs, Ravenhurst. You're the finest specimen of manhood in this family by a long chalk. You've no looks to speak of,' she went on with brutal frankness, thereby eroding her former compliment somewhat, 'but, then, not all women are beguiled by a handsome face.'

He positioned himself before the fire, warming his coat tails, and looked down at her with lazy affection. Apart from the fact that she walked with the aid of an ebony stick, and that the hair beneath the fetching lace cap was completely white, there was little to betray that she had five-and-seventy years in her dish.

Her skin retained a satiny smoothness, her grey eyes were still brightly alert, and she had, much to her eldest son's discomfiture, and his wife's acute embarrassment, a mind as sharp as a meat cleaver and a tongue as corrosive as acid. Many had quailed beneath her blunt manner and astringent comments, but not so Ravenhurst. His grandmother numbered amongst that small handful of people he admired.

'I have never aspired to be an Adonis, ma'am.'

'Just as well,' was the forthright rejoinder. 'But, then, when a man's as rich as Golden Ball, looks are a minor consideration to any discerning female of marriageable age.'

'Not quite that rich,' he countered.

'Don't try to pull the wool over my eyes! You're one of the richest men in the land.' She scowled up at him for several moments before enquiring irascibly, 'And how much longer do you intend standing there, warming the seat of those tight-fitting breeches of yours at my fire, boy? Go get yourself a glass of Madeira! It's from Henry's cellar. The only evidence of intelligence I've ever found in my eldest son is in his ability to pick a wine. And you can pour me one whilst you're about it.'

One dark brow rising sharply, he obediently went

across to the table on which the decanters stood. 'I understood Dr Pringle to say, the last time I was here, that you were to drink only one small glass of wine with your evening meal.'

'A pox on all physicians!' the Dowager responded crudely. 'What does that fool know! And if you think I'm mutilating my insides by drinking a dish of tea at this time of the day, you're far-and-away out.'

Knowing from long experience that to remonstrate further would be futile, Marcus dutifully filled two glasses, handing one to his irascible grandparent before seating himself in the chair placed on the opposite side of the hearth. After sampling the excellent Madeira and settling himself more comfortably in the chair, he enquired politely whether the Earl of Styne was in residence.

'No,' the Dowager responded, not without satisfaction. 'He's taken that whey-faced wife of his to Kent to visit her mother. Don't expect them back for a sennight or, with any luck, two. Why, did you wish to see him?'

'I cannot recall ever having evinced a desire to see my estimable Uncle Henry,' he returned blandly, much to his grandmother's intense amusement. 'But I really think he ought to do something about the trees surrounding this place. They make the interior dratted gloomy, ma'am. And the grounds are a disgrace. Nothing short of an eyesore!'

'I'll thank you not to interfere, Marcus!' she snapped. 'Not one of those trees is being felled whilst I reside in the Dower House. They grant me privacy from all those prying eyes up at the mansion. And Wilkins will soon have the garden in order once he's recovered from his rheumatism.'

As the ancestral home of the Earl of Styne was situated in the centre of the vast park, a quarter of a mile or more away from the Dower House, someone wishing to spy on the Dowager Countess from there would need to possess quite miraculous eyesight. Yet, here again he knew that to argue further would be a complete waste of breath, and so changed the subject by enquiring politely, if with precious little interest, into the health of the other members of the family.

As the Dowager Countess of Styne had seen fit to bless the late Earl with six pledges of her affection, it was some little time before she had finished casting aspersions on her five remaining children and their numerous offspring.

'Agnes was my first chick, and my favourite, Ravenhurst. I've never made any secret of that. Your mother was the best out of the lot of 'em by far.'

'Perhaps I'm prejudiced, but I certainly thought so, too,' he responded, a rare note of tenderness creeping into his voice.

'Never thought I'd outlive any of mine.' She shook her head sadly. 'And it had to be my little Agnes taken from me. I don't think she ever truly recovered from your father's death, Marcus. They were a rare couple, your parents. A real love match.'

He did not respond to this, and after a few moments of dwelling on the deep sadness of loss, which for her had not lessened in six years, she gave herself a mental shake, and looked frowningly back at her favourite child's sole offspring to enquire what had prompted him to pay this unexpected call.

'I'd never hear the end of it if you discovered I'd almost passed your door and didn't pay a visit. I'm on my way to Somerset.'

'Oh?' She cast him an enquiring glance. 'Are you calling on that ward of yours in Bath, by any chance? Strangely, I was only thinking about her the other day. Agnes and her mother were great friends.'

The shapely hand raising the glass to his lips checked for a moment. 'No. I hadn't intended doing so.'

The slight inflection in his deeply resonant voice was not lost on her, and she stared at him for several thoughtful moments before asking, rather censoriously,

'Do you never visit that child, Ravenhurst?'

Placing his glass down on the table conveniently situated by the side of his chair, he rose abruptly to his feet, and took up his former stance before the fire. 'She has been well cared for,' he said in a tone bordering on the brusque. 'I placed her in that seminary in Bath, and then settled Cousin Harriet in Mama's old house in Upper Camden Place to look after the chit. I make her a quarterly allowance. She has everything she needs—my secretary sees to all that.'

The reproachful look remained in his grandmother's eyes, and he found his ready temper coming to the fore. 'Confound it, madam! What more could I have done? I know nothing of schoolgirls.'

'Schoolgirl?' she echoed blankly. 'Where have your wits gone begging, Marcus? Sarah Pennington may have been a schoolgirl, once, but her mother was knocked down by that runaway carriage not four months after your dear mama was taken from us. She must be nineteen, now, at least.'

'Well? And what of it?'

She stared up at him in exasperation. 'She was Agnes's godchild, Marcus. I don't think it would be expecting too much of you to pay some attention to your ward's future well-being. Why not fund a London Season for the girl? Bath is all very well, and I know dear Agnes preferred it to London, but Sarah is far more likely to find a suitable husband if she goes to the capital. And if she favours her mother, I expect she's a very pretty girl. Was she well provided for?'

'She's no heiress, if that's what you mean, but her portion isn't contemptible.'

'There you are, then! I shall speak to your aunt Henrietta when she returns from Kent. She's bringing your cousin Sophia out in the spring, so it wouldn't hurt her to chaperon Sarah as well. Or, I might even do so myself.'

'No need to put yourself out, ma'am,' was his almost indifferent response. 'If I do decide to fund a Season for Sarah Pennington, and I have decided nothing yet, then Harriet can chaperon her. That's what I pay her for.'

'Pshaw! That pea-goose!' the Dowager scoffed. 'If you're not careful, Ravenhurst, you'll have that woman your pensioner for life. She came perilously close to ruining that husband of hers with her gambling, you know.' She looked thoughtfully beyond him to stare down into the fire. 'I suppose, though, at the time you had little choice but to enlist your cousin's aid. I wish I had done more, but it was so soon after Agnes's death. I would have been poor company for the child.'

A tender look erased the annoyance from his eyes. 'Believe me, ma'am, there's no need to suffer pangs of conscience. Sarah is well enough. I've received ample very long and exceedingly boring letters over the years from Cousin Harriet to leave me in little doubt of that. And as far as a Season is concerned. . .?' He paused for a moment, looking thoughtful. 'Of course, I'm not against the idea, but a lot depends on circumstances.'

'Oh?' The Dowager looked questioningly at him again. 'What circumstances?'

'There is every possibility, as you'll no doubt be pleased to hear, that I might be getting myself leg-shackled in the not too distant future,' he confided somewhat crudely.

'And high time you were setting up your nursery, Ravenhurst!' Only a sudden glint in her grey eyes betrayed her delight at the news. 'And who is the lucky gel? Do I know her?'

'You may do. It's Bamford's eldest daughter. She was engaged to be married to my friend Charles Templeton. You may recall he died several years ago in a riding accident, not many weeks before the wedding was due to take place. Broke his neck.'

'Yes, I do remember that. But I cannot say I recall the girl. Is she pretty?'

'Pretty?' he echoed, frowning at an imaginary spot on the far wall, as though having difficulty in bringing a clear image to mind. 'No, I wouldn't call her so. She's handsome enough, and has a deal of self-assurance and reserve. Some think her aloof, but I don't consider that a fault.

'She's six-and-twenty. Not in the first flush of youth, you understand, but then a chit out of the schoolroom who expected me to dance attendance on her all the time wouldn't suit me. We've been acquainted long enough to be sure we'd deal comfortably together. Yes,' he went on as though trying to convince himself, 'Celia Bamford will make an ideal wife. She knows what is expected of her. Once she's provided me with a son or two, there's no reason why we should see very much of each other.'

He sounded so coldly dispassionate that it seemed almost as if he had chosen his future bride with the same impassive discernment as he would have used when selecting a brood mare. The Dowager stared up at her favourite grandchild in silent dismay, her delight, now, ashes at her feet.

'But do you love her, Marcus?' she enquired with unwonted gentleness.

'Love?' His thin-lipped mouth twisted into a cynical smile. 'I don't look for that overblown emotion. I have learned over the years, ma'am, that most members of your sex become extremely loving especially when I am about to loosen the strings of my purse...no, mutual respect will suffice.'

Unlike the Dowager, who passed a very troubled night, Marcus was up early the following morning and, after writing a brief note of farewell to his grandmother, set off on his journey to Somerset.

The wind had dropped considerably during the past twelve hours, and the day was bright, though very cold. Like their owner, the powerful greys were strong and healthy, and they reached the turn off to Trowbridge in good time. Ravenhurst, however, did not take this turning, much to his groom's intense surprise, but continued along the road to Bath.

It was most unlike his master to take a wrong road; those sharp, dark eyes, ever alert, seemed never to miss a thing. The groom debated for a moment, knowing that their eventual destination was a few miles east of Wells, then said,

'Did you not notice the signpost back along, sir? Trowbridge were off to the left.'

'Yes, I saw it, Sutton, but I've decided to make a slight detour,' was the only explanation forthcoming, but the groom, quite accustomed to his master's abrupt manner, was satisfied with that.

Mr Ravenhurst was renowned in polite circles for his sharp tongue and blunt language: traits undoubtedly inherited from the Dowager Countess. But those who knew him well knew him to be a just and honourable man: the sort of solid, dependable individual whom one naturally turned to in a crisis.

All his servants were devoted to him, and with good reason. Since his father's death he had proved himself to be a considerate and caring master who, in return for diligence and loyalty, paid every attention to his employees' well-being. So, naturally, it had irked him immeasurably when the Dowager had been censorious over what she saw as neglect of duty, but later he had had to own, if only to himself, that there had been some justification for the criticism.

He had just turned six-and-twenty when he had found himself in the unenviable position of guardian to a young girl still in the schoolroom. In the swift and decisive manner that characterised him, he had dealt with the situation promptly. Enlisting the aid of a recently widowed distant cousin, Harriet Fairchild, he had installed her in his late mother's Bath residence in order to take care of the orphaned Sarah Pennington, and then had conveniently forgotten the child's very existence, except on those rare occasions when he had taken the trouble to cast his eyes over one of his cousin's exceedingly boring letters.

With very few exceptions he held the entire female species in contempt. He was never vulgar, nor would it ever enter his head deliberately to embarrass any member of the fair sex, but he was a plain-spoken man with little patience for false gallantry.

His astringent comments and heavy scowls had sent many a hopeful young debutante scurrying back to the protection of her fond mama's side. He was impatient of vapours and megrims, and feminine tears rarely moved him. So what good would he have been in the rearing of a young girl?

None whatsoever, he told himself. It had been in Sarah Pennington's best possible interests for him to have kept his distance and not to have interfered. His heavy frown descended. But he could, he knew, at least have taken the trouble to write to the child from time to time, and it would not have hurt him at all to have visited her once in a while.

His conscience smote him. It was a rare experience, and one, furthermore, which he did not care for in the least. Consequently, by the time he had drawn his greys to a halt before a certain house in Upper Camden Place, he was not in the best of humours.

After giving orders to his groom to walk the greys until his return, he mounted the stone steps and rapped sharply on the front door. The young servant girl who answered the summons took one look at the forbidding countenance glowering down at her, and stuttered nervously that her mistress was not receiving any more callers that day.

'Oh, is she not?' he ground out, his tone as alarming as his expression, as he stepped, uninvited, into the hall. 'Well, she shall most certainly receive me. You may tell her Ravenhurst is here.'

After closing the door, the girl disappeared into a room on the right. Marcus, impatiently tapping one highly polished boot on the floor, heard a low murmur of voices before a high-pitched shriek rent the air.

Waiting no longer, he stalked into the room that the young maid had entered to discover his cousin, prostrate, on the *chaise-longue*, the young maid wafting burnt feathers under her mistress's nose and a middle-aged woman, dressed in a very becoming dark blue walking dress and matching fur-trimmed pelisse, kneeling on the floor beside the couch, murmuring soothingly to his highly distraught cousin, who had taken one glance at him and then had promptly dissolved into tears.

'Good heavens, Harriet! What the deuce ails you?'

'You. . .? Here. . .? Today of all days!' came the muffled response from behind the lacy edging of a fine lawn handkerchief. 'Gone, Ravenhurst. Eloped! Oh, the wicked, ungrateful child! How could she do this to me? And after all I have done for her, too!'

'I have already told you, ma'am, that Sarah has not eloped.' The assurance came from the lady kneeling on the floor. She then cast her intelligent grey eyes up at the tall stranger and, easily recognising the signs of a gentleman containing his temper with an effort, hurriedly rose to her feet.

'Sir, you must be Sarah's guardian. May I introduce myself? My name is Emily Stanton.' She held out her hand and found it taken for a moment in a warm, firm clasp. 'Perhaps it might be best if we repair to another room.'

Casting a final impatient glance at his, still, hysterically sobbing cousin, Marcus followed the lady across the hall and into a small parlour overlooking the street.

'Do I understand correctly from my sorely afflicted

relative's somewhat garbled utterance that my ward has eloped?'

Mrs Stanton looked at him consideringly. 'Would it disturb you if she had, sir?'

'Most assuredly it would! She was my mother's god-child. I would be failing in my duties if I permitted her to fall into the hands of some fortune-hunter.'

'Fortune?' she echoed, failing completely to conceal her astonishment. 'Are you seriously trying to tell me that Sarah is a young woman of some means?'

His dark brows rose sharply, betraying the fact that he found the question an impertinence. 'You seem surprised, ma'am? Why should you doubt it?'

'Why, indeed!' she muttered.

He could easily discern the frown of puzzlement before asking her politely to sit down. 'Perhaps you would be good enough to tell me what has been going on here this day? And, if you are able, enlighten me as to the whereabouts of my ward?'

'Be assured, Mr Ravenhurst, that it is not Sarah who has eloped, but my own daughter.'

Again his brows rose, but in surprise this time. 'You will forgive me for saying so, ma'am, but you do not appear unduly concerned.'

She smiled faintly at the dry tone. 'No, sir. I am not,' she frankly admitted. 'My daughter Clarissa and Captain James Fenshaw have known each other since childhood. His family owns the property adjacent to our own in Devonshire. We enjoyed extremely cordial relations with our neighbours until my husband and Mr Fenshaw quarrelled over an unimportant strip of land.

'Since that unfortunate episode, my husband has strictly forbidden Clarissa to have any further contact with James, even going so far as to stop the poor child writing to him.' She paused for a moment, absently twisting the strings of her reticule round her fingers. 'Several weeks ago James returned home from the Peninsular, injured. As soon as he had recovered sufficiently, he travelled with his mother to Bath to benefit from the health-giving waters, you understand.'

He saw the betraying twitch of her lips.

'But I was not fooled for a moment. He struck up an immediate friendship with your ward, and was a frequent visitor to this house, as was my own daughter.'

'Are you trying to tell me, ma'am, that my ward actively encouraged these clandestine meetings between your daughter and this man?'

Mrs Stanton raised her eyes to stare unblinkingly into angry dark ones. 'Yes, she did. Sarah and my daughter have been close friends since they attended the seminary together. Why, they are more like sisters! Your ward has stayed with us in Devonshire on several occasions. I am extremely fond of her. She's a very intelligent and sweet-natured girl.'

'After her involvement in this affair, it shows a generosity of spirit that you still think so, ma'am.' He cast his eyes briefly in the direction of the clock on the mantelshelf. 'Do you wish me to go after the runaways?'

A slight frown creased her forehead as she rose to her feet and stared up at him, almost assessingly. 'Would you do that if I asked?'

'I am at your service. You have only to say the word,' he assured her, and her frown deepened.

'No, sir. I do not wish to stop this elopement,' she surprised him by responding. Moving over to the window, she stared down at the street to see a groom walking a pair of fine horses harnessed to a curricle.

'You must think me a most unnatural parent, but I hope with all my heart that they are successful and reach the border. It was cruel and unjust of my husband to try to keep them apart. They are well suited, and I know James will take good care of Clarissa. I was, unfortunately, duty-bound to adhere to my husband's wishes. Now, thankfully, all that has changed.

'First, I must pay a call on Mrs Fenshaw, and see what can be done to smooth things over here. Unlike our husbands, we have remained on friendly terms. I know she will be of a similar mind. I must, of course, write to my husband and inform him of what has occurred, and if he is foolish enough to go chasing after the pair... Well, so be it!'

She turned round to look at him again. 'But all this is of precious little interest to you, Mr Ravenhurst. Your concerns are for Sarah, only.'

'You may take a light view of her involvement in this affair, ma'am, but I most certainly do not! I shall have a word or two to say to that young woman when she returns here,' he remarked ominously.

'But, sir!' Her expression betrayed her complete astonishment. 'Sarah won't be returning here. She, too, has left Bath.'

'What!' Disbelief was clearly writ across his face. 'Do you mean to tell me that she is accompanying the star-crossed pair on this bolt to the border?' and much to his intense annoyance Mrs Stanton dissolved into laughter.

'Do forgive me,' she apologised when she was able. 'You do not know your ward at all well. That much is certain. Of course she hasn't gone with them.'

'Then where the devil has she gone, ma'am?' he demanded, not mincing words.

As her husband, too, had something of a peppery temperament, she did not bridle at the strong language, and once again regarded him rather considering. 'Before I answer that, I should like to ask you a question. Why, after six years, have you suddenly taken it into your head to visit your ward?'

She smiled at the lofty glance he cast her. 'Yes, naturally, you find it a gross impertinence, and wonder what on earth it has to do with me. Well, sir, as I've already mentioned, I'm very fond of Sarah, and tell you plainly that I shall not help you to discover her whereabouts if your only reason for doing so is to berate the child for her involvement in my daughter's tiresome affair.'

A noise, something akin to a low growl, emanated from his direction. 'Let me assure you, ma'am, that I came here for the sole purpose of ascertaining whether or not my ward would care for a London Season.'

'I see.' Once again Mrs Stanton subjected him to a long, penetrating stare. 'I think there is much that warrants investigation,' she remarked at length, and somewhat cryptically. 'And I think I shall help you.'

'Do you know where my ward has gone, ma'am? And why, if it were not through fear of the repercussions of her involvement in your daughter's elopement, she found it necessary to leave this house?'

'I believe I understand fully your ward's reasons for leaving this place. With my daughter gone there would be precious little joy for her here if she remained. But I am no tale-bearer. You must discover the truth from Sarah yourself. As to where she has gone. . .? I'm afraid she did not see fit to confide in me. I wish I had been in a position to do more for the child, but. . .'

A deep sigh of regret escaped her. 'Sarah left letters for both your cousin and myself, but in neither did she explain where she intended going. In mine she merely begged forgiveness for her involvement in the elopement. Silly, silly child!' she went on, an unmistakable catch in her voice. 'As though I blamed her!'

She paused for a moment, as though striving to regain her composure. 'I have learned already that two ladies and a gentleman left the city early this morning in a hired post-chaise. One of the ladies was my daughter, and the other, by the description given to me, was undoubtedly Sarah. It's my belief she has asked my daughter to take her as far as the Bristol to London road, from where, I sincerely believe, she intends to travel into Hertfordshire.'

His expression betrayed his incredulity. 'What the dev—deuce does she want to go there for?'

Her smile was a trifle crooked. 'You perhaps do not remember, sir, but before you became Sarah's guardian, she was in the charge of a certain Miss Martha Trent, who was employed, so I have been led to believe, as a sort of companion-governess. They were very close.

'After you dispensed with Miss Trent's services, she found employment in Hertfordshire as governess to two motherless little girls. Subsequently, she married her employer. Mrs Alcott, as she is now, visited Bath last year. I have never seen Sarah so happy! I overheard Mrs Alcott say on numerous occasions during her stay that she wished her former charge would make her home with her. And it is my belief that that is precisely what Sarah has decided to do.'

'Do you know Mr Alcott's precise direction, ma'am?'

'I am sorry to say I do not. But what I can tell you is

that he lives in a village not far from St Albans. He owns a sizeable property, and is a well-known figure in those parts. You should have little difficulty locating him.'

'Thank you for your help, Mrs Stanton. You will forgive me if I leave you now, but the need is pressing. I must not delay in searching for my ward.'

'Please do not give me another thought. I shall remain here with your cousin a while longer.' She arrested his progress to the door by the simple expedient of placing her fingers on his arm, and looked up into a face betraying deep concern. 'For some years I have considered you a most neglectful guardian. I am beginning to think my judgement was at fault. Your ward is a capable young woman, but I shall not rest easy until you've found her.'

'Be assured, ma'am, I will!'

'Having now met you, Mr Ravenhurst, I do not doubt that for a moment. But—but, I beg of you do not return her to this house. If you have nowhere suitable to take her, then bring her to me.'

He refused to commit himself on this, but said, 'Be assured I shall not neglect my duties again. Something has induced my ward to leave this house. Why the devil she didn't write to me if she was so unhappy, I don't know. But I mean to find out!'

Mrs Stanton, watching him collect his hat and gloves from the hall table, felt untold relief knowing that dear Sarah was being sought by such a very capable and obviously very concerned gentleman.

Her relief would have been short-lived, however, had she been standing in a certain inn yard not fifteen minutes later to witness the same gentleman stalking into the hostelry with a face like thunder.

The establishment's owner, a conscientious, hard-working man, had, through his own efforts, turned the hostelry into one of the city's finest. Before his marriage to the late innkeeper's daughter, six years before, he had worked since boyhood on the Ravenhurst estate. He had been devoted to the family, but after his beloved mistress's unexpected demise, he had decided to turn his hand to something new, and had never looked back.

He was manfully struggling with a large barrel of ale when he heard a loud voice raised in the tap. Unruly behaviour in his inn was something that he would not tolerate, and had not infrequently been called upon to evict disorderly customers by rough-and-ready means. Breaking off from his task, he strode purposefully into the tap-room, only to stop dead in his tracks, his belligerent look vanishing instantly.

'Why, Master Marcus, sir!' He came forward to clasp Mr Ravenhurst's hand warmly. 'Haven't set eyes on you since. . .well, not since that sad time. How goes it with you, young sir?'

'Well enough, Jeb. But I need your help.'

'Anything, sir. You know that.'

'I had intended travelling to Wells, but have been forced to change my plans. Could you loan me a fresh team and look after my greys until I can arrange for their collection?'

'Course I can, sir! I'll let you have my bays. Wouldn't trust 'em to just anyone, you understand, but I know with you they'll be in safe hands.'

They walked out to the yard and, whilst a young stable lad was harnessing the bays to his curricle, Marcus looked down the long row of stalls. Although the inn was not a posting house, several of Bath's residents stabled their horses here, knowing they would be well cared for.

'Which is my ward's mount, Jeb?' Marcus asked suddenly, his eyes resting on a particularly fine dapple mare. When he had received that letter from his cousin, requesting a horse for his ward, he had not left the matter in the hands of his efficient secretary, but had dealt with it himself.

In his reply he had requested her to seek Jeb's aid in finding a suitable mount. He had thought the price she had paid rather steep, and the cost of a riding habit exorbitant, but had not quibbled, and had increased Sarah's quarterly allowance to cover the costs of stabling. 'Is it that mare?'

'No, sir. Miss Pennington don't stable her horse here. Fact is—' he scratched the side of his head '—don't ever recall seeing her ride. But I 'appen to know that the owner of the mare is wishful to sell her, if you're interested?'

Marcus did not respond to this, but looked at the ex-groom thoughtfully. 'Are you acquainted with my ward, Jeb?'

'Well, I know of her, sir. Naturally, she don't come 'ere, but I've seen her about the city. My wife knows her right enough. Says she's a sweet-natured lass. Not too proud to stop and chat when they bump into each other whilst out doing a bit of marketing.'

'Marketing?' he echoed, not hiding his astonishment. 'But surely my cousin has servants enough to—' He broke off abruptly, his heavy frown descending, as he accompanied the innkeeper outside into the yard once again.

'Don't like the look of that sky, sir,' Jeb remarked, glancing over to the west where dark clouds were gathering ominously. 'Looks as though we're in for a spell o' bad weather. I hope your journey don't prove to be a long un.'

'And so do I!' Marcus responded with feeling as he sat himself beside his groom in the curricle. 'I'll return your bays as soon as I can. Thanks again,' and with that he gave the horses the office to start.

The borrowed team were certainly not in the greys' class, but were, none the less, sturdy animals, and Marcus soon reached the London to Bristol road. Although he had tactfully refrained from divulging the nature of his errand to the innkeeper, Bath being a positive hotbed for gossip, he had explained to his groom the reason behind the change in plans.

Sutton cast a concerned glance at his silent master as the first flakes of snow fell to earth. 'I do hope we find the young person, sir. I reckon we're in for a heavy fall.'

'I'm determined to find her,' Ravenhurst responded grimly. 'Not even a snowstorm, Sutton, will deprive me of the exquisite pleasure of wringing my sweet ward's confounded neck!'

Chapter Two

Sarah Pennington entered the inn's infrequently used private parlour, and sat herself down on the wooden settle conveniently placed near the inglenook fireplace. The homely innkeeper's wife would not hear of a gently bred young woman remaining in the coffee-room where she might be forced to associate with the locals.

'Good enough people in their own way, ma'am,' she had said, 'but a little too rough-and-ready at times.'

She had been all kind consideration for the poor young 'widow's' plight. Sarah's lips curled into a wry little smile. How different her reception had been, here, at this small wayside inn!

When she had entered that busy posting house earlier in the day, she had been subjected to a display of hostile disapproval from the landlady who, after informing her in no uncertain terms that the common stage did not stop at that superior establishment, had begrudgingly furnished her with a cup of coffee before sending her on her way.

Odious woman! Sarah thought angrily, still nettled by the icy treatment meted out to her. How was she supposed to know where the London to Bristol Accommodation

Coaches stopped to change horses and pick up passengers? She had never travelled by that means of transport in her life. But she ought, she knew, to have known that a young unmarried lady, travelling without so much as a maid to give her consequence, would certainly be viewed by many with staunch disapproval.

Fortunately, however, Mother Nature in her wisdom had seen fit not only to bless Sarah Pennington with a very pleasing countenance and a perfectly proportioned figure, but to bestow upon her a sunny disposition, a lively sense of humour and a good deal of no-nonsense common sense. She had, therefore, swiftly rectified the little oversight on her part.

As soon as she had been out of sight of any prying eyes watching her from the windows of that posting house, she had rummaged through her reticule, and had slipped her mother's wedding ring on to her finger. It was, of course, quite respectable for a married lady to be travelling about the country alone. More so a widow! she had decided, quickly placing the handsome husband of her fertile imagination six feet beneath the earth without suffering the least pangs of conscience.

Soon afterwards Fortune had chosen to look favourably on the young 'widow'. Sarah had not walked above a mile or two when she had been taken up by a kindly carrier who had generously offered to convey her to Chippenham to await the arrival of the Accommodation Coach from Bristol or, if she preferred, as far as Marlborough, where he was to have delivered his load of furniture.

As her purse was woefully slim, Sarah had not hesitated in accepting the generous offer of a free ride. Then, of course, cursed ill-luck had seen fit to demand its turn!

They had travelled no more than a few miles past Calne when snow had begun to fall.

The carrier, a seasoned user of the roads, knew the vagaries of the weather, and had predicted a heavy fall. Marlborough, now, was out of the question. He had fully intended to seek immediate shelter with friends, and had advised Sarah to take refuge at the wayside inn clearly visible from the main road.

He had assured her that the landlady kept a good, clean house, so she need not fear damp sheets, nor poor fare; and she was, now, very glad that she had taken his sensible advice, for the snow was falling harder than ever, rapidly adding to the three inches already covering the landscape.

Her reverie was interrupted by the landlord who entered the parlour, his arms laden with several substantial logs.

'Getting mortal bad out there, Mrs Armstrong,' he remarked, piling the logs on the huge hearth. 'You mark my words—there'll be more than one unwary traveller stranded afore this day is over.'

'I dare say you're right. When I arrived at Calne, where my brother was to have met me,' she remarked, her fertile imagination coming to her aid, and not for the first time that day, 'the clouds were, even then, looking rather threatening. It was rather foolish of me not to have remained there, but it's such a busy posting house, and all the noise was giving me the headache, so I thought some fresh air would do me good. I expected, of course, to see my brother's chaise coming towards me at any moment.'

By the sympathetic look on the landlord's craggy, weatherbeaten face, the explanation she had offered for her present predicament, accompanied by a forlorn little sigh, had sounded very convincing.

'I'm so very glad I noticed the smoke billowing from your chimneys from the main road, and had the sense to come here, instead of trying to return to that posting house at Calne.'

'Would that be The White Hart, ma'am?'

'Er—yes, that's right.'

'Did you leave the rest of your baggage there?' he enquired, recalling clearly that the young lady had arrived carrying only a smallish wooden case and a rather old and battered cloak-bag.

'No, my trunk was sent on ahead,' she improvised quickly. 'I've been staying with friends, just a few miles from here. I thought the few clothes I had brought with me would be adequate for my journey home. But I'm afraid I made no allowances for a deterioration in the weather and any possible delays on the road.'

'Don't you worry your head on that score, ma'am. My good lady will provide you with any—er—little necessities you might need. And don't worry about your brother, neither. Stands to reason he won't be travelling far this day. As soon as the weather improves, I'll take you back to Calne in my old gig. No doubt we'll find him awaiting you at the posting house.'

Sarah thanked him, and then watched, a flicker of regret in the depths of her lovely aquamarine-coloured eyes, as he left the room. How she hated lying to these kindly folk! But what choice had she?

She could not bear to be stranded here and be treated with contempt, her presence nothing more than a hindrance, a tiresome burden. She had endured more than enough years of feeling nothing more than a troublesome millstone about someone's neck. No, that wasn't strictly true, she amended silently. She hadn't been made to feel unwanted, at least, not by Mrs Fairchild. And her wretched guardian simply hadn't concerned himself about her at all!

She turned her head to stare down at the logs hissing and crackling noisily on the hearth, and began to recall the events in her life that had led to her present very sorry predicament.

Her father had been a courageous man, a captain in His Majesty's Navy, who had given his life for King and Country during the Battle of the Nile. Sad to say she could hardly remember him at all. She had been just a child when he had died; but she had almost reached the age of fifteen when her dear mother had been so cruelly and unexpectedly taken from her.

Keeping her tears firmly in check, she began to dwell on those idyllic childhood years when she had resided in her father's charming house near Plymouth, and those happy times when she had visited her dear godmother at Ravenhurst, that beautiful stone-built mansion situated in its many acres of Oxfordshire parkland. She retained many fond memories of her kind godmother, but her godmother's son she could not bring to mind at all.

In those early years, whenever she had visited Ravenhurst with her mother, he had been away at Eton, and then, later, at Oxford. The only vague memory she retained of him was on that day he had visited Plymouth shortly after her mother had died.

A hazy vision of a hard-featured face swam before her mind's eye. At the tender age of fourteen, she had been too afraid to look at the tall stranger in whose hands her future well-being had been placed, let alone disagree with any arrangements he may have undertaken on her behalf, and had kept her eyes glued to his highly polished top-boots, and her lips firmly compressed.

Honesty promoted her to admit that she had not disliked the idea of attending a seminary in Bath; she had not even objected to being placed in the care of his cousin, who had turned out to be quite a kindly soul, though slightly scatty and prone to fits of the vapours when things had not gone her way; but she had bitterly resented being separated from her beloved governess.

'No, my dear. It will not answer,' Martha Trent had responded gently, yet firmly, to Sarah's pleas for them to remain together. 'Your guardian is right. It will be much better for you to go to school and have the companionship of girls your own age. And with you attending a seminary, I would have no role to play in your new home. Mr Ravenhurst's cousin will, I'm sure, take very good care of you.

'I cannot live off your guardian's charity, Sarah. I must look about for a new position. And Mr Ravenhurst has very kindly insisted that on no account am I to take the first one offered, but am to look for a situation where I think I would be happy.'

Sarah frowned slightly as Martha's words came back so clearly. Yes, to be fair, she had to own that her guardian had displayed some consideration for her beloved governess. Which was more than he had ever done for her! He was, by common report, a very rich man, and yet he had never seen fit to send her a little money of her own with which to buy a few little luxuries. What dresses she possessed, good quality garments, but sadly unfashionable, had been chosen for her by Mrs Fairchild.

Unlike other girls her age, she had never attended the balls held at the Assembly Rooms, and had rarely been invited to any private parties. The only times she had ever been truly happy were during those few short months each year when Mrs Stanton brought her daughter Clarissa to Bath, and those wonderful summer visits she had made to their home in Devonshire.

The weekday ventures to the Pump Room, where Mrs Fairchild sampled the waters and gossiped with her middle-aged cronies, and the twice-monthly card parties held in the large salon at Upper Camden Place, where Sarah had donned her best pearl-grey gown and had served Mrs Fairchild's guests with wine and tiny sweet biscuits, had proved to be the only slight relief from the tedium of living all year round in that, once, very fashionable watering place.

But it wasn't until Martha had paid that unexpected visit to Bath the year before that Sarah had become totally discontented with her lot. Her ex-governess had assured her that she would be most welcome to visit her in Hertfordshire, and to stay for as long as she wished, and had gone so far as to furnish her with enough money to hire a post-chaise for the journey.

Martha, also, had not attempted to hide her shock and dismay at her ex-pupil's drab, unfashionable attire, giving Sarah reason to hope that, perhaps, she wasn't so poorly circumstanced as she had been led to believe.

'As to that, my dear, I'm not perfectly sure,' had been Mrs Fairchild's vague response to her charge's blunt enquiry. 'Mr Ravenhurst has never seen fit to discuss your financial situation with me.'

'But surely, ma'am, I was left some money?' Sarah had persisted. 'We lived in a charming house near Plymouth. What has become of that? And my mother's family was certainly not poor. My grandfather was, after all, a baronet.'

'Very true, Sarah. But what you, perhaps, do not realise, is that your mother became estranged from your grandfather when she chose to go against his expressed wishes and marry Captain Pennington. Worthy man though your father undoubtedly was, he hardly belonged to your mother's social class. And as far as your old home is concerned. . .? Well, I really couldn't say. Perhaps your mother left debts and Mr Ravenhurst was forced to sell it.

'And I cannot understand just why you have suddenly taken it into your head to concern yourself over such matters,' she had gone on to say. 'You reside in a charming house, have good food to eat and are expected to undertake only the lightest of tasks for your keep.

'I'm sure Mr Ravenhurst has your best interests at heart, my dear. And it most certainly wouldn't do for you to go parading round Bath in a lot of finery and giving the totally wrong impression to any eligible young gentlemen, now would it? But I'm sure that your guardian would not object to purchasing anything for you if it were really needful?'

'In that case, ma'am,' Sarah had retorted, bitterly resentful at what she had deemed an unnecessary slight on her father, 'perhaps you would be good enough to enquire, when next you write to my excessively wealthy guardian, whether he would be willing to furnish me with a suitable mount, so that I am able to accompany my friend Clarissa on her rides whilst she is in Bath. I do not think that that would be too much to ask!'

Of course, Sarah had not left matters there, and had written to Mr Ravenhurst requesting information regarding her circumstances, but had never received a reply, nor had the horse she had craved ever been forthcoming; not that she had been particularly surprised about that. After all, a man who could not even bring himself to respond to the few letters she had written over the years was hardly likely to put himself to the trouble of purchasing a suitable mount for his tiresome ward.

Sighing, Sarah rose from the settle, and went across the room to stare out of the window. The snow was continuing to fall heavily in the rapidly fading late afternoon light. It was impossible, now, to discern the road from the grass verges.

She released her breath in a tiny sigh. Perhaps it had been rather foolish of her to leave Bath at this time of year, but she was not sorry she had. After all, with her friend Clarissa gone, and dear Mrs Stanton no doubt feeling quite out of charity with her daughter's conspiring friend, there was nothing left for her there.

Added to which, in June, when she attained her majority, her indifferent guardian would no doubt be only too eager to wash his hands of her completely. His obligations would then be at an end, and she would be forced to make her own way in the world. So, why wait until the inevitable was forced upon her?

It was as well to be prepared, she told herself, and look for a position as governess, or companion in some genteel household, and she felt certain that her dear Martha would aid her in finding a comfortable situation.

A smart racing curricle, making very slow progress along the road, caught her attention. The driver, his hat and cloak covered in white, put her in mind of a rather large and misshapen snowman; and she might have derived a deal of amusement from the spectacle had it not recalled to mind certain other travellers abroad that day, and she prayed with all her heart that dear Clarissa and James were not stranded on the road but, like herself, had found shelter at some inn.

The door opening broke into her disturbing thoughts, and she turned her head to see the innkeeper's kindly wife enter the room.

'Mrs Armstrong, we've another traveller just arrived wishful to shelter from the weather. Would you object if the gentleman joined you in the parlour for dinner? It's more fitting dining in here, him being a gentleman an' all.'

'Of course I don't object,' Sarah assured her. 'Is he, perhaps, the person I saw just now tooling a curricle?'

'Aye, ma'am. Though what possessed him to go careering round the country in an open carriage in the month of February beats me. Mind, I thought it wisest not to ask. Didn't look in the best of humours when he walked in. But I dare say he'll cheer up and feel a deal better once he's got a decent meal inside him.'

Sarah, her mind still dwelling on the long journey to the border her eloping friends had ahead of them, gave not another thought to the stranded gentleman traveller until, some fifteen minutes later, the parlour door opened yet again.

She watched a tall, broad-shouldered man, immaculately attired in a coat of blue superfine, tight-fitting pantaloons and shining top-boots—whose brilliance, no doubt, was attained from using a secret mixture containing champagne—enter the room. He came purposefully, yet gracefully, towards her, and she found herself staring up at a far-from-handsome and unsmiling countenance.

'I understand from the lady of the house that you have been gracious enough to permit me to share your private parlour, ma'am,' he remarked in the most attractive deep

masculine voice she had ever heard. 'My name is
Ravenhurst.'

Her lovely smile of greeting fading, Sarah sat rigid on
the wooden settle, as though turned to stone.
Ravenhurst. . .? The name echoed between her temples
like some thunderous peal of bells. It couldn't be! Surely
Fate could not be so wickedly capricious as to bring them
face to face this day, of all days!

'Are you all right, ma'am?' The modicum of concern
in his deep voice was lost on her. 'You are very pale. I'll
summon the landlady.'

Sarah could not have responded even had she wanted
to, and could only watch in a kind of trancelike state as
he hurriedly left the room.

Placing a suddenly trembling hand to her throbbing
temple, she tried to make some sense out of her frantically
disordered thoughts. Was it, in truth, 'the' Mr
Ravenhurst? She hadn't recognised him, but that was in
no way remarkable, considering she had set eyes on him
only once in her life before, and then had taken precious
little interest in his outward appearance.

Her finely arched brows drew together in a deep,
thoughtful frown. Even supposing, by some cursed ill-
luck, that the stranger did turn out to be her guardian,
then what in the world was he doing in this part of the
country? Although, she reminded herself, didn't Mr
Ravenhurst have relatives residing in Wiltshire? A grandmother, or uncle, or some such? She felt certain that
Harriet Fairchild had said as much.

If he had not been visiting his relations, then it must
be pure coincidence that had brought him here, surely?
He couldn't possibly have received word so soon of her
leaving Bath. And even if by some mischance he had

discovered her flight, he certainly wouldn't put himself to the trouble of coming after her. . . Or would he?

No, she thought, quickly thrusting this foolish notion aside, and focusing her mind on what course of action to take. Firstly, she must discover if the stranger was, indeed, her guardian; then, if the worst came to the worst, and it turned out to be so, she must try to discover what he was doing in this part of the world. She felt certain he had not recognised her and, given the circumstances, it might be wisest if she allowed him to remain in blissful ignorance.

By the time the object of her thoughts returned, with the very concerned landlady in tow, Sarah had regained full control of herself and was determined not to lose it so foolishly again. After hurriedly assuring the good woman that she was perfectly well, and that her 'queer turn' had no doubt stemmed from a singular lack of nourishment since breakfast, she, once again reverting to her widowed status, introduced herself to the severe-looking man who then drew up a chair, and seated himself.

'Have you far to travel?' she enquired when the land-lady had left them alone together.

His deep-set dark eyes held hers from the opposite side of the hearth. 'As to that, ma'am, I couldn't say with any degree of certainty.'

'You are not from around these parts, sir?'

'No,' was the clipped response, but far from being annoyed by his abruptness, Sarah was amused.

He was, undoubtedly, a man prone to frequent bouts of ill-humour, the permanent crease between those almost black brows being adequate confirmation of this; and she recalled being told, on more than one occasion, that her guardian was a brusque, testy individual, much the same as her friend Clarissa's father.

Unlike Harriet Fairchild, however, who certainly entertained a lively dread of her untitled aristocratic cousin's unpleasant temperament, Sarah, strangely, experienced no such trepidation when in the company of such irascible gentlemen, and could not resist the temptation to goad him a little.

'No doubt you are feeling slightly peevish at having your journey interrupted, sir. Some gentlemen, I know, cannot brook the least deviation from their original plans, and fly into the boughs at the slightest hitch,' and it took every ounce of self-control she possessed to stop herself from bursting out laughing as he regarded her much as he might have done a rare specimen in some fairground freak-show.

'But as there is nothing either of us can do to improve the weather,' she continued, her voice not quite steady, 'I suggest we try to make the best of our enforced stay here.'

A sound, somewhere between the noise a gentleman makes when clearing his throat and that of a predatory beast's suppressed growl, reached her ears before he said, still with an unmistakable trace of annoyance in his voice, 'Forgive me, ma'am, if I seemed—er—peevish, but the day has not turned out at all as I had expected. There hasn't been so much a small hitch in my original plans as a total abandonment, instigated by the completely unwarranted and feather-brained actions of my—'

He stopped abruptly, his lips for a moment compressed into a thin, angry line, though when he spoke again it was in a distinctly milder tone. 'But as you correctly surmised, I do not reside in this part of the country, although I do have relatives living not far from here. My home is in Oxfordshire.'

Oh, God, no! Sarah could have screamed in vexation. There wasn't a doubt about it. The wretch was her guardian!

It was perhaps fortunate that the landlady and her buxom rosy-cheeked daughter chose this auspicious moment to enter the room: one laying covers on the table; the other going about the room lighting the various candles and closing the curtains, offering Sarah time to calm herself down and rethink her strategy.

From what he had let fall, it was abundantly obvious that he was searching for her. But how on earth had he discovered, so quickly, her departure from Bath? There was only one possible explanation: against all the odds, he must have visited Upper Camden Place that morning. Wretched man! Why, today of all days, had he suddenly taken it into his head to visit Bath?

Not that that was of any relevance, she told herself, turning her head to stare down into the fire once more, blissfully unaware that he was studying the play of different emotions flit across her face. It was unlikely that Harriet Fairchild would have realised where her charge had intended going and, to be fair, Sarah knew she had given little away in the note she had left her. But Clarissa's mother might well have guessed Sarah's destination.

If Mrs Stanton had happened to be present when Ravenhurst arrived, how much information had he gleaned from her? Certainly enough to bring him thus far. Therefore, it stood to reason that he had learned of Martha Alcott's home in Hertfordshire. What beastly ill-luck!

'Something appears to be troubling you, Mrs Armstrong.'

'W-what?' Sarah drew her head round with a start. 'No, not really, sir,' she managed in a moderately convincing voice, while silently cursing his astuteness. She forced herself to stare into those intelligent dark brown eyes. No, her guardian was certainly no fool.

Ought she to tell him who she really was? She dismissed the notion in an instant. His sole purpose in trying to locate her must be to return her to Bath. And she would not go back there! she thought determinedly. But she would need to be so very careful from now on, giving away no clue as to her true identity.

Had she mentioned that her destination was Hertfordshire to either the innkeeper or his wife? No, she felt certain she had not. Therefore, her destination now, if anyone should enquire, would be. . . Surrey. Yes, Surrey would serve very well, but she must ensure that she stuck to her original story, for if she made one slight slip, and he learned something different from either the innkeeper or his wife, she felt certain he would be on to her like a cat after a hapless mouse.

'I was just thinking about my brother. My friends left me at The White Hart in Calne where I was to have awaited his arrival.'

'Then why didn't you?'

It was on the tip of her tongue to tell him to mind his own business, but she refrained, and said, instead, 'I grew tired of waiting. I expected to see him at any moment coming along the road towards me in the chaise, but in the end was forced to seek shelter here. It was foolish of me not to have remained in Calne, I suppose.'

'Exceedingly so, ma'am,' he returned bluntly, the

forlorn little voice that had gained the sympathy of the innkeeper earlier having no such effect on him. 'Quite feather-brained, in fact!'

The green in her eyes became more prominent. 'Yes, as totty-headed as driving about the country in an open carriage at this time of year, I dare say,' she parried, and was astounded by the appreciative smile that curled his lips and completely erased the hard lines of his face, turning him into a most attractive man.

'*Touché*, madam.' He rose to his feet. 'I believe we are served.'

Sarah accompanied him over to the table, not quite knowing what to make of him. He was certainly abrupt, and exceedingly rude, but he was not totally ill-mannered, for he did pull a chair out for her, and then proceeded to carve several slices of chicken on to her plate.

'I'm relieved to see that you have a healthy appetite, ma'am,' he remarked after watching her help herself to the various contents of several dishes. 'I cannot abide females who insist upon chasing morsels of food around their plates for the duration of a meal, and then have the crass stupidity to wonder, after eating so little, why they are prone to fainting all over the place.'

She could not forbear a smile at his scathing tone. 'Then you must be relieved to see that you are not in the company of such a one. I enjoy my food, and can assure you that I have never fainted in my life.'

'You came perilously close to doing so earlier,' he countered, and she cast him a wary look, but gained her composure almost at once.

'And that is precisely why I am rectifying that near-transgression on my part. I really could not bear the humiliation of having you step over me whilst on your way about the inn.'

Once again she was privileged to see that rather wonderful smile. 'I would never do anything so ungentlemanlike, I assure you.'

He surveyed her for a moment over the rim of his glass, noting the strands of gold in her rich brown, plainly though neatly arranged hair, and the finely arched black brows and long black curling lashes that framed her lovely and unusually coloured blue-green eyes.

There was nothing classical in the lines of her small straight nose, but her lips were pleasantly formed and curled up slightly at the corners, and there was certainly more than a hint of determination in that softly rounded chin. All in all she was an exceedingly pretty young woman who, he suspected, possessed a great deal of lively wit and charm.

'Your husband must be concerned about you, ma'am. Were you expected home this day?'

'I'm a widow, sir,' she responded evenly, and just for an instant thought she could detect a flicker of sympathy in his eyes as they rested for a moment on her plain grey gown. 'Are you married, Mr Ravenhurst?'

For some reason his dark straight brows snapped together, and his tone once again was clipped as he said, 'No, ma'am, I am not!'

'No, I didn't think so.'

'Oh? And what gave rise to that assumption?'

'Because you had not long entered this room before I became fairly confident that I was in the company of a confirmed misogynist.'

His deep rumble of laughter filled the air. 'My word, but you're forthright, ma'am! If that were, indeed, true,

I think I can safely say that I'm rapidly losing my hatred.'

For one dreadful moment she suspected him of flirting with her, but then he changed the subject, and she felt certain she must have been mistaken.

Unlike his cousin Harriet Fairchild, who rarely cast her eyes over a printed word, and then only those set between the hard covers of a Gothic romance, Sarah was an avid reader who scanned the daily newspapers from cover to cover, and so kept abreast of happenings in the world. She was, therefore, able to converse with Mr Ravenhurst on a wide variety of topics, from the progress of the war with France to the Prince of Wales's inauguration as Regent the previous year.

It transpired that her guardian had been amongst the two thousand guests who had attended the celebration party held at Carlton House; but from his scathing condemnation of the traffic blocking many of the capital's busy streets that day, and his caustic remarks on the oppressive warmth and the cluttered and vulgar opulence of the Regent's town dwelling, it was quite apparent that he had not enjoyed the experience very much.

They had no sooner eaten their fill of the excellent dinner than the landlady's daughter returned, carrying a bottle and a glass on a tray.

'Ma said as how you being a gentleman, sir, you'd be wanting this after your meal,' she offered nervously, setting the tray down on to the table.

'What's your name, girl?' Marcus asked, reaching for the port and pouring himself a glass.

'Daisy, sir. . . Daisy Fletcher, sir.'

'Be good enough to convey my thanks to your mother, Miss Fletcher. That was an excellent dinner.'

'Oh, thank 'ee, sir! Ma do know how to look after

gentlemen, right enough. She were in service when she were a girl. She do keep a good, well-stocked larder, so you needn't afear to go 'ungry whilst you're 'ere. And if the weather do stay bad for a few days to come, Pa be willing to slaughter the goose, and his favourite suckling pig, which'll do for several meals if you make use of the innards an' all. No, you won't be going 'ungry, sir.'

Marcus, a look of comical dismay on his face, watched her leave the room, and then turned once again to his dinner-companion to see her shoulders shaking with suppressed laughter.

'Has no one ever told you, ma'am,' he said in a voice of mock censure, 'that it shows a decided lack of breeding to laugh at rustics?'

'I was not laughing at her!' Sarah refuted hotly, but not quite steadily. 'It was you who very nearly sent me into whoops. If you could have seen the look on your face when she mentioned slaughtering the pig.'

'Dear me, yes. She spoke as though it were a pet. And do people consume the insides of a pig?'

'Some parts of it, certainly. The liver, and the chitterlings, I believe.'

'Oh, God spare us! Let us hope it doesn't come to that. Though I'm sure if you're willing to tackle such fare, I can steel myself to do so. Where are you going?'

Sarah, who had risen, placed her chair neatly beneath the small table. 'I was up very early this morning, sir, and am rather tired. So, I'll bid you good-night, and leave you to your port.'

Picking up a candle, Mr Ravenhurst surprised Sarah by escorting her to the door, and then across the deserted coffee-room to the foot of the narrow staircase where he handed her the candle.

'Good-night, Mrs Armstrong,' he said, his features once again softened by that warm smile. 'I look forward to the pleasure of your company at breakfast.'

Feeling not just a little confused, Sarah made her way up the narrow staircase and along the passageway to the spotlessly clean, low-ceilinged bedchamber that she had been shown into soon after her arrival at the inn.

At some point, while she had been in the parlour, some-one had entered the room to fold down the bedcovers and to pull the floral-patterned drapes across the window. The candle on the small table in the corner had been lit and the fire had been made up, making the room pleasantly warm and cosy.

After going about the room lighting the other candles, she set the light Mr Ravenhurst had given her down on the chest of drawers by the bedside, and then went across to the table in the corner on which she had placed her wooden writing-case. She had been able to bring so few possessions with her—not that she had that many to bring—but she had refused to leave this, the last present her mother had ever given to her, behind in Bath.

She ran one finger lovingly over the delicate gold leaf of her initials, exquisitely carved into the fine wood, before flicking the catch and opening the lid. It was so beautifully made, having sections for ink bottles and pens.

There were two small drawers, one set in each of the back corners: the right quite inocuous; the left hiding a cunningly made secret compartment for billets-doux. There was also ample room in the centre of the box for several sheets of paper, the top one of which already contained several lines in Sarah's neatly flowing hand.

Lifting the sheet from off the pile, Sarah ran her eyes over the letter to her guardian that she had begun to write, ironically enough, shortly after her arrival at the inn, and groaned inwardly. The cool formality had seemed just the correct tone to adopt, but now, having met Mr Ravenhurst again after so many years, it seemed totally inappropriate, rude almost.

She raised her eyes to stare blindly across the comfortable room. And what an enigma the man had turned out to be! She had been given every reason to suppose, from remarks Mrs Fairchild had made over the years, and from snippets of information gleaned from visitors to Bath who were acquainted with her guardian, that Mr Ravenhurst was nothing more than an abrupt, unfeeling individual who had no consideration for his fellow man.

A wry smile curled her lips. He was most certainly abrupt, but his caustic remarks, far from giving offence, had amused her. She had enjoyed his company very much during dinner; and the simple thanks he had offered to the landlady's daughter had afforded a glimpse of his true character. He was far from the care-for-nobody she had thought him. Which made his seeming indifference towards her over the years even more puzzling.

She shook her head, genuinely perplexed. Something just didn't ring true. Added to which, he had come searching for her. Was that the action of an indifferent guardian? No, of course it was not! And, now, having come to know him a little, she felt she ought to tell him who she really was. After all, sooner or later he was going to discover the truth; and she felt certain that, once he understood her reasons for leaving, he would not force her to return to Bath.

Yes, first thing in the morning, she decided firmly, she would confess all. And who could tell, he might even be kind enough to escort her the rest of the way to Hertfordshire!

A sudden commotion below reached her ears. She could clearly hear the sound of several raised voices, and wondered what on earth was going on.

Curiosity got the better of her and, quickly thrusting the letter back into the writing-case and closing the lid, she picked up a candle and made her way back down the stairs to discover that a strange assortment of dishevelled travellers had invaded the coffee-room: some arguing amongst themselves; others calmly watching proceedings; and the very distraught landlord trying desperately to make himself heard above the din.

'What the devil is going on out here?'

The authoritative voice had an immediate effect. The hubbub ceased instantly as all eyes turned to stare at the imposing figure framed in the parlour doorway.

'Sir!' The landlord hurried towards Mr Ravenhurst, realising at once that here was a man born to command and, unless he was very much mistaken, accustomed to having those commands obeyed.

'These be the passengers from the London to Bristol Accommodation Coach. From what I can make out their vehicle be in a ditch, sir, a mile or so back along the main road. The driver and guard are walking the horses to Calne. And I been trying to tell 'em that that's what they should o' done, instead o' coming 'ere. We ain't a posting house, sir. We can't cater for such a large number.'

'Now, Frederick—' his wife came forward '—you can't send these poor folk back out on a night like this. Why, it's blowing a blizzard out there. It would be positively unchristian!'

'And I for one won't walk another step!' declared a very fat woman who, much to Sarah's amusement, substantiated the statement by plumping herself down in the middle of the coffee-room floor.

Marcus, not so easily diverted by the action, shot the woman an impatient glance before casting his eyes over her fellow-travellers, his gaze coming to rest on a sandy-haired young man who was gaping back at him in astonishment.

'Ravenhurst! What the deuce are you doing in this out-of-the-way place?'

'I should have thought that that would have been patently obvious to anyone of the meanest intelligence, Nutley,' he responded dampingly before addressing himself to the innkeeper's wife. 'How many of these persons are you able to accommodate?'

'Well, sir, if some wouldn't mind sharing, I dare say we can fix them all up.'

'One of the ladies could, perhaps, come in with me,' Sarah offered kindly.

'No, there's no need for you to put yourself out,' Marcus intervened before the landlady could accept the generous offer. Unlike Sarah, he had taken stock of the passengers.

Apart from the fat lady, who was still stubbornly seated on the floor, and who looked to be travelling with the thin man hovering nearby, there were only two other females amongst the passengers: a spinsterish-looking woman who bore all the appearance of a governess, and whose face was hidden by a large and rather ugly bonnet; and a twinkling-eyed female in a dashing red confection, whose saucy smile gave him a fair notion of what her particular calling might be.

'If you would be willing to change rooms with me, ma'am, I shall be happy to share with one of these gentlemen,' he continued, raising a questioning brow at the tall young man whose broad shoulders were propped against the wall, and who had been silently viewing proceedings with an amused glint in his tawny-coloured eyes.

'Very decent of you, sir,' he said coming forward. 'My name is Carter—Captain Brin Carter.'

Marcus acknowledged him with a nod before turning to the innkeeper again. 'I leave the rest of the arrangements to you and your good lady.'

Although having been granted little say in the matter, Sarah did not object to the new arrangements, and accompanied Mr Ravenhurst back up the stairs.

It took but a few moments to repack her meagre belongings into the cloak-bag and carry it across the narrow passageway into her newly allotted and much smaller bedchamber. She was genuinely fatigued after the events of the day, and long before the harassed innkeeper and his wife had the remainder of their unexpected guests accommodated, she had fallen sound asleep.

Marcus did return downstairs for a short while. He joined Captain Carter and one of his fellow travelling-companions in the tap to sample a tankard of the innkeeper's excellent home-brewed. The Captain, it transpired, was on his way to Bristol to board the next vessel leaving for Spain, and Mr Stubbs was merely paying a visit to the city to stay with his daughter.

Mr Stubbs's explanation for travelling at such a time of year sounded plausible enough, and Marcus might have accepted the reason at face value had the middle-aged, stockily built individual not betrayed an inordinate interest in the other customers: locals who had braved the elements for their evening tipple.

'An odd character, Stubbs,' the Captain remarked later, when they entered their bedchamber. 'Friendly enough, but a mite inquisitive, wouldn't you say?'

Marcus's lips twisted into a crooked smile. 'Yes. Our friends at Bow Street do travel far and wide these days.'

'A Runner?' The Captain's brows rose. 'That would account for it, then! He was very chatty during the journey, asking a great many seemingly innocent questions. In fact, that weasel-faced fellow in the black coat, who started all the commotion earlier, was quite put out when Stubbs asked him what he did for a living. Can't imagine why. Turns out he's only some damned clerk in a lawyer's office.'

Marcus did not respond to this, for his attention was focused on the gold letters carved into the lid of the very handsomely made wooden box resting on the small table in the corner of the room. Without experiencing the least qualms he calmly opened the lid, ran his eyes over the unfinished letter lying on top and, much to the Captain's unholy amusement, suddenly uttered a string of decidedly colourful and unrepeatable oaths.

Chapter Three

Sarah awoke with a violent start the following morning when the daughter of the house, entering the bedchamber, thumped a pitcher of warm water down none too gently on the top of the wash-stand.

'Sorry, Mrs Armstrong, did I wake you?'

'Oh, that's all right.' Rubbing the sleep from her eyes, Sarah watched the flat-footed Daisy stomp across the room to draw back the curtains. The morning looked remarkably bright, and for a few elated moments she retained the hope that she might be able to continue her journey, until assured that nothing had passed along the road that morning.

'I overheard one of the locals saying last night that there be drifts ten foot deep in parts, blocking the main road,' Daisy voiced dampingly. 'Although the sun be shining, there be precious little warmth in it, and Pa reckons there'll be more snow afore long. You won't be leaving 'ere today, Mrs Armstrong. Nor tomorrow, I don't reckon.'

'Never mind. It cannot be helped,' Sarah responded, resigning herself quickly to remaining at least one more day at the inn. Fully awake, now, she sat up and pushed her tousled brown hair away from her face. 'Did you manage to accommodate all those passengers off the stagecoach?'

'Aye, we did that, ma'am, but it were a bit of a squeeze. I had to give up my bed to that farmer and his wife. The young sprig and another man had Ma and Pa's room, and Mr Ravenhurst's groom kindly agreed to share with our Joe, so the lady in the pretty red bonnet could 'ave 'is old room. And the spinster lady and that man who be forever carping on 'ad to make do with the smallest rooms down the far end of the passageway.'

Having always taken an interest in the welfare of others, Sarah looked up in some concern. 'But where on earth did you and your parents sleep?'

'We bedded down in our parlour next to the kitchen. But from tonight I'm to sleep at me aunt's 'ouse, just down the road. And we're to 'ave me cousin Rose 'elping out.' She pulled a face. 'She be a right flighty little wench. And as sly as bedamned. I'd never trust 'er. She'll come to a bad end one o' these days, ma'am. You see if she don't.'

So, Daisy evidently didn't care for her cousin very much, and most certainly wasn't looking forward to her presence at the inn. Sarah regarded her with an understanding smile. 'I expect you could do with the extra pair of hands, though.'

'Aye, we could that. Ma's been up since daybreak, baking and the like. Which reminds me. She wants to know if you'd like your breakfast brought up on a tray, or are you wishful to eat in the parlour again?'

'Definitely in the parlour, Daisy. You will have enough to do without running up and down the stairs with breakfast trays all morning.'

After washing in the contents of the pitcher, Sarah donned her detested grey gown, and stood before the wash-stand mirror to tidy her hair, twisting it in a long plait before securely pinning it to the back of her head. Vanity, thankfully, had never been one of her failings.

Yet she was feminine enough, as she stood there staring at her reflection in the mottled glass, to crave pretty dresses to wear and to long for the ministrations of an abigail, whose skilled fingers could arrange those silky brown tresses in a more becoming style.

A sigh escaped her. Elaborate hairstyles and elegant gowns were not the hallmarks of a governess, she reminded herself and, desperately trying to resign herself to her possible future station in life, left the bedchamber, blissfully unaware that her unfashionable attire and plainly arranged hair did not diminish her prettiness one iota.

Young Captain Carter was most certainly favourably impressed with what he saw, and cast an appreciative eye over both face and figure as Sarah entered the parlour a minute or two later. Unlike Mr Ravenhurst, who remained seated and merely acknowledged her with a curt nod, the Captain politely rose to his feet and, after introducing himself, thanked her for so generously giving up her bed-chamber the night before.

'Not at all, sir. It was no inconvenience, I assure you.' She sat beside Mr Ravenhurst at the table but, after a quick glance at his forbidding profile, decided to address herself to the far more amiable Captain. 'I trust you both slept well?'

Captain Carter shot a wicked glance in his bedfellow's direction. 'I'm quite used to sharing, ma'am. In Spain one is forced to adapt to many things, but I don't think our friend, here, is similarly accustomed.

'And it certainly didn't improve matters by being awakened this morning by a young lass who threw open the door so violently that it crashed against the wardrobe, and then added insult to injury by tripping up over the mat at the bottom of the bed and very nearly drowning us both with the contents of the water jug she was carrying.'

'Clumsy wench!' Ravenhurst muttered, his eyes narrowing fractionally as he detected the slight movement of slender shoulders shaking in suppressed laughter. 'By the by, Mrs—er—Armstrong, I believe you left that box in our room last night.' He gestured to the small table by the window on which he had set the writing-case a little earlier. 'At least I assume it's yours. It has the initials S.P. carved in the lid.'

'Oh, yes. It is mine,' Sarah confirmed after casting the briefest of glances at her most treasured possession, and cursing herself silently for leaving it behind in the room for him to find. 'My maiden name was Postlethwaite,' she managed after only the briefest of pauses. 'Serafina Postlethwaite.'

Marcus very nearly choked on his coffee, and hurriedly got to his feet. 'If you will both excuse me, I think I shall take a wander outside and see for myself just how bad conditions are.'

The Captain, frowning slightly, watched him leave. 'He's an odd fellow. Don't quite know what to make of him. One minute he's as considerate as can be, and the next—' He broke off abruptly, and cast Sarah an almost apologetic smile. 'I'm sorry, ma'am. Are you well acquainted with the gentleman?'

'No, sir, I am not,' she responded truthfully. 'He arrived here late yesterday afternoon, and we dined together. He is certainly a puzzling creature, though. I cannot make up my mind whether I like him or not.' She considered the point as she bit into a deliciously warm buttered roll. 'Last night he was a charming companion, and yet, this morning. . .'

'Temperamental, I should say.'

'Oh, he's most certainly that, Captain. I suspect he was thoroughly spoiled as a child,' she went on, experiencing no qualms whatsoever at discussing her guardian with a complete stranger. 'Needless to say he belongs to the aristocracy and is incredibly wealthy. So, I suppose, he's accustomed to having his way in all things.'

'Ah, yes. Our privileged aristocracy. Where would we be without them?' he responded bitterly, but then seemed to collect himself and hurriedly rose to his feet. 'I hope you'll not think me rude if I leave you to finish your breakfast in peace, ma'am. I think I, too, shall take a wander out of doors to indulge in a reprehensible habit I picked up in Spain.'

'Not at all, sir.' Sarah watched him leave, wondering why he should bear such an ardent grudge against a certain social class. There had certainly been more than a touch of acrimony in the attractive Captain's pleasant voice.

Shrugging, she quickly dismissed it as her own immediate problems came to the forefront of her mind and, rising from the table, went over to her writing-case, once again silently cursing for leaving it behind in that room.

Could her guardian possibly suspect? she wondered, staring down at those beautifully carved initials. After all, S.P. could stand for—well—almost anything. More importantly, thought, why hadn't she been honest with him when the opportunity had arisen? She shook her head. No, she couldn't have confessed, then, not with the Captain present. Added to which, Mr Ravenhurst had not been in the best of moods, most unlike the convivial companion he had been the evening before.

She was still determined to tell him the truth, but she must choose just the right moment, catch him in a more agreeable frame of mind. In the meantime, though, it wouldn't do to add to any suspicions he might already be harbouring by hiding the case away. No, it made sense to leave it in full view for the time being, but she must certainly remove that damning evidence.

Quickly opening the box, she screwed the half-written letter into a tight ball and threw it into the fire.

The once intended recipient of that, now, burning missive was at that precise moment standing just inside the stable block, with his faithful groom beside him, gazing frowningly at the depth of snow in the yard. Captain Carter, who had emerged from the inn a few moments before, was standing by the door leading to the kitchen, enjoying a cheroot, and the innkeeper's massive son was busy with a shovel, trying to clear a path round the hen-coop.

'Not a hope in hell of us getting away this day, sir,' Sutton remarked, gazing up at the sky. 'Nor tomorrow, neither, by the looks o' them clouds yonder.'

'No, there's certainly more to come. We must resign ourselves to remaining here for two days, possibly more.' Marcus glanced down at his trusted, middle-aged henchman. 'How did you manage last night?'

'What a carry on, eh, sir? Never seen the likes before! You'd think folks'd be thankful to find shelter anywhere rather than be out on a night like that.' He looked across at the innkeeper's son. 'Joe be a big beef-witted lad, but there's no 'arm in 'im. And how did you cope, sir?' he asked casting his eyes in the young Captain's direction.

'Well enough. But I don't doubt we'll all be sick and tired of one another's company before too long, and be more than ready to leave here when the time comes. Which reminds me. . .' Ravenhurst stared down in silence at the stable's earth floor for several thoughtful moments, then went on, 'I've changed my plans, Sutton. When the roads do become passable, I want you to go to Sir Henry Bamford's place with a letter of apology from me. I most certainly shan't be staying with him now.

'You'll no doubt be able to get a seat on the stagecoach with this lot. Take it as far as Chippenham, from where you should have no difficulty hiring a horse to take you the rest of the way. Bring Quilp and my carriage to my grandmother's house.'

The groom's brawny shoulders shook with wicked amusement. He had scant regard for his master's pernick-ety valet. 'I reckon old Quilp must be miffed 'cause we ain't turned up, sir.'

'I do not pay Quilp to question any change of plan I may choose to make,' was the curt response. 'I employ him to take care of my gear.'

Sutton cast his master a surreptitious glance. 'Will you be going after the girl again, sir?'

A not-unpleasant smile erased Marcus's heavy frown. 'Be assured, Sutton, my darling ward isn't so very far away.'

'Aye, sir. But where?' He shook his head, genuinely perturbed. 'I don't like to think of the young lady about on 'er own. Why, anything might 'appen to 'er!'

'Come on, man! Use your head! How far away can

she be? You know full well that that farm labourer saw a young female getting out of a post-chaise at the junction. The coach turned north on the road to Stroud, and she, on foot, went east.

'The landlady at that posting house gave us an accurate description, and we know a female answering that description was seen in a carrier's cart by that toll-gate keeper at Chippenham. We traced her as far as Calne. The carrier couldn't possibly have gone much farther.'

'Aye, sir, but supposing it weren't your ward, but some other little lady riding in that cart.'

'It was extremely remiss of me, before leaving Bath, not to have attained an accurate description of my ward and what she might possibly be wearing. But I harbour no doubts whatsoever, Sutton, that the young woman in the grey cloak and bonnet and my ward are one and the same person. Believe me, I shall have Miss Sarah Pennington safely installed in my grandmother's house long before you arrive there with the carriage,' and with that positive assurance Marcus went back into the inn.

He was halfway across the tap when he was accosted by the innkeeper, who kindly enquired whether he would care to browse through a copy of the *Morning Post*. Marcus accepted politely and, with the briefest of nods to acknowledge the stagecoach passengers consuming a hearty breakfast in the coffee-room, carried the journal into the private parlour to discover Sarah still there, seated at the small table near the window, busily writing a letter.

She didn't look round to see who had entered, and for a few moments he studied her, his expression a strange mixture of exasperation and gentle appreciation.

'It's good to see you are able to keep yourself occupied,

Mrs Armstrong,' he remarked, seating himself at the dining-table.

'I think boredom will prove to be the malady of us all.' She looked out of the window. The snow was so deep that it almost came up as far as the window-sill. The only tracks were those of tiny birds, braving the elements to search for scraps of food. Nothing, not even a farm cart, had risked travelling along the road. 'How long do you think we shall be stranded here, sir?'

'By the look of the sky, I should say we're in for a further fall.' No sooner had he spoken than the first flakes began to flutter to earth. 'Certainly not tomorrow. Perhaps the day after, if we're lucky.'

'Ah! May we join you?' The stylishly attired young gentleman who, Sarah noticed, had addressed Mr Ravenhurst by name the evening before entered the room, accompanied by a stockily built middle-aged man with penetrating grey eyes set in a kindly face. 'Or do we intrude?'

'Not at all, sir.' Sarah's warm, friendly smile encompassed them both. 'I did not hire this parlour for my private use. You are welcome to use it whenever you wish.'

'That is most gracious of you, ma'am,' the younger man responded. 'Ravenhurst, be kind enough to introduce me to this charming young lady.'

His dark eyes appeared above the printed page. 'Mrs Armstrong, the Honourable Mr Cedric Nutley and Mr—er—Stubbs. Mrs Armstrong, I should mention,' he went on after the gentlemen had made their bows, 'ought not to be here at all. But as she chose to go jaunting about in a snowstorm, found herself, like the rest of us, stranded here.'

Sarah, wisely, ignored the gibe, and merely satisfied herself with casting him a darkling look before resuming her seat at the small table. After exchanging a few pleasantries with Ravenhurst, Mr Nutley came over to her.

'What a charming writing-case, Mrs Armstrong!'

'Yes, it is, isn't it.' Sarah surreptitiously covered the letter that she had just begun writing with a plain sheet of paper. It was destined for an elderly lady, whom she had been in the habit of visiting regularly, and she did not wish him to catch sight of its contents, which might give rise to mention of a certain city.

'It's beautifully made, and has a secret compartment, here,' she explained, pressing one of the tiny carved squares that decorated the sides of the drawers, and a small flap sprang open, revealing the hidden section. 'Needless to say, it is empty. I never use it. In fact, the spring is a little stiff, I notice.'

Mr Nutley looked at it keenly for several moments. 'Why, unless one knew its secret, one would never suspect it was there! Which little square did you press?'

'This one—third from the end.' Closing the flap, Sarah obligingly repeated the procedure before putting away her letter and closing the case.

'Heavens above!' Marcus ejaculated suddenly, drawing everyone's attention. He turned to the front cover of the journal. 'This newspaper's over a week old. I thought the articles seemed familiar. Wait a moment, though. . . I've not read this before.'

His eyes scanned the few lines at the bottom of one of the columns. 'The Felchett diamonds have gone missing. There's a reward being offered for information leading to their return.' He raised his head, fixing his eyes on Mr Nutley. 'Did you know about this, Cedric?'

'I thought everyone knew,' the young man responded casually, before joining Mr Stubbs on the settle. 'Their disappearance was discovered on the morning after the betrothal party. You were there, Ravenhurst. Surely you cannot have forgotten?'

'I attended the party, yes,' he concurred, 'but I left early for London the following morning, and haven't been back to Oxfordshire since.'

'Oh, well, in that case——' Mr Nutley shrugged one slim shoulder '——you probably wouldn't have heard. Deuce of a to-do about it the following day when the maid discovered the necklace wasn't in her mistress's jewellery-case. Been left open all night, apparently, on the dressing-table.

'My beloved sire had gone off with Lord Felchett and a few of the other gentleman guests for a spot of shooting. By the time they returned to the house, Lady Felchett had already sent poor Harry hot-foot to London to call in the Runners. Old Felchett was furious when he discovered what his good lady had done. Well expected him to burst a blood vessel the way he went ranting on. Didn't want any fuss, you see.'

'That seems rather odd, Mr Nutley, don't you think?' Sarah remarked, frowning in puzzlement. 'You would have thought Lord Felchett would have applauded such swift action on his wife's part.'

'Perhaps. But half the gentry in the county had been invited to their son Harry's betrothal party. Some of them were staying on for the weekend, my family included. Wouldn't do to have the Runners sniffing round, asking a lot of fool questions. Might give offence. One cannot go about accusing one's neighbours, ma'am.'

'No, I suppose not,' she agreed. 'Is the necklace very valuable?'

'Lord, yes! Worth a small fortune, wouldn't you say, Ravenhurst?'

'It is certainly reputed to be very valuable, yes,' he responded, gazing fixedly at an imaginary spot on the floor. 'I wonder if there's a connection?'

He looked up to find three pairs of eyes regarding him questioningly. 'Several valuable and well-known items of jewellery were stolen in London during the Season last year. And the famous Pelstone pearls were taken when the family was in Brighton during the summer. I was just wondering if the same person or persons were involved in the robberies.'

Sarah frowned. 'But how do they dispose of the items, sir? If they are all well-known pieces, surely they would be easily recognisable?'

Marcus looked directly into the grey eyes of Mr Stubbs, who had been listening intently to the conversation. 'Now, there's an interesting point, sir, do you not think?'

Mr Stubbs's gaze did not waver. 'No honest merchant would touch 'em, of course, so I would very much think that the items must find their way into the hands of some unscrupulous dealer who would, then, either sell them abroad, or separate the stones, melt down the gold, or whatever, and have them made up in some other form.'

'I, for one, think that is monstrous!' Sarah exclaimed, appalled by the mere thought of such callous actions. 'Those jewels have probably been in the respective families for years. They must be of great sentimental value, too.'

'But not to the thieves, my dear lady,' Marcus countered, getting to his feet. 'It's turned out to be only a small flurry this time. Looks as though the sun is trying to come out again. I think I'll lend a hand at clearing the yard.'

'What an odd fellow he is!' Mr Nutley remarked when the door had closed behind Mr Ravenhurst. 'Helping servants to clear away snow? Whatever next! Do you know, Mrs Armstrong, I've known that man all my life, and yet I still don't understand him at all.'

'You live near him in Oxfordshire, Mr Nutley?' she enquired.

'Yes. My father's Sir Giles Nutley. Our home is some four miles from Ravenhurst.' Slightly effeminate arched brows drew together above insipid blue eyes. 'Deuced odd his being here, though.'

'I don't see why, sir,' Sarah responded in what she hoped was an indifferent tone. The last thing in the world she wanted was for Mr Nutley to start asking awkward questions. 'I'm sure Mr Ravenhurst mentioned that he has relatives living not too far away from here.'

'That's right, he has! I'd forgotten that.' He giggled suddenly like a schoolgirl. 'Lord! He must be smarting, having to put up at a place like this. Ravenhurst's accustomed to the very best. Well, he can afford it, not like some of us,' he went on, his tone decidedly resentful. 'Lucky dog! He's independent. He isn't forced to travel on the common stage because of the miserly allowance his father gives him.' A glinting sparkle brightened his eyes. 'But it won't be like that for much longer.'

Evidently Mr Nutley was expecting to come into money. Sarah cast a brief glance over his fashionable, yet slightly dandified attire. He was certainly able to clothe himself in the first style of elegance on his miserly allowance, if nothing else. She decided she didn't care for this sulky young man very much, but masterfully disguised her feelings as she made an excuse to leave the gentlemen to their own devices, and went out into the coffee-room to find Daisy busily clearing away the breakfast dishes.

'Here, let me help,' she offered.

'Oh, no, ma'am. There's no need for that. We've plenty of 'elp, now. Me cousin's 'ere. And that farmer and 'is wife offered their services if Pa could see 'is way to knocking a bit off their bill. They expected to be back in their own 'ome by now, and are a bit short of the readies. They've turned out to be good workers. Which is more than can be said for 'er,' she added, gesturing to the archway by which one gained access to the stairs.

Sarah caught a glimpse of a golden-haired girl in a blue dress and white apron. From what she could see of her, the slender girl appeared to be rather pretty, and Sarah could quite understand, as she looked back at Daisy's plump figure and homely face, from where poor Daisy's dislike of her cousin stemmed.

Jealousy seemed a common affliction amongst certain inhabitants of this inn, she mused as she mounted the narrow flight of stairs. Mr Nutley was definitely envious of Mr Ravenhurst's wealth, and Daisy, Sarah suspected, her cousin's good looks. Captain Carter, too, had certainly betrayed a deal of resentment, earlier, to a certain class of persons.

As she reached the top of the staircase, she saw the spinsterish-looking female who had been among the passengers off the stagecoach hurrying purposefully down the passageway towards her.

'Good morning. I am Mrs Armstrong.' Sarah stood at the head of the stairs, effectively preventing the woman's further progress. 'I, too, have been forced to seek shelter here.'

'Grimshaw. Miss Tabatha Grimshaw. Pleased to meet you,' she responded in clipped tones. Which betrayed the fact that she was anything but!

'I find all this most vexing, Mrs Armstrong,' she went on in a most agitated manner. 'As I particularly asked for peace and quiet, I did not object to being placed at the very end of the passageway in what is, I suspect, the smallest room in the house, but when I requested that no one should enter my room on any pretext, and find upon my return from breakfast that my belongings have been tampered with. . . Well, it is just too much!'

'Oh, dear. Have you discovered something missing?'

'Missing? On, no, no! Everything is there.' The icy-blue eyes behind the pince-nez shot Sarah a furtive glance. 'It is just that I have not been well of late. An irritation of the nerves, you understand. The slightest little thing seems to overset me. I am better on my own. I shall insist upon all my meals being brought up to me on a tray from now on. I must have my solitude. And I won't have my belongings touched!'

Sarah had come across many highly strung people during her years in Bath, and Miss Grimshaw gave every sign of belonging to their number. She was a tall, thin woman, whose greying hair was confined in a tight bun at the back of her head, and whose pallid complexion was evidence of poor health, as were the dark circles round the eyes.

Moving aside, Sarah cast her a sympathetic smile. 'I'm sure when you explain that you have been unwell, Miss Grimshaw, the landlady will be only too pleased to send your meals up to your room.'

'Dried-up old stick!' a voice behind her snapped, and
Sarah, after having watched Miss Grimshaw scamper
down the stairs with quite remarkable agility for a middle-
aged woman who professed to be unwell, swung round
to find the female who had been wearing the bright red
bonnet the evening before regarding her from one of the
bedchamber doorways.

Sarah's eyes began to twinkle. 'Who. . .? Me?'

The woman gurgled with laughter, a light tinkling
sound which instantly brightened the atmosphere. 'No,
Miss Grimstone, or whatever 'er name is. She never spoke
a word to anyone from the moment she entered the stage
at Marlborough. And when I asked, friendly like, if we'd
met before, she deliberately snubbed me. Miserable old
fossil!'

'Well, perhaps there's some excuse for her behaviour.
She hasn't been well.' A sudden frown creased Sarah's
forehead. 'And I don't think she's as old as she appears.'

'She's certainly a lot older than you or me. My name
is de Vine, by the way. Dorothea de Vine.'

Sarah went smilingly towards her. 'Mrs Serafina
Armstrong.'

'Is that your real name?'

'W-what?' Sarah was rather taken aback. 'Of course
it is! Why do you ask?'

The young woman entwined her arm round Sarah's
and drew her into the bedchamber. 'My name ain't really
de Vine,' she confessed in a conspiratorial whisper.
'That's me stage name. Me real name's Dottie Hogg.'

'Oh, you're an actress. How exciting!'

'It ain't all it's cracked up to be,' Dottie confessed
with a plaintive sigh. 'I'm between jobs at the moment,
as you might say. Tried me 'and in London, but it didn't

work out, so I'm going back to Bristol. Me old mother still lives there, so I'll move back in with 'er until I can gets m'self fixed up, like.'

'How I envy you! You must meet some interesting people,' Sarah remarked, accepting the invitation to sit down beside Dottie on the bed.

'You come across all sorts, that's for sure. Like that lot off the stage. Mr *Stubble* is a good sort. Nice and friendly, not like old Grimlock and that weasel-faced clerk.'

'I haven't met him yet.'

'You ain't missed much, Mrs *Armitage*. What a fuss he were creating last night! The young sprig's not so bad. Kept giving me the eye, though, but I'm used to that. And I ain't just anyone's for the asking,' she confided, much to Sarah's puzzlement. 'But that 'andsome Captain, now. Cor! I bet he could show a girl a good time. Like that gentleman friend of yourn. He's a bit stern-looking. But I like a man to be a man, if you knows what I mean. I bet he knows 'ow to treat a girl, eh?'

'Gentleman friend?' Sarah echoed, still somewhat confused by Dottie's perplexing utterances. 'Oh, you mean Mr Ravenhurst! He isn't a friend of mine. He arrived late yesterday afternoon, and we dined together.'

Dottie looked slightly nonplussed. 'Well, if that's so, you watch out, Mrs *Armshaw*. He's right taken with you. Believe me, I know the signs. The way he looked at you just before you went off to bed last—'

'You're mistaken, Dottie,' Sarah cut in. She found herself, unaccountably, blushing and hurriedly rose from the bed. 'Mr Ravenhurst isn't interested in me in the least.'

'No offence intended, I'm sure.' Dottie, too, got to her feet. 'Anyone can tell you're a lady. It was just. . . Oh, well, never mind.' She began to rummage through the contents of her cloak bag, which she had scattered across the bed. 'Here, would you like to read this? A friend give it me. Trouble is, me eyes ain't what they were, and I can't make out the print too well.'

Sarah accepted the well-thumbed volume with genuine gratitude. 'Thank you, yes. It will certainly help to pass the time.'

'And I've a letter, somewhere,' Dottie announced, arresting Sarah's progress to the door. 'Drat the thing! Where the devil did I put it?' She delved into the pockets of a rather garishly coloured red-and-green striped gown. 'I know I brung it with me. Oh, well, when I do come across it, will you be kind enough to read it to me? It's me dratted peepers, you see.'

'Of course I shall. And thank you again for the book.'

Sarah wandered along the passageway to her own room, which had been tidied in her absence. The fire had been made up, and she was about to draw the chair nearer to its comforting warmth when the sound of voices caught her attention. As her bedchamber was at the front and very end of the house, she thought at first the voices were filtering up from the private parlour situated directly below, but then she realised that they were coming from outside.

Curious, she went over to the window to discover Mr Ravenhurst, Captain Carter and two other men she did not recognise busily clearing a path along the front wall of the inn. By the deep rumbles of masculine laughter that from time to time reached her ears, the four were enjoying their task hugely. She gazed at each man in turn before her eyes became fixed on one head of dark, slightly waving hair.

Discourteous and surprisingly thoughtful by turn, Mr Ravenhurst was, as his young neighbour had remarked, a very perplexing man. Unlike Mr Nutley, however, who evidently thought it beneath his social standing, Mr Ravenhurst did not hesitate to lend a helping hand at clearing away snow or, she reminded herself, to say a simple 'thank you' to an innkeeper's daughter for a meal enjoyed.

She experienced a sudden feeling of deep regret that they had not become better acquainted during those years of his guardianship. It was unlikely now, given the over-crowded confines of the inn, that this omission would be rectified. But somehow she must contrive to attain a few precious minutes alone with him in order to declare her true identity.

The opportunity was destined not to be granted that day, however. Mr Ravenhurst was not among those who partook of a light luncheon, and Sarah did not see him again until the evening, when she entered the coffee-room to join her stranded fellow-travellers just before dinner.

She had spent most of the afternoon in the company of Dottie who, after skilfully arranging her own blonde tresses in a riot of bouncy curls, had contrived to arrange Sarah's hair in a more becoming style.

Donning her best pearl-grey gown, which she had worn on the occasions of Mrs Fairchild's exclusive little card parties, Sarah thought she looked quite presentable until Mr Ravenhurst, breaking off his conversation with Captain Carter and Mr Stubbs, came over and greeted her with,

'Oh, God! Not half-mourning again!'

She flashed him a look from beneath her long curling lashes. 'You forget, sir, I am a widow, after all.'

'You err, child. I forget nothing.' His dark, intelligent eyes looked her over from head to foot. 'The hair is a definite improvement, though.'

'Why, thank you!' Sarah felt inordinately pleased by this mild compliment. 'Miss de Vine arranged it for me. She's very clever with—'

'Miss who?' he cut in sharply.

'Miss Dorothea de Vine. Haven't you been introduced yet, sir?'

He clapped one shapely hand over his eyes. 'No, I haven't. And you can spare yourself the trouble of introducing me to the "Divine" Dorothea. Pure fabrication if ever I heard it! Still,' he tutted, 'there's plenty of that going on here.' He removed his hand and cast a brief glance at the lively and not unattractive damsel who had positioned herself at the Captain's side. 'What's her real name, by the way?' he asked, not giving Sarah the opportunity to assimilate his former remark.

'Dottie Hogg.'

'Oh, dear me, yes. I suppose there's some justification for it, then. Only slightly worse than Serafina Postlethwaite, I should say.'

This time Sarah couldn't mistake the underlying implication, and looked at him sharply, but his expression gave nothing away. In fact, he stared down at her with such a depth of warmth in his dark eyes that for some obscure reason her pulse became quite erratic, and she swiftly forgot her suspicions.

Whether or not by his contrivance, Mr Ravenhurst was seated beside her at dinner. She had suggested to the landlady earlier in the day that it would be more convenient, and involve less work, if everyone ate together in the coffee-room, after which they could all repair to the parlour, enabling the staff to clear away in peace.

The landlady had welcomed the idea, and had placed two tables together to accommodate everyone. Only the farmer and his wife, whom Sarah assumed were eating in the kitchen, and Miss Grimshaw did not join the group.

Mr Ravenhurst, as had happened the night before, proved to be an ideal dinner companion, and only twice came close to oversetting her. The first occasion was when he asked Mr Nutley, who seemed for some reason in a very subdued frame of mind, to move the branch of candles further along the table as the light was catching his young neighbour's brightly coloured waistcoat and dazzling him.

The second occurred when the middle-aged clerk, Mr Winthrope, whom Sarah had met for the first time at luncheon, began to bemoan the fare, declaring the beef overcooked and the chicken tough. Mr Ravenhurst turned his head and spoke just one soft and very idiomatic sentence. Sarah did not quite catch what he had said, but knew it must have been extremely rude, for Mr Winthrope coloured to the roots of his sparse, greying hair, and said not another word throughout the remainder of the meal.

Apart from the chastened clerk, who sought immediate refuge in his bedchamber, everyone else repaired to the parlour once the enjoyable meal was over. The innkeeper had managed to provide them with a pack of decidedly sticky and dog-eared playing cards, and Sarah found herself making up a foursome at whist.

Mr Ravenhurst elected himself her partner, leaving Mr Nutley to join forces with Captain Carter as their opponents. Sarah and her partner won the first rubber, and then went on to win the second very comprehensively, which won her a modicum of praise from Mr Ravenhurst.

'However,' he went on to say, his tone decidedly censorious, 'it does lead one to suppose that your upbringing
was not all that it might have been, Mrs Armstrong, if
you were permitted to while away your formative years
in the pursuit of gaming.'

'Oh, yes. Such wanton dissipation! You cannot imagine
to what extent I indulged myself. I became thoroughly
depraved, in fact,' she responded airily, much to the
Captain's amusement and Mr Nutley's astonishment.

'The lady is but jesting, Cedric,' Ravenhurst assured
him. 'Your deal, I believe.'

'I'll sit this one out.' Mr Nutley rose from the table,
offering his place to Mr Stubbs. 'I think I'll track down
that rascally landlord. I have a fancy for a glass of
rum punch.'

When he returned to the room, after what seemed a
very long absence, he was bearing a tray upon which
stood several glasses and a large bowl. Pushing Sarah's
writing-case a little to one side, he set the tray down on
the small table by the window, and began to ladle out
the warm liquor. 'Who'll join me?'

Only Sarah and Mr Ravenhurst declined, but the others
were happy to imbibe in the warming drink, though the
Captain, Sarah noticed, grimaced at his first mouthful.
She offered her place to Mr Nutley, who seemed far more
convivial than he had earlier in the evening, and for a
while she sat talking with Dottie before being the first to
retire for the night.

She could hear, quite clearly, the murmur of voices
from the room below as she curled up in the comfortable
bed. She found the sounds reassuring, and was soon
fast asleep.

*   *   *

She awoke with an almost violent start sometime later. What on earth was that? A table being overturned. . .? A chair, maybe? For a few moments she lay there, not daring to move, her frightened eyes darting about the room, expecting at any moment to see a shadowy movement, but all remained still, all was quiet; not even the murmur of voices, now, from the parlour below.

Then, as the grandfather clock near the foot of the stairs struck two, she understood why. She had been asleep for several hours, not the few minutes she had first thought.

Cautiously, she eased herself into a sitting position, and felt for the tinder box. It took a moment before she had the candle on the bedside table lit; then she cast her eyes about the small bedchamber once more, just to reassure herself that there was truly no one there. All was as it should be, and yet she felt certain she had heard something. . .but what?

Wide awake now, she abandoned the notion of trying to get back to sleep for the time being, and decided to finish the letter she had begun writing the previous morning, but recalled that she had left her case downstairs in the parlour. She hesitated only for a moment then, throwing the bedcovers aside, she slipped her woollen shawl round her shoulders, and picked up the candle.

Her bare feet made hardly a sound as she tiptoed lightly along the passageway, but she was powerless to prevent the eerie creaking of the narrow stairs during her descent to the coffee-room. She had never been afraid of the dark, not even as a small child, and yet, without quite knowing why, something in the atmosphere of the place unnerved her.

It did not help matters when she bumped into one of the chairs, sending it scraping across the wooden floor, but when she began to imagine every shadow had a life of its own, and a dozen pairs of villainous eyes were watching her every move, she took herself roundly to task for such childish fancies.

Consequently, when she opened the parlour door to discover a darkly cloaked figure standing by the window, she was disinclined to believe the evidence of her own eyes, and it was only when a sudden blast of cold air blew out her candle, and the shadowy figure perched itself on the sill and swung its legs out of the open window to disappear into the night, that she realised her imagination had not been playing tricks on her after all.

Her first impulse was to turn tail and run, but she checked it, and with the self-possession that characterised her she flew across to the windows and securely fastened them, lest the intruder return.

The terrifying possibility that she still might not be alone, that the intruder might have had an accomplice, now waiting in the shadows, ready to pounce on her at any moment, crossed her mind, and she stood perfectly still, not daring to move, hardly daring even to breathe; but the only sounds she heard were the heavy pounding of her own heart, and the solemn ticking of the grand-father clock in the other room.

Slightly reassured, she very slowly turned her head, darting quick glances about the room, trying desperately to pierce the gloom. The only faint light came from the dying embers of the fire and, after taking several deep breaths in a desperate attempt to steady her fraught nerves, she made her way cautiously towards it, very nearly tripping over something lying on the floor.

With trembling hands, she felt along the high shelf until her fingers came into contact with a taper. It was

her duty to rouse the landlord, but she flatly refused to
venture one more step without the aid of a light to guide
her way.

Quickly thrusting the taper into the embers, she relit
her candle and only just managed to stifle the hysterical
cry that rose in her throat. It was not a chair leg that she
had almost tripped over, but a man's leg, a thin leg
encased in fashionable primrose knee-breeches, and she
instinctively knew, even before she had edged her way
round the end of the settle, and had forced herself to look
down into those strangely staring insipid blue eyes, that
Mr Nutley was dead.

Chapter Four

For a few moments it was as much as Sarah could do to stop her knees from buckling and to remain standing, then without conscious thought she made all haste back up the stairs and along the passageway to the room situated directly opposite her own. Pausing only a second or two to catch her breath, she scratched lightly upon the door.

'Mr Ravenhurst. . .? Mr Ravenhurst, are you awake?' she called softly, her heart pounding against her ribcage, but only silence answered her. She raised her hand, about to knock again, when she detected the distinct sound of a bed creaking. The next instant the door opened a fraction, and that heavily scowling countenance, blessedly, appeared in the crack.

'What is it? What's wrong?'

How comforting, how reassuring that curt voice sounded! 'It's Mr Nutley, sir. He's downstairs in the parlour. He's dead. . .I'm certain he's dead'

His heavy frown, if possible, grew more pronounced. 'Wait there! I'll be but a moment.'

The door closed, but opened again almost at once, and Mr Ravenhurst, looking surprisingly younger with his dark hair tousled by sleep, emerged from the room, dressed in a strikingly patterned brocade robe; and it was only by exercising the firmest self-control that Sarah suppressed the almost overwhelming urge to throw herself on that broad expanse of chest.

'Hold the dratted thing steady, girl!' he scolded, after trying unsuccessfully to light his candle from hers.

She had not realised she was trembling. She suddenly felt so very cold, and so very vulnerable standing there in just her nightdress and shawl, and with her hair tumbling down her back, but managed to gain control of herself sufficiently for him to achieve his objective at the second attempt. Then, without another word, he stalked along the landing, and Sarah almost had to run to keep up with his massive strides.

She followed him down the stairs and across the coffee-room, but flatly refused to re-enter the parlour and remained by the door, watching anxiously as he knelt down by Mr Nutley's body.

'He's dead right enough,' he confirmed, after a brief examination. 'His neck is broken.' He turned his head, saw Sarah still hovering by the door, her face as white as her nightgown, and went slowly towards her, shielding her gaze from Nutley's body.

'What happened, child?' he asked in the gentlest tone she had ever heard a member of his sex use.

'I—I came in here to collect my writing-case.' She remembered everything in minute detail, and yet it seemed so unreal, like a terrible dream. 'There was someone standing over there by the window. Before I knew what was happening, he'd disappeared.'

'Where? Through the windows?'

'Yes. I closed them. The draught blew out my candle,

you see. That's why I went across to the fire. And it was then—it was then that I saw. . .'

As her voice trailed away, Marcus went over to the windows, checked that they were securely fastened and then drew the curtains. He came back towards her, his expression thoughtful. Then he suddenly became aware of her state of dress.

'Where the devil is your dressing-gown? And you've nothing on your feet!' he admonished.

'W-what?' The scolding tone did manage to penetrate that veil of unreality which seemed to be shrouding her, but she still felt somewhat dazed by it all. 'Oh, no, I know. There wasn't room in my cloak-bag for things like that.'

He muttered something under his breath as he placed his candle down on one of the tables, and before Sarah could utter more than a stifled protest, he had lifted her into his arms.

'What on earth do you think you are doing, sir?' she demanded, indignation bringing colour back to her cheeks and restoring her self-possession with a vengeance.

'I'm putting you back to bed where you belong,' he ground out, striding purposefully back across the coffee-room, and sublimely ignoring her continued demands to be put down at once. 'And that is precisely where you are going to stay, my girl! And, for heaven's sake, hold that candle steady! I don't want covering in hot wax.'

He carried her effortlessly up the stairs and along the passageway, just as though she had weighed no more than a child, and he was not even breathing heavily, she noticed, as he lay her gently down on her bed.

'You're absolutely frozen, girl!' he continued scolding, after briefly clasping one slender foot in his warm fingers, which had the effect of sending her pulse rate soaring. Casting her a far from approving look, he straightened the bedcovers, relieved her of the candle, and then went over to light the one on the wash-stand.

'Now, I'm going to leave you for a while, but I'll be back. And don't concern yourself if you hear people moving about.'

'What are you doing?' she asked in some agitation as he removed the key from the door.

'I'm going to lock you in.' Both expression and voice were much softer now. 'But don't be alarmed, child. I shan't forget you.' He made to leave, but turned back to ask, 'You don't happen to know which room Stubbs is in, do you?'

'It's down the far end. First door on the right after the stairs, I think.'

She heard the rasping of the key being turned in the lock, the reassuring sound of his firm tread moving along the passageway, and then nothing more for what seemed an interminable length of time, but was perhaps no more than a few minutes.

Then all was action: doors opening and closing; heavy feet descending and mounting the stairs; and a continual muttering of voices. The sounds of people talking below in the parlour eventually reached her ears, but she could not discern just what was being said. She felt certain, though, that one of the voices belonged to Mr Ravenhurst, and smiled to herself as she lay her head back against the pillows.

She felt, oddly, very comforted knowing that he was there. He was so capable, so dependable. It was strange, too, the way she had instinctively gone to him in those moments of panic and confusion after she had discovered poor Mr Nutley, as though to do so were the most natural act in the world. She closed her eyes, trying ineffectually to blot out the memory of Mr Nutley's twisted body and wildly staring eyes.

Her hand trembled as she gripped the bed covers. Reaction, at last, was beginning to set in. She wished desperately that Mr Ravenhurst would return, but the grandfather clock in the coffee-room had chimed three before she heard the blessed sound of the key being fitted back into the lock, and turned her head on the pillow to see him, a cup in one hand and her writing-case in the other, enter the room.

'Ah, good! You're still awake,' he remarked in an almost conversational way, just as though nothing untoward had occurred. 'Here, sit up and drink this.'

Sarah automatically obeyed. Taking the cup of warm milk he held out, she took a large swallow, and then grimaced at its taste. 'What on earth have you put in it? It's vile!'

'Only a little brandy, my dear.' He placed the writing-case down on the floor and then sat himself on the edge of the bed. 'Now drink it up. You've had a nasty shock, and it will do you good.'

He could not prevent a smile at the suspicious glance she cast the cup's contents as she tentatively raised it to her lips. 'Why, anyone would think it was drugged!' His smile faded. 'Drugged. . .' he murmured. 'I wonder?'

'What do you wonder?'

'Nothing, child. I was merely thinking aloud. Come, down with that milk.'

Feeling fairly sure that he would not let her get away with leaving any, and that he wouldn't balk at forcing the issue by pinching her nose and tossing the contents down her throat himself, Sarah gulped down the rest, and shuddered as she placed the empty cup on the bedside table.

'What has been going on?' She lay her head back down on the pillow once again, perfectly composed, as though it were quite the norm for her to be alone with a man in her bedchamber. 'I heard a lot of moving about downstairs.'

'Nutley's body has been removed and placed in one of the outhouses,' he explained. 'The parlour has been tidied, and a thorough search has been made of the down-stairs rooms, and those bedchambers we were able to enter.'

She frowned up at him. 'Why? Surely the intruder wouldn't be foolish enough to return?'

'I should think that highly unlikely, child.' His voice was very reassuring, as was his smile. 'So rest easy. What we were endeavouring to discover was just how he managed to get in here in the first place. Although we found no sign of a break-in, the landlord freely admits that several of the window catches do not fit properly and could quite easily be forced.'

'Then, if he did not break in,' she said after a moment's thought, 'he must have been in the inn already, or. . .'

'Or someone let him in,' he finished for her. 'Yes, child. They seem the only logical alternatives. In the ordi-nary course of events, a magistrate would have been summoned without delay. Unfortunately, the nearest lives some three miles from here. Getting a message to him is out of the question for a day or two, so we are obliged to deal with the investigation ourselves.'

'Oh, dear.' A wickedly mischievous twinkle brightened her eyes. 'How tiresome for you, sir! You didn't expect to have anything like this thrust upon you when you sought shelter here, did you?

'No, I most certainly did not! Nor have I any intention of taking responsibility for the unfortunate affair,' he said determinedly. 'And that, my child, is precisely why I did not hesitate to rouse Mr Stubbs.'

'Mr Stubbs?' she echoed, perplexed.

A wry smile curled his lips. 'Our friend Mr Stubbs is none other than a Bow Street Runner.'

'Good heavens!' Sarah was astounded. 'Well, it just goes to show one should never take people at face value.'

'It does indeed,' he concurred, his twisted smile returning. 'He wanted to question you tonight, but I wouldn't hear of it. But if you're not too tired, perhaps you could explain to me exactly what happened, precisely what you saw?'

Sarah was silent for several moments, her brow furrowed in deep thought.

'Something woke me,' she began. 'At first I thought there was someone in my room, but now, of course, I realise the sound must have come from the parlour directly below. I heard the grandfather clock chime the hour, and lit my candle. I knew I wouldn't go back to sleep, so I decided to finish a letter I had begun yesterday morning. Then I remembered I had left my writing-case in the parlour and went down to collect it.'

'Go on,' he prompted when she fell silent.

'It might have been my imagination, but there was something in the atmosphere of the place. . .something eerie.' She shuddered at the memory. 'I kept imagining there were people lurking in every shadow. So, by the time I did enter the parlour, and saw someone by the window, I was fully convinced I was seeing things.'

'Were the windows open at this point?'

She frowned in an effort to remember. 'Yes. Yes, they must have been, because the draught blew my candle out.'

'I imagine, then, our intruder must have heard your approach.'

'Well, I'm not surprised,' she responded frankly. 'I bumped into one of the coffee-room chairs, sending it skidding across the floor.'

'That must have been what I heard. Go on,' he urged again.

Sarah shrugged. 'You know the rest, sir. He escaped through the window, I relit my candle, and then. . .and then discovered Mr Nutley.'

'You said "he", child. Are you sure it was a man?'

'Oh!' Sarah fixed her eyes on the strong column of his neck. Some detached part of her brain registered that there were dark hairs clearly showing between the lapels of his dressing-gown, but so hard was she concentrating on trying to conjure up a clear vision of the intruder that she paid little heed to this rather startling discovery. 'I assumed it was a man. Whoever it was was certainly not as tall as you, sir, more Mr Nutley's height, or maybe an inch or two taller. I cannot be sure because he was wearing a dark cloak with the hood drawn over his head, which might have made him appear taller. He was certainly wearing boots and breeches—which, of course, would suggest a man—and yet. . .and yet something struck me as rather odd at the time, but for the life of me I cannot think what it could have been.'

'All right, my child, that's enough for tonight.' Marcus rose to his feet. 'You'll need to repeat what you've told me to Stubbs in the morning, but do not worry—I fully intend to be present when he questions you.'

The fact that he should insist upon being with her during the interview did not occur to her; she was just grateful that he was offering his support. She watched him move across to the window to check that it was securely fastened. 'What's Mr Stubbs doing here, sir? Is he on the trail of some villain?'

'In a manner of speaking, yes.' He picked up the candle on the wash-stand before moving back over to the bed, and looked down at her with his attractive smile. 'But, unless you are a jewel thief, my dear, you've nothing to fear.'

'Oh, I see.' Her eyes glinted like those of a child who was about to indulge in some new and exciting game. 'The diamond necklace you were discussing yesterday, I should warrant.'

'Amongst others, yes. He's learnt of a certain gentleman in Bristol who doesn't bother asking too many questions about items brought to his establishment. Now, that really is enough for tonight!' he said authoritatively, like a strict uncle dealing with a recalcitrant child. 'Try to get some sleep. I shall lock your door again, but don't worry. I shall sleep with mine open, and shall hear you if you should call.'

It never entered her head to protest. The brandy was beginning to take effect, and she had no troubling in dropping off to sleep.

When she opened her eyes again it was to discover that it was morning and to find Daisy standing beside the bed.

'Ooh, ma'am, what dreadful goings on, eh? That poor young gentleman. Me and Rose learned all about it when we arrived. Ma and Pa's right upset. Never 'ad anything like this 'appen 'ere afore.'

'Yes. It will be a shock to everyone.'

'Aye. And you most of all, I'll warrant. It must of been terrible finding 'im that way. How are you feeling, Mrs Armstrong?'

'Dreadful!' Sarah placed her hand to her throbbing temple. 'Mr Ravenhurst laced my milk with brandy. And now I have the headache!'

'You ain't the only one, ma'am,' Daisy informed her, her plump face breaking into what Sarah considered an extremely callous smile. 'Apart from Mr Ravenhurst, everyone seems to 'ave a sore 'ead this morning.'

Sarah watched Daisy draw back the curtains, and then screwed up her eyes against the painfully bright light. 'What time is it?'

'Getting on for ten, ma'am. Mr Ravenhurst said as how you weren't to be disturbed any earlier.'

The dratted man seemed to be taking an awful lot upon himself! Sarah felt quite out of charity with him as she eased herself into a sitting position so that Daisy could place the tray on her lap. She found she had little appetite, but managed to force down a buttered roll and to drink a cup of coffee before placing the tray back on the bedside table.

When she went down to the coffee-room, half an hour later, it was to find Mr Ravenhurst and Captain Carter seated at a table. Mr Ravenhurst had his face buried between the printed sheets of a newspaper, but raised his head at her approach, and rose to his feet, his dark eyes scrutinising her face.

'How are you feeling this morning?' he enquired gently, and could not mistake the flash of annoyance in her eyes before she seated herself at the table.

'But for you, sir, I think I would have been perfectly well. He took it upon himself to force brandy down my throat,' Sarah explained in response to the young Captain's puzzled look.

'If it's any consolation, child,' Marcus drawled, sounding sublimely unconcerned, 'there are others similarly afflicted.'

'So I have been reliably informed. But it is scant consolation.'

He smiled at the pettish tone as he turned his attention once again to the journal. 'How riveting!' he remarked in an attempt to change the subject. 'It would seem the Fair Langley is rivalling Sarah Siddons in popularity.'

'I have never been to the theatre, so have never been privileged to see either of them,' Sarah admitted, placing her elbows on the table and resting her chin on her hands. 'But I believe Mrs Langley is considered a very handsome woman.'

'Like yourself, ma'am, I have never seen the lady perform,' the Captain responded, 'so cannot comment on her degree of beauty, but can safely say that although men may appreciate handsome women, we much prefer pretty ones. Eh, Ravenhurst?'

'Infinitely,' he answered, his eyes resting on Sarah's delicately featured profile.

It wasn't necessary to look at him; she instinctively knew those dark eyes were turned in her direction, and could feel the heat glowing in her cheeks. There had been an unmistakable teasing quality in the Captain's voice, but not in Mr Ravenhurst's, and she felt untold relief when there was the sound of a door opening, and Dottie emerged from the parlour, holding a highly perfumed handkerchief to her temple.

'Oh, Mrs *Armitage*! What a to-do, eh?' she wailed. 'It were bad enough waking up with the worst 'ead I've 'ad in years, but then to be questioned as though I was a common criminal. And 'ere I thought Mr *Stebbs* were such a nice man, too!'

'He is only doing his duty, madam,' Marcus responded, displaying not a ha'p'orth of sympathy.

'I know that, Mr *Ravenleigh*, but the whole business 'as sent me quite unnecessary, and I think I'll lie down for a bit.' She cast an appealing glance at the more sympathetic younger man. 'Would you assist me up to my room, Captain? Me legs feel all queer.'

Rolling his eyes in Mr Ravenhurst's direction, the Captain rose from the table. 'It will be my pleasure, Miss de Vine.'

Sarah frowned in puzzlement as her eyes followed their progress towards the stairs. 'Do you know, sir, I do not think Dottie can be a very good actress. She cannot even remember people's names. So how on earth does she memorise her lines?'

His lips twitched as he rose from the table. 'I think the theatre plays only a small part in our "Divine" Dorothea's life, my little innocent. Her talents, unless I'm very much mistaken, lie in quite another direction. Now, do not let us keep Mr Stubbs waiting.'

Only for an instant, as Sarah entered the room, and stared briefly at that portion of floor where Mr Nutley's body had lain, did she experience any slight trepidation. Mr Stubbs, looking very efficient, sat at the table with several sheets of his hand-written notes in front of him. She answered all the questions he put to her clearly and without hesitation, but she was unable to tell him any more than she had told Mr Ravenhurst the night before.

'And nothing else has occurred to you?'

The question came from her guardian, and she turned her head to look directly into his eyes. 'Yes, sir, it has. Why do so many people appear to be suffering from the headache this morning? Mr Stubbs, here, appears similarly afflicted.'

The Runner had, indeed, been massaging his forehead on several occasions, but his perceptive grey eyes had remained fixed on Sarah throughout the interview. He turned his gaze on to Mr Ravenhurst, one greying brow rising. 'I think we can tell her that, sir, don't you?'

'I don't think there's any need,' Sarah put in before Mr Stubbs could explain. 'With the exception of Mr Ravenhurst, everyone was drugged.'

'Clever girl!' Marcus's lips curled into an appreciative smile. 'Stubbs and I had come to that conclusion.'

'Normally, ma'am, I am a very light sleeper. It is essential in my line of work. But last night I slept heavily. I heard nothing. In fact, it took Mr Ravenhurst, here, a full five minutes to rouse me.'

'The drug could not have been in the wine,' Sarah voiced after a moment's intense thought, 'because I had a glass with my dinner. Therefore, it must have been. . .'

'In the punch,' Marcus finished for her. 'I did notice yesterday evening that although Nutley poured himself a glass, it remained on the table by his elbow, untouched. It's a pity, in this instance, that the lady of the house is such a diligent person. She cleaned both bowl and glasses before retiring for the night, so we are unable to confirm our theory.'

'I see.' Again Sarah became thoughtful. 'Wait a moment, though. What about Miss Grimshaw and Mr Winthrope? They did not join us yesterday evening.

Have you had the opportunity to question them?'

'Yes, I have, ma'am.' Mr Stubbs referred to his notes. 'Miss Grimshaw is in the habit of taking a few drops of laudanum in water last thing to help her sleep, and so heard nothing. And Mr Winthrope came down to request more candles, as he'd been reading throughout the evening, and was accosted by Mr Nutley who, having just finished preparing the punch in the coffee-room, persuaded the gentleman to sample a glass.

'Mr Winthrope assures me that ordinarily he doesn't imbibe in strong liquor, but isn't averse to the occasional glass of rum punch. And as for the others. . .' Again he referred to his notes. 'Not one of them heard a thing until roused by Mr Ravenhurst and myself. Although Mr Ravenhurst's groom mentioned that Nutley did try to persuade him and the innkeeper's son to sample a glass of the punch whilst they were keeping each other company in the tap, but they both declined.'

Sarah's frown returned. 'But why should Mr Nutley have attempted to drug everyone? Unless, of course, he had arranged to meet the man in the cloak and didn't want anyone to witness that encounter.'

'A distinct possibility, child,' Marcus agreed. 'Or his intent was quite otherwise, and he was disturbed by our mysterious cloaked figure. But whether or not his death was accidental, we can only speculate at this juncture.'

Sarah shuddered convulsively as she rose from the table. 'Unless you've any further questions, Mr Stubbs, I think I shall return to my room.'

She closed the door behind her, leaving the two men in private. Although Mr Ravenhurst had flatly refused to take any responsibility for the enquiry into the sad affair until a magistrate could be summoned, it was evident that, perhaps because he was acquainted with Mr Nutley's family, he felt obliged to take some interest in the proceedings.

And as Mr Ravenhurst had proved, beyond a shadow of a doubt now, he was not a man to shirk any obligation. So why, then, a tiny voice reminded her, had he behaved so out of character during his guardianship of her? It just didn't make sense.

Sarah pondered anew over this rather puzzling circumstance as she made her way back to her room. At the head of the stairs she heard one of the bechamber doors close, followed by the sound of humming, and turned to see Daisy's pretty golden-haired cousin tripping lightly along the passageway towards her.

The girl cast her a rather furtive glance as she brushed past and Sarah's eyes narrowed suspiciously as she watched her progress down the stairs. Perhaps Daisy's dislike of her cousin was well founded, after all: there was something decidedly sly about that girl.

Dismissing the thought from her mind, she went along the passageway and into her own room. Although there were no signs, yet, of a thaw, there had been, thankfully, no further falls of snow during the night, and the day was dry and bright.

Sarah decided that she had had more than enough of being cooped up in the inn, and collected her cloak from the wardrobe. As she swirled it about her shoulders, the folds caught Dottie's book, which had been placed on the bedside table, sending it tumbling to the floor.

Bending to retrieve the volume, Sarah noticed a folded sheet of paper lying beside it and, believing it to be her own, cast her eyes over the few lines written in a rounded childish scrawl: *I am glad you did that to the little worm,*

Dottie. He had it coming to him. Hope everything turns out well for you. Eliza.

Why, this must be the letter that Dottie had been searching for the previous day! She must have slipped it inside the back cover of her book for safekeeping, and then forgotten where she had put it, Sarah decided, and so took it along to Dottie's room.

After scratching lightly upon the firmly closed door, and waiting in vain for her summons to be answered, Sarah pondered on what she should do, for she could clearly detect soft moaning sounds and the creaking of bedsprings, so knew there was someone within.

Fearing Dottie might be unwell, she very gently turned the doorknob, opening the door sufficiently for her to poke her head into the room, and then promptly coloured to the roots of her hair at the sight that met her naïve, incredulous gaze.

She had often pondered with her friend Clarissa on the mysteries of the marriage bed, those untold, secret dealings between men and women that married ladies carefully avoided discussing with their younger and less experienced counterparts. Sarah realised in those few brief moments of acute embarrassment and stupefaction that she was witnessing, first-hand, those veiled relations between the sexes.

Then, before either Dottie or Captain Carter could detect her presence, she quietly closed the door, thrust Dottie's letter beneath, and flew down the passageway, only to collide moments later with a solid, immovable object at the head of the stairs. Strong fingers grasped her arms, steadying her, and she found herself staring up into laughing dark brown eyes.

'Anyone would imagine the devil himself were after

you. Steady, child!' Marcus then noted the heightened colour and slightly erratic breathing, and his smile faded. 'What is it? What's occurred to distress you?'

'Why, nothing! Nothing at all,' she managed, but not very convincingly. 'I'm just going out for some air,' and before he could detain her further, she broke free from his gently steadying hold and rushed headlong down the stairs.

The cold air on her burning cheeks was refreshing, and it was such a relief to be out of doors after the previous day's confinement. The day looked set to remain dry and bright, giving one reason to hope that the thaw would not be long in commencing. No vehicle, though, had braved a journey along the road; the snow remained a furrowless thick blanket of white, sparkling brightly like some glinting bed of crystals.

A sudden gust of the biting northerly wind sent the brightly coloured inn sign swinging to and fro on its rusty hinges, drawing her attention, and she looked up to see the painting of an old man making his weary way towards a building whose windows were ablaze with welcoming light.

'The Traveller's Rest,' she murmured with a wry little smile. There had been precious little rest for the weary travellers who had sought shelter beneath this roof, and she certainly didn't envisage that state of affairs changing after the tragic events of the previous night.

'Ah! So there you are.'

Sarah swung round to see Mr Ravenhurst, seemingly oblivious to the icy conditions underfoot, striding towards her. Evidently, he had doubted her assurances that she was perfectly all right, and had come out in search of her. How very thoughtful! She felt strangely touched by this obvious concern for her welfare.

'Not that we can walk very far, but permit me to show you round the outside of our temporary dwelling place,' and without giving her the opportunity to acquiesce or not he reached for her hand.

In those moments when those long shapely fingers, strong yet gentle, curled about hers to entwine her arm through his, a vision of yet another long-fingered, shapely hand fondling a large white breast flashed before her mind's eye. What must it feel like to be caressed like that? she wondered, as Dottie's image was replaced suddenly by one of herself lying on a bed, a lean, muscular frame stretched out alongside her.

She was aware of a strangely powerful craving developing deep within. Only it wasn't the image of the tall Captain's well-muscled frame pressed against her soft white nakedness that aroused this frighteningly powerful yearning, but that of the man beside her.

A further gust of icy-cold wind brought her out of her reverie with a start. What on earth had come over her to imagine such things? she wondered, appalled at having had such abandoned thoughts. Surely she couldn't possibly be attracted to this man? No, unthinkable! Ravenhurst was her guardian, for heaven's sake! He stood in place of a. . .a father.

She cast a tentative glance up at that hard-featured profile. The trouble was, though, she just couldn't bring herself to see him in that light; and only hoped, as they set off on their stroll round the rambling old building, that if he should happen to notice the renewed scarlet flush mounting her cheeks he would put it down to nothing more than the frosty nip of the cold north wind.

The men had stuck to their task the previous day, and

had managed to clear a path all round the inn, but Sarah's
stout boots slipped occasionally on the exposed stones,
and she was glad of that supporting arm. They inspected
the exterior of the many outhouses, but Sarah carefully
avoided enquiring into which Mr Nutley's body had been
placed, and they ended their tour in the long stone-built
barn, which contained only three horses and one cow.

They sat themselves down on the wooden stools placed
near the open doorway, and after a few minutes Sarah
realised that Mr Ravenhurst, who had been conversing
quite amicably during their short tour, had grown very
quiet as his dark eyes scanned the rear aspect of the inn.

'What are you studying so thoughtfully, sir?'

'That lean-to roof.'

Sarah turned her attention to the single-storey construction, which had obviously been added to the original
building at some later date, and which ran along the whole
length of the inn's back wall. Its sloping roof was tiled,
and at its highest point was only a matter of a foot below
the four bedroom windows.

'Are you thinking the intruder might have entered the
inn that way?'

'It's a possibility, certainly. Climb on that water butt
at the end there, and you can get on the roof without any
trouble. Why, even a child could do it! If there is a loose
catch on any one of those windows, it would be a simple
matter to insert a knife or some other thin implement and
flick open the catch.

'It's a great pity the landlord and his son cleared the
snow off that roof yesterday. We would have seen footprints and known for sure, then. But as some of the
timbers are not too sound, it's quite understandable why
they did so.'

'Supposing our intruder did enter by one of those windows, he was taking an awful risk. After all, he wasn't to know that most of the occupants of those rooms had been drugged,'

'Very true.'

'And if that were, indeed, the case, surely the motive for doing so must have been robbery, and not to meet Mr Nutley.'

'It certainly looks that way.'

'More importantly, though, where did he go after climbing out of the parlour window? Travel is nigh impossible, even on a horse. Nothing has passed along that road for a day and a half. I know one can manage to walk into the village because Daisy and Rose have done so, but—' She gave a sudden start. 'Oh, Lord! You don't think it was one of the local inhabitants, do you?'

'That, too, is a distinct possibility.'

She looked searchingly at him. 'But you don't think so, do you?'

'I'm not sure what I think, child. But Nutley drugged the rum for some purpose. And if we could uncover why he did that, it might give us the answers to a great many questions.' He stood up and assisted Sarah to her feet. 'Come, let us return indoors. It will soon be time for luncheon.'

Leaving Mr Ravenhurst to quench his thirst with a tankard of the landlord's excellent home-brewed, Sarah made her way up the stairs, blushing slightly as she hurried past Dottie's room. She had only just hung her cloak back in the wardrobe when there was a knock on the door, and she turned, surprised, to see Miss Grimshaw quietly enter the bedchamber.

'Mrs Armstrong, I thought it my duty to come and see

you. How are you feeling? What a terrible thing to have happened!' She slumped down, uninvited, on to the only chair. 'Why, we might all have been murdered in our beds!'

'I'm fine, ma'am,' Sarah assured her. 'It was kind of you to take the trouble to enquire.'

'You saw who killed poor Mr Nutley, so I've been told.'

'I certainly saw the intruder, ma'am. But whether or not he was responsible for Mr Nutley's death. . .'

'Yes, yes. I suppose it might have been an accident, but. . . Oh, dear! My poor nerves won't stand much more of this. I can hardly wait to be away from this wretched place!'

'I think we all feel the same.'

Miss Grimshaw cast her a rather penetrating glance before staring fixedly down into her lap. 'Yes, yes. I dare say. But I expect you will need to stay to see the magistrate or—or someone. After all, you're the only one who saw the intruder.'

'I saw a figure, yes, but I didn't see his face. I could pass him in the street and wouldn't recognise him.'

'Oh, I see! Well, in that case, there would be little point in your remaining.' Miss Grimshaw placed a hand to her temple. 'I long to be with my sister in Bristol, Mrs Armstrong. Even though I didn't really know the young gentleman, I'm afraid this dreadful business has quite overset me. Did you know Mr Nutley at all well? Did you become acquainted yesterday?'

Sarah thought this rather an odd question to ask, but didn't hesitate to respond. 'Naturally we had some conversation. It is rather difficult to avoid one another in this inn. But we had never met before. Mr Ravenhurst knew

him, however. I believe he lives not too far away from
Mr Nutley's parents. I suppose that is why he has taken
an interest in proceedings.'

'A very proper attitude!' Miss Grimshaw remarked,
rising to her feet. 'Well, I shan't detain you further, Mrs
Armstrong. It will soon be time for luncheon, and you
are no doubt eager to join the others downstairs.'

'Why not eat with us yourself, ma'am?' Sarah suggested. 'It might help to keep your mind off things.'

'That is kind of you, but I'm not very good in mixed
company. I think gentleman find me a little trying. No,
I'm better on my own.'

Sarah, watching the woman leave the room, experienced the most peculiar feeling of unease. Had that visit
really been made out of the purest motives? She could
not help thinking that it was quite otherwise.

Chapter Five

Sarah was rudely awoken not by Daisy this time, bringing in the morning pitcher of warm water, but by a bedroom door being slammed, quickly followed by the sound of heavy footsteps hurrying along the passageway. It was in all probability only the farmer and his wife rising early as usual in order to help in the kitchen. In which case, it would be quite some time before the pitcher arrived, she thought and, turning on to her side, promptly went back to sleep.

When she awoke again, it was to see a bright ray of sunlight filtering though the chink between the patterned drapes. Swinging her feet to the floor, she padded across to the window, and could have wept for joy at the sight that met her eyes as she drew back the curtains.

Some time during the night the wind had changed direction from a biting-cold northerly to a much friendlier westerly. Although the landscape was still covered in its blanket of white, droplets of water were running down the window panes. The thaw had begun!

Deciding not to wait for Daisy, Sarah washed in the contents of the previous day's pitcher. It was unpleasantly cold, but she didn't care. The only thing that mattered was that she would soon be able to leave this place; perhaps not that day, but certainly the next, providing, of course, the wind continued to blow from its present direction and, perish the thought, there were no fresh falls of snow.

She refused, however, to be pessimistic and, hurriedly finishing her toilet, went downstairs, expecting to join the other no doubt equally jubilant stranded travellers, only to discover the coffee-room, surprisingly, deserted.

She frowned as she went over to the table at which they usually ate their meals. Not even the covers had been laid. How very odd! Although her stay at the inn had been far from pleasant, she had no fault to find with the landlady, who always had meals prepared on time. A quick glance at the grandfather clock, solemnly ticking away in the corner, confirmed that she was far from late in coming down to breakfast. So where was everyone?

It was then that she detected the sound of voices in the parlour. Surmising that breakfast for some reason was once again being served in there, she was about to enter when a noise behind her caught her attention and she turned to see Daisy, carrying a large tray, enter the coffee-room. One swift glance at those red-rimmed eyes was sufficient to warn Sarah that all was not as it should be.

'Why, Daisy! Whatever's the matter?'

'Oh, ma'am!' Depositing the tray on the table and herself down on a chair, Daisy sniffed loudly. 'It—it's our Rose. She—she were found behind the hen-coop this morning by our Joe. She's been done for. . . Her throat's been cut!'

Sarah, joining her at the table, could hardly believe it, didn't want to believe it. 'When did it happen?'

'During the night, they reckon.' Daisy drew out her handkerchief and blew her snub nose vigorously. 'I overheard Mr Stubbs say as 'ow she'd been dead for several hours.'

Sarah frowned. 'But I understood that you and Rose walked back to the village together, directly after serving dinner here in the evening.'

'Aye, Mrs Armstrong, that be right. And we walked back to me aunt's house together last night. I been sharing Rose's room. We ate our supper, and then went to bed at the usual time, but when I wakes this morning she weren't there. I thought it odd, but didn't pay it much mind. I thought she'd just got up early and come 'ere by 'erself. Our Joe found 'er when he went out to collect the eggs for breakfast.'

'So, at some point during the night,' Sarah remarked after a moment's intense thought, 'Rose got out of bed, dressed and came here. She must have arranged to meet someone, surely?'

'Aye, ma'am, that's what we all thinks. I know its wrong to speak ill of the dead, but she were a right flighty piece. There be no getting away from it. Our Joe were right fond of 'er, but she weren't interested in 'im. Kept calling 'im a slow-top and the like. You can bet your life she came 'ere to meet some man. She were forever teasing the village lads, setting one against the other. I reckons one of 'em 'ad 'ad enough, and did for 'er.'

It was certainly a possibility, especially if Rose's disposition was flirtatious. But why arrange to meet someone here? Sarah wondered. It just didn't make sense. Surely if Rose had wanted the meeting with this man kept secret, she would hardly select directly outside her aunt's house as a trysting place?

Reaching for the coffee-pot, Sarah was about to pour herself a cup when the sound of hysterical sobbing reached her ears, and she turned her head in the direction of the parlour's closed door.

'Who on earth is in there?'

'Mr Stubbs carted Miss de Vine in there quite some time ago, ma'am,' Daisy disclosed in a conspiratorial whisper. 'Summat to do with a letter found on our Rose. Though what Rose were doing with it, I can't imagine. Couldn't read a word, she couldn't!' The pathetic sobs continued. 'Sounds right upset, don't she? Wonder what they're doing to 'er in there?'

'I don't know, but I mean to find out!' Without a moment's hesitation Sarah stormed into the parlour to discover not only Mr Stubbs, but Mr Ravenhurst too, and poor Dottie, her elbows resting on the table, and her face buried in her hands. 'What on earth is going on?' she demanded, the light of battle in her eyes.

'You should not be here, child.' Marcus's tone betrayed his annoyance at the interruption, but Sarah stood her ground.

'I have as much right to be in here as you have,' she countered and, ignoring that, now, all-too-familiar low growl, calmly closed the door and moved towards them.

Dottie grasped Sarah's hand in pathetically trembling fingers. 'Oh, Mrs Armstrong!' she wailed, for perhaps the first time in her life remembering someone's name correctly. 'They say I done it, but I didn't. I swear I didn't!'

'We're saying nothing of the sort, you foolish creature!' Marcus snapped as he continued to stare in a far-from-friendly fashion at Sarah. 'We are merely trying to discover why a letter written to you was in that servant girl's possession.'

'And I keep telling you it ain't mine!' Dottie cast her blue eyes up to Sarah in wide appeal. 'They won't believe me, but I ain't never seen it before in my life.'

Sarah turned to Mr Stubbs. 'May I see this letter?' and without the least hesitation he handed it across to her. The ink was smudged, but the writing was still legible, and she had no difficulty in recognising it as the letter that had fallen from the book, and which, subsequently, she had slipped beneath Dottie's door. As the note had her name clearly written on it, it was extremely foolish of Dottie to deny ownership, unless. . .

Sarah gave a sudden start as a suspicion crossed her mind. Raising her eyes, she held Mr Ravenhurst's angry gaze above Dottie's head, and then quite deliberately turned the letter the other way up before handing it to Dottie. 'Just have one more look to make sure. I know your eyes aren't too good, and the ink is rather smudged. But, just to be certain.'

Sarah saw enlightenment dawn on the men's faces as Dottie, without turning the letter the right way up, cast her eyes over its contents, just as though she were reading every word.

'No, I ain't never seen it before,' she confirmed.

'No, but I most certainly have,' Sarah astonished them all by admitting. She calmly took the letter from Dottie and handed it back to Mr Stubbs, who was regarding her with intense interest now. 'Dottie loaned me a book the day after we all arrived here. Yesterday morning I accidentally knocked the book on to the floor, and that letter fell out. It wasn't until after I had apprised myself of its contents that I realised it wasn't mine, and so took it along to Dottie's room.'

'But you never gave it to me!' Dottie stated flatly.

'No, I know I didn't. You—er—were not alone at the time. I believe Captain Carter was with you, so I pushed it under your door.' Sarah could feel the heat rising in her cheeks, and carefully avoided looking in Mr Ravenhurst's direction.

'There are one or two other rather important facts you ought to be aware of, Mr Stubbs. . .I have it on the best authority that the poor dead girl was illiterate. Furthermore, how did that letter come to be in her possession? More interestingly, though, the letter, I noticed, has been deliberately altered. It was signed by someone calling herself Eliza, not A Well-wisher.'

'Eliza Cooper!' Dottie exclaimed. 'She were working at that theatre with me.'

Sarah cast a look of comical dismay at Mr Ravenhurst. 'You're certain her name is Cooper?' she asked tentatively, knowing all too well the lively damsel's propensity for getting names wrong.

'Course I am!. . .or it might be Hooper,' Dottie amended after a moment's thought. 'Something like that, anyhow.'

Sarah could not prevent a twitching smile. 'And the—er—little worm your friend Eliza refers to is. . .?'

'Oh, 'im! He were the boss o' that rubbishing place. Dirty old demon! He were always after us girls. Wouldn't leave us alone.'

Tears forgotten, Dottie gurgled with laughter. 'I got 'im a bit tipsy one afternoon, took off all his clothes and got one o' the lads to 'elp me carry 'im on to the stage. Brought the house down, it did, when he stood up stark naked in the middle of the first act.' She raised her shoulders in an indifferent shrug. 'Course, he gave me the push afterwards, but it were worth it.'

'I dare say all this can be confirmed, Mr Stubbs,' Sarah remarked airily. She felt rather pleased with herself for coming so successfully to Dottie's aid and, although Mr Ravenhurst's brows remained fixed in a disapproving scowl, Mr Stubbs, before she went out, looked far from displeased with her interruption.

Her appetite having deserted her completely, Sarah went directly up to her room to collect her cloak. As she stepped outside the inn, the rapidly melting snow squelched beneath her boots. There were large puddles everywhere, and several wheel tracks, now, along the road. Life, it seemed, was getting back to normal.

But would life ever be the same at The Traveller's Rest? she wondered, walking across the yard. Certainly not for some considerable time. She shook her head in disbelief. It seemed incredible that such grisly events had taken place in this idyllic rural setting. Two deaths in as many days! A frisson of fear feathered its way down the length of her spine as the gruesome thought of who might be next crossed her mind.

'Oh!' She gave a sudden start as she walked into the stable. 'I didn't see you standing there, Captain.'

'Sorry if I startled you, ma'am.' He stepped out of the shadows. 'Came out to blow a cloud, as there were no signs of breakfast being served.'

'It is ready now,' she informed him, sitting herself down on one of the low stools. 'What do you make of this sad business, Captain? I must confess it has me puzzled.'

Flicking the cigar butt into the yard, he sat beside her on the other stool. 'I don't know, ma'am. Nutley's death

might well have been an accident. He might have fallen
awkwardly, and hit his head on the edge of the settle,
and it was that which broke his neck. But the young
girl. . .?' He shook his head. 'That was murder. . .cold-
blooded murder.'

'But why on earth should anyone want to murder a—
a servant girl?'

'She might well have discovered something about
Nutley's death. When Stubbs examined the body, he
found a fragment of a five-pound note clutched in the
dead girl's fingers.'

'Blackmail?' Sarah's eyes widened for an instant, then
she became thoughtful. 'Yes. Yes, I should say Rose
would have been capable of that. After all, where else
would she have come by such a large sum of money? I
wonder just what she had discovered. . .and, more importantly, about whom? Surely not someone staying at
the inn?'

'It certainly looks that way, Mrs Armstrong. The
weapon used in the attack was lying in the snow beside
the body. The landlady recognised it as one of her own
kitchen knives.'

'Oh, my God!' Sarah's stomach lurched violently at
the mere thought of someone at the inn being the culprit.
'I know Dottie's letter was found in the dead girl's possession, but. . . No, I cannot believe Dottie would ever
do such a thing!'

'Oh?' His russet-coloured brows rose. 'And why not?
Women are as capable as men of committing dastardly,
underhanded deeds.'

Sarah stared at him sharply. His tone had been flat,
indifferent almost, as though it would not have mattered
a jot to him if the murderer did turn out to be none other

than Dottie. Yet, how could he remain so impassive after what had taken place between them only yesterday? Surely he must care something for the woman? Or could a man share those experiences with a female and remain totally unemotional. . .? Apparently, yes.

She felt, unaccountably, annoyed, and found herself saying, a touch of censure creeping into her voice, 'But I thought you liked Dottie, Captain Carter?'

'I neither like, nor dislike her, ma'am,' he responded with brutal frankness. 'I have learnt the hard way that people are not always what they seem. And have been given little reason to trust your sex.'

Sarah's annoyance faded and she regarded him thoughtfully. His voice had remained level enough, but she had easily detected the bitterness and underlying hurt. She gazed at his strong, attractive profile.

She had liked Captain Carter from the first and, had circumstances been different, had she not been forced to play the part of a recently widowed young woman, friendly but slightly aloof, wary of every word lest she give her true identity away, she would not have objected to getting to know him a little better. He was still a young man: twenty-four; twenty-five at most. Yet, already, life had begun to etch unmistakable lines of cynicism in his young face.

'So, you have been let down by a lady, Captain. And rather badly, I suspect. And now you have scant regard for the rest of my sex.' She saw his strong hands clench, the knuckles growing white. She had no intention of prying, and was tolerably certain that he would not satisfy her curiosity if she did, but could not prevent herself from adding, 'There is a great deal of bitterness in you, sir.

And, I suspect, it does not all stem from unhappy dealings with women.'

He looked at her then, his tawny eyes questioning. 'What do you mean?'

'You made it abundantly clear, the very first morning we met, that you bore a grudge against our privileged class.'

His well-shaped mouth twisted into a begrudging smile. 'And with good reason, ma'am. Although, I suppose, you might say I number amongst them.'

'Oh?'

'My father was a younger son of a Viscount. But my mother, God bless her, came from rather different stock.'

'Really? Then we have something in common, sir,' Sarah responded, completely forgetting to put a guard on her tongue. 'My mother was a baronet's daughter, and my father a naval captain.'

'Well, well!' There was not a trace of bitterness, now, in his pleasant voice. 'Tell me, ma'am, do you ever feel that you belong in neither one class nor the other?'

She shrugged. 'To be honest, I've never given it much thought. I am what I am, sir, and there is nothing that can be done to change that. But it does anger me sometimes when people suggest that my mother married beneath her. My father was a courageous man. And I'll not hear a word said against him!'

'Good for you, ma'am!' His smile was full of appreciative warmth, and there was more than just a hint of respect in his tawny-coloured eyes, too. 'And you are wrong, by the way. . .I do not hold all members of your sex in contempt.'

'Do I intrude?' Mr Ravenhurst suddenly appeared in the doorway, his expression anything but warm. 'Stubbs is looking for you, Carter,' he informed him curtly. 'Wants to ask you some questions.'

'Lord! It's worse than the Spanish Inquisition in this place! In fact, I'll be glad to return to that country. It's a dashed sight more restful.' The Captain reluctantly rose to his feet. 'May I escort you back inside, Mrs Armstrong?'

'I am more than capable of performing that courtesy!' Marcus snapped out. 'Therefore, do not let us detain you.'

Sarah saw the Captain's smile fade and his eyes narrow, and hurriedly intervened. 'You go on ahead, sir. I shall be along presently.' For a few moments Sarah watched his progress across the yard, and then turned a reproachful look up at the man glowering above her. 'Are you always in such a disagreeable mood before noon?'

'Only when I'm put into one by damnably foolish actions!' he retorted. 'What do you mean by remaining out here alone with that man?'

How dared he adopt such a high-handed tone with her! Sarah rose from the stool, her bosom heaving. 'And what, pray, has that to do with you, sirrah?'

'God give me strength!' he rasped through clenched teeth and, before she knew what he was about, he took a firm hold of her upper arms and shook her none too gently. 'You brainless creature! A young female has been brutally murdered here within the last twelve hours, possibly by someone residing at this inn, and you wander about aimlessly, just as though nothing untoward had occurred.'

'Oh, how dare you!' Sarah gasped, breathless from the shaking. She had never been so ill-used; nor could she ever recall feeling so angry with anyone in her life before.

'Kindly remove your hands from my person. I dislike it excessively!'

Her lofty tone drew a ghost of a smile to his lips. 'You might need to accustom yourself, my girl.'

'Now you are being ridiculous! As ridiculous as suggesting Captain Carter is the murderer.'

'I was suggesting nothing of the sort!' He released her then, his smile vanishing as he ran an impatient hand through his dark hair. 'But, unlike you, I possess some discernment, and do not accept people at face value.'

'And neither do I. But unlike you,' she mimicked him with wicked sarcasm, 'I try to look for the best in people.'

'In the circumstances, my girl, that is singularly foolish. You would do better to cultivate the opposite standpoint. What do you know about Captain Carter? What do you know about any of them?'

'Not very much, I'll admit. But I know I am as safe with Captain Carter as I am with. . .with you.'

'Oh, is that so?' he purred silkily. The sudden glint in his dark eyes should have warned her, but she took little heed. 'So, you think you are safe with me,' and before she knew it, she was in his arms and his lips had fastened securely on to hers.

Only for an instant did she struggle against the pressure of his mouth and the firm clasp of those muscular arms, then quite suddenly, unexpectedly, she found herself responding. Of their own volition her lips parted beneath his, and his kiss deepened, demanding and receiving a response.

Her imaginings of the day before were becoming a reality. That powerfully exhilarating sensation deep within began to stir once again, and her body seemed suddenly to have acquired a will of its own.

Her young breasts, pressed against that broad expanse of chest, grew hard, and she experienced an almost overwhelming desire to raise her arms, to entwine them round his neck, to run her fingers through that dark waving hair and to keep those tantalisingly disturbing lips securely fastened to her own, but his arms continued to encircle hers, restraining, keeping her his firm, but far from unwilling, captive.

When at last he released her, she was achingly aware that her traitorous body yearned to be pressed against that hard muscular frame once again, and could only stare up at him in wonder, in disbelief, almost.

'Now, let that be a lesson to you,' he said in strangely hoarse tones, his breathing as ragged as hers. 'It is unwise to be alone with any man. No matter how honourable he may be, given enough provocation, he might not always behave as he ought.'

Sarah did not wait to hear more. Reality had returned with a vengeance, and she felt the red-hot heat of shame rising rapidly to the roots of her hair. Swirling round, she hurried back inside the inn, not stopping to catch her breath until she had attained the relative sanctuary of her bedchamber.

Slumping down on to the bed, she placed her hands to her burning cheeks. What must he think of her? She had behaved no better than a wanton! And yet she seemed, even now, powerless to quell that strange yearning in her newly awakened young body. If she were to grant the opportunity, could any man have such a devastating effect on her? She quickly thrust this disturbing thought aside, for she knew it couldn't possibly be true.

On one occasion when she had been staying at her friend Clarissa's home, she had been caught in the shrubbery by a neighbour's son. She had found his advances repugnant, and had boxed the spotty youth's ears soundly when he had tried to kiss her.

Yet Mr Ravenhurst's kiss had aroused no desire for such retaliatory actions, a taunting little voice reminded her. He, of course, was a man of experience. He had probably kissed scores of females, and had no doubt enjoyed the charms of many a beautiful mistress over the years, she thought bitterly, experiencing for the first time in her life that gnawing pain of jealousy.

She released her breath in a heartfelt sigh. It was a lowering realisation, but one much better faced—he had kissed her merely to teach her a lesson. It had meant less than nothing to him. And yet, her brows drew together in a deeply puzzled frown, if that was, indeed, the case, why then had he seemed just for one unguarded moment as disturbed by the experience as she had herself?

As no logical explanation came readily to mind, Sarah tried not to dwell on the disconcerting interlude, but this proved no easy task. In the end she decided she could not possibly come face to face with Marcus Ravenhurst again until she had herself, mind and body, well in hand. She remained incarcerated in her room for the remainder of the morning, and for the first time since her arrival at the inn requested a meal brought up on a tray.

Having not partaken of breakfast, she consumed every last morsel on her plate, and had only just set the tray back down on the bedside table when there was a knock on the door, and her tormentor, himself, walked boldly into the room, just as though he had every right to do so and, what was worse, as though he hadn't a care in the world.

'Over your sulks yet?' he enquired with a wickedly

provoking smile, and that was all it needed to restore Sarah's equilibrium.

She glowered across the small room at him. 'I have not been sulking!' she retorted. 'And kindly close the door again on your way out,' she added pointedly.

'Now, that is most impolite, my girl. Especially as I came here to see if you would care to leave.'

'Leave?' she echoed, forgetting to be angry with him. 'Do you mean the roads are passable?'

'Certainly. The Mail was spotted travelling along the main road quite early this morning. The local magistrate is here now, and I've cleared it with him for us to be on our way.'

'How wonderful!' She was on her feet in an instant. 'The landlord very kindly offered to return me to—'

'I know all about that,' he cut in. 'I've already told him I'll escort you. Do you think you can be ready in half an hour? I'll meet you downstairs.'

Without giving her the opportunity to disagree with the arrangements he had undertaken on her behalf, he left the room. Not that Sarah had any intention of wrangling over who took her back to Calne. She was too excited at the prospect of continuing her journey to worry her head over such an insignificant detail, nor did it cross her mind to wonder why the magistrate had not insisted upon seeing her before she left.

It took no time at all to pack her meagre belongings, and after returning Dottie's book and bidding her farewell, she went down to the coffee-room where she discovered Captain Carter sitting quite alone.

'It would seem, sir, that I have been given permission to leave, and Mr Ravenhurst has kindly offered to escort me back to Calne. So, I must bid you farewell.'

He rose to his feet and took her outstretched hand in both his own. 'Godspeed, ma'am. I hope the remainder of your journey may pass without incident.'

'I sincerely hope so, too.' She looked earnestly into his attractive tawny-coloured eyes. 'But do you know, Captain, I should dearly love to discover just what has been going on here.'

'Probably no one ever will. But if by some chance the truth is ever unearthed, Ravenhurst has promised to write and let me know. Apparently he is acquainted with my commanding officer, Colonel Pitbury. So a letter should reach me.'

Sarah's smile was full of gentle warmth. 'Well, good-bye, Captain Brin Carter. Don't get yourself killed, will you?'

'I shall do my utmost not to.' His smile was a carbon copy of her own. 'And let us say, rather, farewell. Who knows, my dear lady, our paths may cross again. . . I, at least, sincerely hope so.'

He made to pick up her cloak-bag, but she forestalled him by grasping the handle first, and as she walked away, she had the oddest feeling that they would meet again, and perhaps more than once, in the not too dim and distant future.

The landlord, awaiting her in the tap, informed her that Mr Ravenhurst had paid her shot, and then insisted upon carrying her belongings out to the curricle. Sarah thanked him for his hospitality, said all that was proper in respect of the death of his niece and then, after requesting him to pass on her farewells to the other members of his family, scrambled up beside her escort while the landlord placed her belongings beneath the seat.

'Is it not wonderful to be on our away again, sir?'

Sarah remarked, as Mr Ravenhurst gave the bays the office to start. 'But where is your groom? Surely you're not leaving him behind?'

'Sutton is taking a seat on the stage as far as Chippenham, and then hiring a horse. I've sent him on an errand.'

'Oh, I see!' Sarah, then, bethought herself of something else, and began to rummage through her reticule. 'You paid my bill, sir. How much do I owe you?'

He cast her an impatient glance. 'Nothing.'

'But, sir, I cannot possibly permit you to——'

'If you think I'm stopping this carriage,' he cut in sharply, 'so that you can grease my palm with a few paltry coins, you can think again. Put that confounded purse away, child!'

For some reason, best known to himself, he had fallen into one of his more disagreeable moods. Sarah cast him a furtive sidelong glance. Ought she now, at this the eleventh hour, to divulge her true identity? It wasn't that she had deliberately avoided doing so; it was simply that just the right opportunity had never presented itself. Which was hardly surprising, considering the tragic events that had taken place in the past days.

A tiny sigh of indecision escaped her. He was hardly in a particularly approachable mood, and yet. . .

She was still debating with herself when they arrived at the main highway. Instead of turning right, which would have taken them to Calne, Mr Ravenhurst confounded her by turning in the opposite direction.

'Sir, you have gone the wrong way!' she pointed out in some urgency.'

'No, I haven't.'

'But, sir, Calne is the other way,' she reiterated,

slewing round in the seat to look back at the signpost.

'I'm fully aware of that, child. I know this part of the country very well.'

'Then why have you come this way?' she asked, not unreasonably, and watched a wickedly slow and infuriatingly smug smile curl his lips.

'Because, Mrs Serafina Armstrong, *née* Postlethwaite. . .alias Miss Sarah Pennington, my troublesome ward, I am taking you to a place where I can keep my eye on you!'

Chapter Six

For several moments it was as much as Sarah could do to gape at him, hoping against hope that she had misheard, but his smugly satisfied smile was proof enough that she had not. The wretch had deliberately tricked her into going with him! And she, idiot that she was, had climbed willy-nilly into his carriage like a trusting fool!

'How long have you known?' she asked at length, striving to remain calm.

'Since that first night,' he answered truthfully. 'And I cannot tell you how relieved I am that you are not foolishly trying to deny it.'

A little late for that, now, she thought wretchedly before cursing herself silently for a fool. What a complete and utter ninny-hammer not to have realised long before! Almost from the moment of his arrival at the inn he had shown such marked consideration for her welfare, and she had foolishly put it down to nothing more than a gentleman's concern for a young widow.

She raised puzzled eyes to stare blindly at the road ahead. But how on earth had he discovered her true identity? Had she foolishly given herself away? She cast her mind back, trying to recall in detail all of their many conversations, but could think of nothing she had said that might possibly have betrayed her. Curiosity got the better of her and she found herself asking outright how he had found out.

'The instant I saw those initials on your writing-case I became suspicious,' he did not hesitate to admit. 'And, of course, that damned impertinent letter confirmed it.'

'What? You mean you read. . .?' Sarah regarded him in silent dismay for a moment, remembering all too clearly the pompous, not to say condescending, tone she had adopted when composing that half-finished missive, but then the sheer effrontery of his actions brought her temper to the fore. 'How dared you rifle through my belongings, sir! How dared you! Stop this carriage at once!'

'No,' he responded with infuriating calm. 'And do not attempt to jump out,' he continued while expertly overtaking a lumbering coach. 'You might achieve your objective without suffering a sprained ankle, but you'll certainly end up with a sore rear. I'll see to that!'

He caught the tiny gasp of outrage, but missed the calculating look she cast him.

'That you would stoop so low as to lay violent hands on a defenceless female does not surprise me in the least,' she informed him loftily. 'But don't you think you've left it rather late to play the heavy-handed guardian? Or to take on the role at all, come to that?' she finished bitterly.

'So that rankles, does it?' He did turn to look at her then, and noted the stubborn set of the softly rounded chin. 'Believe it or not, child, I refrained from interfering in your upbringing because I believed you would go on much better without it. But I see, now, I was wrong.' He cast a scowling glance over her dull grey garb. 'Confound it, girl! Have you no dress sense at all? That dratted colour don't suit you in the least!'

'Dress sense?' she echoed, anger stirring once again at the unjustified criticism. 'How was I supposed to dress anywhere near decently on the paltry allowance you gave me?'

'Paltry. . .?' His brows snapping together, he drew the curricle to a halt at the side of the road, and then turned in the seat to face her squarely. 'Right, it's high time you and I sorted a few things out, young woman. Why did you suddenly take it into your head to run away?'

'I didn't run away!' she refuted staunchly. 'I left. . . well, I left because I saw little point in remaining. I shall attain my majority in June, in case you have forgotten,' she reminded him, a hint of sarcasm edging her voice. 'Your guardianship will then be at an end, and I shall need to make my own way in the world. I thought to seek some genteel occupation—a companion, or governess.'

'Governess?' he echoed, not hiding his consternation. 'What foolishness is this?'

'It might seem foolish to you, sir,' she retorted, flashing him an angry look from beneath her long, curling lashes, 'but not everyone is blessed with a vast fortune. Most of us need to work in order to live.'

'And what makes you suppose that you number amongst them?'

'I should have thought that was obvious!' she snapped. 'I have no money.'

'Who told you that?'

Sarah opened her mouth, closed it again, and regarded him questioningly. 'Are you trying to tell me that I do have money of my own?'

'Of course you have, you silly chit! Surely you cannot have forgotten your home near Plymouth? Which I have rented out, incidentally, on your behalf. And I suppose you have in the region of twenty-five thousand pounds on top of that, or perhaps a little more.'

'Twenty-five. . .?' Sarah's jaw dropped perceptively. It was a fortune! And all these years she had assumed she was little more than a pauper. 'Why didn't you tell me?' she queried, a touch of censure creeping into her voice now. 'Surely I had the right to know my financial situation, sir?'

'You had only to ask.' he responded airily.

'Ask? I did ask! Well, I wrote to you,' she amended. 'But you never once bothered to take the trouble to reply to any of my letters.'

He did not respond to this, and after a few moments Sarah turned her head to look at him. There was a strange intensity in his gaze. He was looking directly at her, but she sensed that he was seeing something else. Then suddenly she saw it too. Everything became crystal clear. He had never received her letters, not one, simply because Mrs Fairchild had never sent them.

She realised, too, in those moments of astonishing enlightenment, that the allowance he had made her over the years must have been a generous one, but most of it had gone into Harriet Fairchild's pocket or, rather, had been squandered on her ruling passion—gambling.

The woman had been so very cunning, keeping her charge away from the assemblies, and denying her the pleasure of attending many parties where she might just possibly meet some eligible young man, because her comfortable existence would then have come to an end. As long as Sarah had remained in Bath, Mrs Fairchild could continue to indulge in her vice at her wealthy cousin's expense.

'The lady I met in Upper Camden Place told me there was much that warranted investigation,' he said ominously. 'And she wasn't far wrong!'

'So, you did meet Mrs Stanton,' Sarah remarked, instinctively knowing to whom he referred. 'I thought you must have done. Your cousin wouldn't have realised where I intended going.'

'Yes, I met your friend's mother.' His expression was one of staunch disapproval as he gave the bays the office to start again. 'And I shall have a word or two to say to you in the not-too-distant future, young woman, regarding your involvement in that elopement.'

You carry on, then. See if I care, Sarah thought blithely before a thought struck her. 'Why did you suddenly take it into your head to visit Bath? Did you go there especially to see me?'

'Of course I did, silly chit! Why else should I go to that confounded place?'

'Well, there's no need to snap my nose off! How was I supposed to know?' she retorted, having come to the conclusion long since that there was little point in trying to hold a polite conversation with him. 'You've never bothered to pay me a visit before. Did you have a specific reason for doing so?'

'I intended asking whether you would care for a Season in London.'

'Truly?' Sarah was startled by the admission.

'Yes. But, given your recent conduct, I'm not so sure the offer is still open.'

For a few elated moments Sarah allowed her mind to dwell on the heady delights of a London Season, but then realised that it might be best if she didn't accept his offer. She had been confined for so many years, and the thought of being encumbered with yet another chaperon did not appeal in the least. During the past few days she had experienced the sweet taste of freedom, and had no desire to relinquish her new-found liberty.

No, she told herself, it would be better to stick to her original plan and stay with the Alcotts in Hertfordshire. Thankfully, having money of her own, she would not now need to seek a position, and once she had attained her majority, she could return to her home near Plymouth.

'It's kind of you to offer, sir, but I don't think I shall go to London.'

'I-beg-your-pardon!' he ground out, turning the curricle off the main road and down a narrow twisting country lane. 'What makes you suppose that you'll be given any say in the matter? If I say you'll go to London, you'll go, my girl! And that will be an end to it!'

'I have decided on exactly what I am going to do,' she returned, completely unruffled by the autocratic tone. 'And why have you turned down here?'

'Because I'm taking you to my grandmother's house until I can make more suitable arrangements.'

'No, I won't go there!' Determination was very evident in her voice. 'I am going to Hertfordshire.'

'Sarah,' he said with careful restraint, 'you will do exactly as I tell you.'

'Oh, do you really think so?' she parried sweetly. 'I wouldn't be too sure of that if I were you.'

He gave vent to one of his low growls, but managed to bite back the threatening retort that rose in his throat.

They continued the journey in chilling silence, but from time to time Marcus cast a suspicious glance in her direction. She kept her gaze firmly fixed on the road ahead, and her hands in her lap, looking for all the world quite innocently angelic, but he was not fooled. They had not spent those three days in close proximity without his gaining a fair knowledge of her character.

His eyes narrowed. The little minx was definitely plotting something: how to give him the slip, no doubt. He would need to watch her like a hawk for the next few days, he decided grimly.

Entering his uncle's vast Wiltshire estate by the north gate, Marcus turned the curricle on to the driveway leading to the Dower House. As soon as he had brought the team to a halt in the stableyard, and an aged groom had taken a hold of the horses' heads, he leapt out the curricle and, before she had time to alight herself, grasped Sarah's slim waist and swung her to the ground.

Ignoring the indignant look she cast him, he took a firm grasp of her wrist and almost hauled her behind him along the path to the front entrance; and only when Clegg had opened the solid oak door in answer to the summons, and they had stepped into the hall, did he release his hold.

'I take it my grandmother is in her sitting room, Clegg? Good,' he went on in response to the nod. 'This is my ward, Miss Sarah Pennington. And I should be grateful if you would keep an eye on her while I have a brief word with her ladyship.'

While he was speaking he removed his hat and coat, and promptly handed them to the bemused butler, who was regarding the very pretty, but indignant young lady with considerable interest. Then, without so much as a glance in Sarah's direction, Marcus mounted the stairs, and went directly to his grandmother's private apartments. He entered the room without knocking to find her seated in her favourite chair near the hearth.

'Ah, good! You're awake.'

The Dowager gave a start. 'Heavens above! Must you creep up on a body like that!' she greeted him crossly, but with unmistakable warmth in her grey eyes, as he came towards her chair. 'Well, and am I to congratulate you? Am I looking at a betrothed man?'

'What?' He looked nonplussed for a moment. 'Oh, no. Never got as far as Bamford's place. Been careering about the country after that ward of mine. Little baggage had the temerity to run away from Bath! Caught up with her, though. She's here now. And that's what I've come to speak to you about.'

'And so, too, have I.'

They both turned to see Sarah framed in the doorway: the Dowager's expression one of surprised interest; her grandson's one of scowling disapproval.

'I thought you knew to await me below!'

Sublimely ignoring the reproof, Sarah turned and calmly closed the door before taking several paces into the room. She had removed her grey bonnet and cloak, and was embarrassingly conscious of the Dowager's shrewd eyes scrutinising the plain grey gown, but did not betray her discomfiture, and even lifted her chin slightly.

'Your grandson, ma'am, has brought me here for some perverse reasons of his own and, I might add, against my will. Unless I am very much mistaken, he was about to persuade you to house me under your roof—an arrangement, I'm sure, which would please you as little as it would please me.'

The Dowager tapped her ebony cane on the floor. 'Hoity-toity, miss! I shall say what pleases me and what does not.' She looked up at her grandson. He was still staring fixedly across at his ward. There was more than a touch of annoyance in that gaze, but something else, too.

She looked back at Sarah. 'Come here, child. Let me look at you.' Sarah meekly obeyed, and stood before the Dowager, gazing solemnly down at her. 'Why, you do look like your mother! Except prettier, I think. And you certainly did not get those lovely eyes from her, nor those dark brows. What unusual colouring!'

'No, ma'am. From my father, so I understand.' Her lips curled into a shy smile. 'Did you know my mother well?'

'Yes, child. Your mother and my Agnes were great friends since the days they both attended the seminary together. Your mother frequently stayed with us when she was a girl, but I saw little of her after she married your father.' She turned to her grandson. 'I cannot imagine why you are still standing there, Marcus. Go away and leave me to talk to Sarah in peace. You'll find brandy in the library.'

'I could certainly do with one after what I've had to contend with during these past days!' he responded with feeling. He went over to the door, but turned back to add, 'And don't you dare try to slip away, my girl! The library is downstairs. And I fully intend to keep the door open.'

'Infuriating man!' Sarah muttered, much to the Dowager's intense amusement, as the door closed behind him.

'Has my obnoxious grandson been giving you a hard time? Do sit down, child, and tell me all about it. What induced you to run away from Bath?'

Sarah raised her eyes heavenwards as she settled herself in the comfortable chair opposite. 'As I told your grandson, though he seems determined not to believe me, I did not run away, ma'am. I simply chose to leave.'

She then went on to explain the reasons for her actions. The Dowager leaned back against the chair, listening quietly for the most part, but occasionally interrupting to ask a question. Her shrewd grey eyes never wavered from the lovely, expressive face as she learned a little of those years Sarah had endured in Bath.

Her grandson's arrival at the inn, and the subsequent events, brought more than one wickedly amused chuckle to rise in her throat, and Sarah's astringent comments on her guardian's perfidy at tricking her into accepting a ride in his curricle afforded the Dowager unholy amusement.

'The cunning wretch!' she exclaimed when she had learned all. 'Little wonder you feel quite out of charity with him, my dear. But he is right, you know,' she went on seriously. 'You cannot go wandering about the country on your own. Look at what has befallen you already!'

There was a clearly discernible glint in Sarah's eyes. 'Naturally, I was saddened by the tragic deaths, but I could not help being excited by it all,' she freely admitted. 'Nothing like that has ever happened to me before!'

'You poor child. You did have a very dreary time of it all in Bath, didn't you?'

Sarah could feel the colour rising in her cheeks, and was unable to hold that shrewd gaze. 'Well, I—I. . .'

'There is no need to explain,' her ladyship said gently. 'That is all in the past. Now, we must look to the future. But first, you may go across to the decanters over there, and pour me a glass of Madeira. And pour yourself one whilst you're about it,' she added as Sarah rose gracefully from the chair 'It won't do you a mite of harm.'

The Dowager watched her intently, scrutinising every fluid movement of the slender young body, and was more than satisfied with what she saw.

'My dear child, I'm beginning to like you already,' she remarked, taking the glass held out to her. 'You have a steady hand and you can fill a glass. Which is more than can be said for some people.' She sampled the wine, then continued, 'Now, we must decide what is best to be done with you. I can fully understand your being piqued at my grandson's high-handed attitude. Sadly, it is his way, and you must grow accustomed.

'For my part I see no reason why you shouldn't stay with your old governess. It is evident that you have a great fondness for each other. I shall certainly have a word with Marcus about it. But it is out of the question for you to travel to Hertfordshire alone, and on the common stage. So, until some arrangements can be made, would you object very much to remaining here with me?'

Sarah had the grace to blush. 'I'm sorry if I appeared rude when I came in here, ma'am, but I thought Mr Ravenhurst might try to, well, bully you into housing me here.'

A wicked cackle answered this. 'Oh, my dear child! When you come to know me better, you will realise that even my dictatorial grandson is incapable of that feat.'

She became serious again, and looked across at Sarah intently. 'We are very alike, Ravenhurst and I. There are those who might disagree, but I believe I have mellowed over the years, and my grandson might well do so, given the incentive. But we're both plain-spoken, and spoilt enough to want our own way in all things. You might not find it easy staying here with me, and I shall not force it upon you, but I should very much like to have you as my guest, Sarah Pennington.'

Sarah did not doubt the sincerity, and felt touched by the invitation. 'Well, I—'

'Decide nothing yet, child,' the Dowager interrupted. 'Take a little time to think it over. Now, be good enough to go over to the bell-pull.'

Sarah obeyed and, at the Dowager's request, gave it several sharp tugs. A few minutes later a gaunt middle-aged woman, with the most frighteningly piercing and almost black eyes, entered the room. She cast Sarah the briefest of glances before turning to her mistress and enquiring, quite disrespectfully, Sarah thought, what she required.

'Sarah, my child, this obnoxious creature you see before you is my personal maid, Buddle,' the Dowager informed her with wicked amusement. 'Don't be alarmed. She might not appear so, but she is quite human, I assure you. She has been with me for more years than I care to remember.'

A loud snort answered this, and her ladyship turned to her maid without any visible signs of having taken offence. 'Has a bed chamber been prepared for Miss Pennington, Buddle?'

'Naturally.'

'Which one?'

'Master Marcus always has the largest guest chamber, as you very well know,' the maid answered impatiently. 'Miss Pennington's belongings have been placed in the other guest room.'

The Dowager was silent for a moment, then said decisively, 'Then remove them! Put Miss Sarah in the room next to mine. See that she has everything she needs, then come back here to me.'

Only for one unguarded moment did the maid betray surprise. 'Very good, my lady.' She turned to Sarah. 'If you would care to come with me, Miss Pennington, I'll show you the way.'

Sarah wasn't so very sure that she did care to go with the forbidding-looking woman but, after hurriedly finishing the contents of her glass, rose to her feet, and followed Buddle down the narrow passageway and into a room where the drapes had been pulled halfway across the window. She was immediately aware of the delicate fragrance of lavender and rose petals sweetening the air, and turned her head to see a good fire burning welcomingly in the grate.

Buddle went over to the windows, and opened wide the drapes, allowing the fading afternoon light to filter fully into the room, and then turned to see an unmistakable look of delight on Sarah's face as her eyes wandered over the room's decor, picked out in delicate shades of blue.

'It is a pretty room, isn't it, Miss Pennington?' she remarked, with a modicum of warmth in her voice.

'Yes, it is,' Sarah answered, running her fingers lightly down the pale blue velvet bed hangings.

'I'll just go along and collect your things from the other room. Now, is there anything else you'll be wanting?'

'If it isn't too much trouble,' Sarah replied, casting the abigail an apologetic smile, 'I'd dearly love a bath. I've not had one since leaving Somerset.'

As soon as the door had closed behind Buddle, Sarah examined her surroundings more closely. The drapes at the windows matched the bed hangings exactly, and the pale blue wallpaper was patterned with delicate bunches of flowers in shades of pink, and white. A beautifully made lace cover with scalloped edging adorned the dressing-table, on which stood several dainty scent bottles, a comb and a silver-backed hair brush.

It was undoubtedly the boudoir of a lady of fashion. And she was anything but! She grimaced at her reflection in the dressing-table mirror, disliking more than ever the dull grey gown and her plainly arranged hair. Her appearance seemed even dowdier in these lovely surroundings. But why, suddenly, did it matter so much to her how she looked? Her appearance had never worried her unduly before.

She was still pondering over this when Buddle re-entered, carrying the battered old cloak-bag and writing-case. As a result of the hasty packing back at the inn, her best pearl-grey gown was badly creased, and she looked at it in dismay. Everything, but everything seemed to be going wrong for her that day!

'Don't you worry your head over that, Miss Pennington,' Buddle said, noting the forlorn expression. 'I'll soon have it pressed. The bath is on its way. Ring when you've finished, and I'll come back to you.'

Later, when Sarah emerged from the rose-scented water, clean and refreshed, and having washed her hair, she felt slightly less disgruntled. Wrapping herself in the robe a young maidservant had brought with the towels, she rang for Buddle, and then sat at the dressing-table and studied her reflection in the glass.

The Dowager Countess had said that she had unusual colouring. Sarah turned her head on one side, considering this, as she dragged a comb through her long wet tresses. She had never given it much thought before, but she supposed she had. The finely arched dark brows and long dusky lashes made a striking contrast with hair that looked more golden than brown when touched by sunlight or a candle's glow.

Her features were regular and, looking at them dispassionately, she supposed her blue-green almond-shaped eyes were her most striking feature. She did not consider her small straight nose anything out of the common way, nor did she realise that many men found her sweetly curving lips very provocative and extremely kissable. But she had been given reason to suppose that Mr Ravenhurst considered her a pretty young woman.

She found herself, unaccountably, blushing, and was angry with herself for the unalloyed pleasure his appreciation gave her, especially as she still felt completely out of charity with him for his duplicity and high-handed treatment earlier in the day.

Buddle entering the room, accompanied by the young maid carrying several dresses over her arm, gave Sarah's thoughts a new direction, and she gazed across at the vibrantly coloured garments in wonder as the maid laid them very carefully down on the bed.

'Her ladyship said you were to make use of these, miss, until you have more suitable garments of your own to wear,' Buddle informed her, picking up the blue velvet gown and casting an expert eye over Sarah's slim, shapely figure. 'Yes, I think this will do nicely for this evening. Her ladyship has decided to eat downstairs in the diningroom, miss. So we'll need to look lively. The mistress has always kept early hours when in the country.'

'But——but who do they belong to, Buddle?' Sarah asked, gazing longingly at the dark blue velvet gown with its high neck and long tight-fitting sleeves, and wishing fervently that it was hers.

'They belong to Miss Caroline, one of her ladyship's

granddaughters. She visits every year, and left a trunk full of her belongings here after her last visit. More hair than whit, that one, Miss Pennington, but she does know what suits her. Now, while Betsy's bringing the rest of the things in, I'll see to you.'

Sarah had grown accustomed to doing most everything for herself during the past six years, and found it more than a little embarrassing to have someone else in the room while she scrambled into freshly laundered underthings. Buddle, however, seemed not to take the least notice, and set about drying the long hair on a fluffy towel.

'You have very pretty hair, miss, but it's rather heavy and is in desperate need of cutting,' the abigail remarked in her usual forthright manner and, without giving Sarah the opportunity to acquiesce, or otherwise, whipped out a pair of sharp scissors from the pocket of her starched white apron and made several judicious snips.

Sarah glanced down apprehensively at the growing pile of prettily waving long strands of hair about her feet, and earned herself a severe reprimand, much as her old governess had given her on more than one occasion when she had been a child; but she could not prevent a reluctant smile as she sat obediently rigid on the chair.

For the next few days, at least, she would find it difficult not to be in the company of at least one of three very domineering people; and unless she was prepared to make a stand right from the start, she would no doubt find herself scolded and bullied and far from gently persuaded into doing precisely what she had no earthly desire to do.

So, it would be far more comfortable in the long run if she made it abundantly clear, right from the start, that she was a young woman with a mind of her own, and had no intention whatsoever of becoming submissively docile and kowtowing to the unreasonable demands of the members of what could only be described as a despotic household.

Raising her eyes from the contemplation of the dressing-table's lacy covering, she promptly forgot her resolve to be assertive as she gazed in astonishment at her reflection in the mirror.

Buddle had gathered her hair high on her head, twisted and pinned a large portion of it into a tight circlet, and then had pulled the remaining hair through, so that it hung over one white shoulder like a silken pony's tale. She had also cut several strands very short at the front, and tiny curls now feathered across her forehead and on to her cheeks.

'Oh, Buddle, what clever fingers you have!' she enthused, still somewhat in awe over the result. 'I could never achieve anything half so elegant.'

The compliment had been spontaneous, and had sounded so sincerely meant that a suspicion of a smile hovered about the abigail's thin-lipped mouth. 'It's quite a simple style, Miss Sarah, but effective. And it's as much as I can do for you this evening. Now, let us get you into that dress. They will be awaiting you downstairs.'

Quickly hooking up the velvet gown, Buddle barely gave Sarah time to cast her eyes over the finished result in the full-length mirror before she whipped a blue-and-white silk shawl about her shoulders, and then showed her the way downstairs to the drawing-room where the Dowager and her grandson sat talking.

As the door opened, Marcus broke off what he was saying to turn his head, and for one unguarded moment could only stare in rapt admiration of his ward's transformed appearance as she moved gracefully towards them.

He rose to his feet. 'Certainly an improvement,' was the only mild praise he offered, however, before turning to his grandmother. 'Where did the dress come from?'

'It belongs to your cousin Caroline. She left one of her trunks behind the last time she paid me a visit. I doubt the silly chit has missed it.' She smiled up at Sarah. 'My dear, you look charming. Don't feel uncomfortable about making use of the other things, but we must not delay too long in purchasing some new garments of your own. There's quite a respectable little establishment in Devizes that might be worthwhile visiting.'

'I should dearly love to, my lady. Unfortunately, I have only sufficient funds to cover the rest of my travelling expenses to Hertfordshire.' She bestowed a rather sweet, but slightly provocative smile on her, now, frowning guardian. 'Unless, of course, I may have a little of the money my mother left me.'

'No, you may not!' was the unequivocal response. 'You secure your inheritance upon marriage, or attaining the age of five-and-twenty. Whichever comes first.'

'But—but that is monstrous!' Sarah was hard pressed not to scream at the injustice of it all. What had her mother been thinking of? Under the terms of the will she had been effectively prevented from becoming an independent young woman. And, what was worse, she would be virtually tied by the caprice of another for a further four years. It really didn't bear thinking about!

The Dowager could easily discern the resentment in Sarah's eyes, and cast her a sympathetic smile. 'It is in no way unusual, my dear, for matters to be settled thus.

But it need not prevent us from acquiring a new wardrobe for you.'

Scant compensation! Sarah thought bitterly, but it was not in her nature to agonise over what could not be altered, and resigned herself very quickly to making the best of it.

During dinner the Dowager and her grandson kept up a lively conversation. It soon became abundantly clear to Sarah that they were very fond of each other, and their pithy remarks and bantering exchanges caused more than one chuckle to rise in her throat.

As soon as the meal was over the ladies returned to the drawing-room. The Dowager wasted no time in extracting a promise from Sarah that she would be willing to remain at the Dower House for the time being, and then her ladyship made plans to go on the shopping expedition the following day.

'Of course, you cannot expect a provincial dressmaker to rival a London modiste, Sarah, but I do not think you will be disappointed.'

'Oh, I shan't, ma'am. I assure you. Anything has to be better than what I have at present.'

'That much is certain,' Marcus concurred, earning himself one of his ward's darkling looks as he came back into the room. 'In fact, I think I shall accompany you when you go on this trip to Devizes, just to ensure that you do not continue to tog yourself out in half-mourning.'

'If I thought that by doing so I could annoy you, I would be almost tempted,' Sarah retaliated.

'Now, now, Marcus,' the Dowager intervened quickly. 'You are not to tease the child. Sarah has agreed to stay with me for a while. But what plans have you for her future?' She saw a ghost of a smile hovering about his mouth. 'Do you intend that she should go to London for the Season?'

'Perhaps,' was his non-committal response.

'Well, you had better hurry and make a decision, my boy. It will soon be March. Precious little time to organise everything.'

At this he turned to his ward. 'Would you care for a Season, Sarah?'

His polite enquiry surprised her: she wasn't accustomed to such courtesy from him. Then her eyes began to twinkle rather wickedly. 'The object of a Season being to find a suitable spouse, I rather think I would, sir. If I am successful in my endeavours, I shall then be free of your pernicious influence.'

'Hornet!'

Sarah rose to her feet, and merely curtsied in response before turning to the Dowager. 'If you will excuse me, ma'am, I think I shall retire early. What with one thing and another, it has been a rather trying day.'

'Oh, Sarah,' Marcus said in suspicious tones, arresting her progress to the door, 'do I need to lock you in your room tonight to prevent a furtive midnight departure?'

She turned her head on one side as though giving the question due consideration. 'No, I do not think there is any necessity for that. I rather have a fancy to lull you into a false sense of security, and then abscond when you're least expecting it. That would be far more rewarding.'

'Little baggage!' he muttered after the door had closed behind her.

'Do you know, Marcus,' the Dowager remarked, highly amused, 'that gel ain't in the least afraid of you.'

'Of course she isn't! Why the devil should she be?'

'Well, you're not exactly renowned for your polite drawing-room conversation, you know.'

He dismissed this with an impatient wave of his hand. 'Sarah's not such a wigeon as to boggle at a bit of plain speaking.'

'Just as well,' responded the Dowager, eyeing her grandson for a moment with a mocking glint in her eyes, but then she became serious. 'What has been going on, Marcus? From the snippets Sarah let fall earlier, the child has had a pretty poor time of it all in Bath. And those dreadful clothes she brought with her...they are positively dowdy! Why, even my servants are better clad!'

'You may well ask,' he responded grimly.

She looked at him with interest, but when he offered nothing further, she changed the subject by remarking, 'I'm glad Sarah has agreed to a Season. I don't think you'll have the least trouble in getting her off your hands, Marcus. She's a lovely, prettily behaved young woman.'

'Prettily behaved?' he echoed, incredulous. 'It's quite evident that you do not know her very well, ma'am. You've no notion of the worry she's caused me. She's the most outrageous little minx! She's friendly to a fault, she'll mix with any raff and scaff and she's as trusting as bedamned! And when I think I shall need to keep an eye on her every minute throughout the Season, just to make sure she doesn't fall into any more scrapes, I'm almost tempted to retract the offer!'

The Dowager considered his remarks a trifle inflated, but refrained from further comment. In fact, during the rest of the time she remained downstairs with him, she did not mention Sarah's name again, but that night as she lay in her bed, sipping her customary cup of warm milk, she had a very thoughtful expression on her face.

Buddle, who was in the process of hanging her mistress's gown back in the wardrobe, looked suspiciously across at her. 'I know that look of old,' she remarked, coming across to the bed to relieve the Dowager of the cup. 'You're up to something.'

The Dowager did not so much as blink; her eyes remained glued to an imaginary spot on the far wall. 'What do you think to Sarah Pennington, Buddle?'

'Ah! So that's it, is it! I knew as soon as you wanted her put in Miss Agnes's old room you were up to no good. If you want my advice, you'll leave well alone, and not interfere in Master Marcus's concerns.'

'But he likes her, Buddle,' the Dowager murmured, almost to herself. 'There is that in his eyes when they rest upon her. . . There is such—such tenderness there. It is unmistakable. I've never seen him look at anyone that way before.'

Her lips curled into a satisfied smile. 'And he hasn't offered for that Bamford chit,' she went on to divulge to the woman who was not only her personal maid but also a friend and confidante. 'And I cannot say I'm sorry. Sounds a cold, heartless chit to me. Wouldn't suit him at all!'

'Be that as it may, Master Marcus still wouldn't thank you none for meddling in his private concerns. And you know it!'

The Dowager's brows snapped together as she fixed her gaze on her maid. 'Do you know, Buddle, you are becoming quite testy in your old age. Cannot imagine why. Now, go away, and leave me in peace! I need to think.'

Chapter Seven

Sarah, too, had much to ponder over before she eventually fell to sleep that night. Her main concern was not her immediate future. The Dowager Countess seemed genuinely eager to have her as a guest, and Sarah was not unhappy at the prospect of remaining in a place where she knew her presence would be welcome. But her stay here could not be an indefinite one.

Once she had attained her majority, of course, she could seek shelter with the Alcotts, and her guardian would be powerless to remove her from their sphere, but he still retained control of her fortune for a further four years. Curse him! That still rankled, but she forced herself to swallow her chagrin and concentrate her thoughts on the options open to her.

She was still determined to go to Hertfordshire and remain with dear Martha and her family for a few weeks, but, here again, to impose upon the Alcotts' hospitality for any great length of time was unthinkable. Independence had effectively been denied her until she had attained the age of five-and-twenty.

So, unless she stuck to her original plan and tried to

seek employment as a governess, or was prepared to bind herself to Mr Ravenhurst's will, which would no doubt involve living quietly somewhere with yet another female of his choosing acting as chaperon, the only other course open to her was marriage.

Sarah frowned as she stared up at the velvet canopy above her head. Strangely enough, she had never considered marrying. She didn't quite know why this should be, because all the young females of her acquaintance thought of nothing else. Perhaps, she mused, it was because she had had precious little experience of men.

Her father had died when she was very young and, with the exception of James Fenshaw, whom she had liked very much, but who had never figured in her thoughts as a prospective husband, the only other men with whom she had ever had any real dealings were the middle-aged husbands of Harriet Fairchild's friends.

Naturally, she had come into contact with many young men during her years in Bath. The Pump Room was a favourite meeting place for ladies of all ages, many of whom were dutifully escorted by some young male relative; but with very few exceptions, Sarah had considered those budding sprigs of fashion empty-headed nincompoops, who had little thought for aught else other than the latest vogue in tying a cravat, or the way to achieve a looking-glass shine on a pair of boots.

Her frown grew more pronounced. Perhaps the only man she had ever been attracted to on sight was Captain Brin Carter, and yet her feelings for him had been— well—more sisterly, really, like her feelings towards her friend Clarissa's beau... And the only other man, of course, with whom she had ever had more than a passing contact was. . .

Sarah's frown grew so heavy her brows almost met above the bridge of her nose. No woman in her right mind would ever consider Marcus Ravenhurst as a prospective husband! He was rich, certainly, but all the wealth in the land could never compensate for being joined in wedlock to such an arrogant, dictatorial creature! He was without doubt the rudest man she had ever met in her life. It would be impossible to find another ruder! And yet. . .

A soft, reminiscent little smile erased the scowl as her mind returned to those days spent at that inn. Her guardian could be quite kind at times, touchingly so in his little acts of thoughtfulness. Beneath that hardened exterior lay a benevolent, generous spirit. The right sort of woman, one who would not be cowed by his sharp-tongued brusqueness, could, she felt certain, mellow him in time, allowing the real essence of the man to surface.

She could do it; she felt certain of it! His caustic remarks never upset her; annoyed her sometimes, certainly, but for the most part she found his acerbic tongue highly diverting. Yes, she mused, she most certainly could sweeten the masterful Marcus Ravenhurst's vinegary disposition, and. . .

Releasing her breath in an almost imperceptible gasp, Sarah brought her wayward thoughts to heel sharply. What on earth was she thinking of? Marry Marcus Ravenhurst. . .? Why, it was unthinkable! Ludicrous! Besides, he would never take to wife someone so beneath his own station in life. Only the daughter of a duke or marquis would be good enough for him. Added to which, she didn't even like the man. . .did she?

Dressed in another borrowed gown, a pale blue dimity this time, with a high neck ending in a tiny frill, and long sleeves buttoned at the wrists, Sarah went into the room where they had dined the evening before to find her guardian sitting alone at the table, consuming a hearty breakfast. He acknowledged her with a nod, and then politely enquired whether she had slept well.

After responding that she had, which wasn't strictly true, but rather better than admitting that thoughts of him had kept her awake until the early hours, she proceeded to place several wafer-thin slices of ham on her plate and pour herself coffee; but each time she raised her eyes from the food on her plate, it was to discover her guardian staring at her in a rather disconcerting and quite unreadable way.

She tried her best to ignore him, and carried on eating in silence, but after several more minutes of this continued scrutiny she found herself asking, rather testily, 'What on earth is the matter with you now? I know more often than not you're in a churlish mood in the mornings, but must you keep staring at me as though—as though I'd a smut on my nose?'

His lips twitched in response to the waspish tone. 'You've no smut, but you do have two or three rather pretty freckles. No, no! Don't rip up at me, you little shrew!' he went on hurriedly when she looked about to do just that. 'Instead, tell me if you've a riding habit amongst those borrowed clothes of my cousin's?'

She was rather taken aback by the unexpected enquiry. 'I'm not certain. Why?'

'You can hardly go riding without one.'

'I can hardly go riding without a horse, either, come to that,' she parried, sweetly sarcastic. 'And as I do not possess a mount, the question of whether or not I can lay my hands on a habit is completely irrelevant, wouldn't you say?'

Leaning back in his chair, he regarded her from beneath hooded lids. 'Remind me to beat you some time.' He saw the slender shoulders shaking with suppressed laughter, and could not prevent a twitching smile himself. 'You really are the most provoking little witch at times, Sarah Pennington,' he informed her with gentle censure. 'Now, do you think we could possibly continue this conversation with a little less flippancy? Can you ride, child? If not, would you like me to teach you?'

For a moment Sarah regarded him in astonishment, then quickly lowered her eyes. If she had needed more proof of Harriet Fairchild's artfulness, she had been given it now. His cousin had never written to him requesting a mount for his ward, or if she had, the money had been squandered elsewhere. Sooner or later he was going to discover the full extent of his cousin's chicanery, but she had absolutely no intention of turning informer.

After quickly searching her mind for a suitable response, she said, 'Yes, I do ride, sir, but I'm a little out of practice, I'm afraid.' Which was true enough, as she had not been in the saddle since staying at her friend Clarissa's home in Devonshire during the previous summer.

'Never mind that,' he replied dismissively, rising from the table. 'I'll see what cattle my uncle's got in his stable. He's bound to have something suitable for a lady to ride. We'll soon have you up to scratch. Meet me outside in an hour. And if you cannot lay your hands on a habit, wear that deplorable grey gown of yours. It won't matter a whit if that gets ruined. In fact, it'll be a blessing if it does!' was his parting shot on closing the door.

Sarah was too excited at the prospect of riding again to concern herself over that completely unnecessary gibe. She did not linger long over her breakfast, and hurriedly made her way back up the stairs, but stopped outside the Dowager's room.

Her guardian might be quite mannerless at times, but she was not prepared to allow his shortcomings to rub off on her. She was a guest in his grandmother's house, and it was only polite to enquire if there was anything required of her before setting off on her ride.

Buddle answered the summons, admitting Sarah with a modicum of warmth in those almost black eyes which, had Sarah but known it, meant that the highly discerning middle-aged servant had made her assessment of Ravenhurst's ward and had already awarded the young person the stamp of approval.

The Dowager, still abed and propped up against a mound of frothy while pillows, was sipping a cup of sweet hot chocolate.

'Good-morning, child. I trust you slept well?'

'Quite well, thank you, ma'am.' Sarah came to stand beside the elaborately carved four-poster bed. 'Your grandson has kindly offered to take me riding this morning, but I wondered if there was any service I might perform for you before I leave?'

'My dear, you are not here to dance attendance upon me,' her ladyship responded gently, yet firmly. 'You are a guest in my house and, as such, may do precisely as you wish. Besides,' she went on, her grey eyes twinkling with wicked amusement as she cast them briefly in her formidable abigail's direction, 'Buddle might become jealous if I conferred her privileged duties on to another.'

'Ha! Privileged, indeed!' Buddle scoffed before turning

a much friendlier countenance on to Sarah. 'You'll be
needing a habit, miss. I believe there is one hanging in
the wardrobe in the spare bedchamber. Hardly ever been
worn, as I recall. I'll go and fetch it and bring it along
to your room.'

'Yes, that is something else we must attend to when
we go shopping later, Sarah,' the Dowager remarked as
Buddle went out. 'We'll order a habit made, and a few
other gowns, but I'm sure you would much prefer to wait
a while for the bulk of your new clothes, and deck yourself
out in the latest fashions when we go to London.'

'We?' Sarah echoed, lips twitching. There seemed to
be much the Dowager had decided upon since the evening
before. 'Are you proposing to act as my duenna, ma'am?'

'Yes, my dear, I rather think I shall.' Her ladyship,
looking for all the world like a very contented cat, patted
the bed, and Sarah dutifully sat herself down on the edge.

'I haven't been to London for some years—not since
your godmother passed away, so it's high time I bestirred
myself and did a little socialising whilst I'm still able to
get about reasonably well. I shall enjoy visiting my old
friends. I had considered asking Henrietta to chaperon
you, as she is bringing Sophia out this year, but I think
you'll find it more amusing with me.'

Sarah frowned slightly. 'I'm sorry, ma'am, but I do
not perfectly understand. Who is Henrietta?'

'She is the Countess of Styne, my dear, my son Henry's
wife. And Sophia is their eldest daughter. Their eldest
son, Bertram, is up at Oxford. The boy's an impertinent
nincompoop, but harmless enough. And I shall not bore
you with details of the four other children who are all
still in the nursery and all equally silly.'

'I look forward to meeting them,' Sarah responded

politely, though slightly unsteadily.

'They are due home at the end of the week, so I don't expect it will be long before I receive a visit from them,' the Dowager remarked with scant enthusiasm. 'Henrietta's a wigeon, but a kind-hearted soul. I expect you'll like her—most people do. But I don't relish the prospect of spending several weeks under the same roof as my daughter-in-law. I'll have a word with Ravenhurst. I'm sure he'll grant us the use of his town house in Berkeley Square for the duration of the Season.'

The Dowager glanced across the room at the clock as she placed her empty cup on the bedside table. 'You run along now, my dear. You don't want to keep my grandson waiting. And don't be late back from your ride. I want to leave for Devizes directly after luncheon.'

Buddle was awaiting her in the bedchamber, and it took Sarah no time at all to change into the stylish gold-coloured habit, and to have her hair neatly confined in a snood before a beaver hat, dyed the exact same shade as the habit, was placed at a jaunty angle on her head. From somewhere Buddle had acquired a pair of black gloves and a riding crop, and as Sarah emerged from the house, she felt for the first time in her life quite the young lady of fashion.

She found to her surprise that the stableyard was deserted, and so decided to fill the time while awaiting her guardian's arrival by inspecting the exterior of what was to be her dwelling place for the next few weeks.

The late February sun was doing its best to brighten the setting, picking out the pinkish hues in the Dower House's grey stone and striving to cast its rays into those numerous shadowy areas of what could only be described as a very neglected, overgrown garden, but it was battling against overwhelming odds. Sarah cast a frowning glance up at the tall trees. Even now, still bared of their greenery, those stately beeches and elms managed to make their presence felt by blocking out most of that much-needed light.

She had noticed the evening before that Clegg had gone about lighting the candles very early because the rooms on the ground floor were so gloomy. It was such a shame, really, Sarah thought, looking along the front aspect of the fine Elizabethan building.

It was a charming house, not large, but elegantly appointed and very comfortable. Two or three industrious men would soon have the gardens in order, and if a few of those trees were felled the light could filter into the rooms, making them much more cheerful.

The sound of hoofbeats reached her ears, and she turned to see Ravenhurst, astride a large bay and leading another mount, disappear under the archway. Picking up her skirts, she hurried along the path to the stables to catch him in the act of dismounting.

'Ah, so there you are!' His expression was one of approval as he watched her approach. 'I was just about to go searching for you. I cannot tell you how relieved I am to discover you're a female who can be on time!'

'I came out a few minutes ago. I've been taking a look at the garden.'

His expression changed dramatically. 'It's damned disgraceful!' he declared, not mincing words. 'I've already told the Dowager she ought to have these confounded trees chopped down, but she won't listen.'

Sarah could not prevent a smile at this. 'And what would you say, sir, if people tried to tell you what you should do with the gardens at Ravenhurst?'

'Tell 'em to mind their own business!'

'Precisely! You are very like your grandmother, you know.'

'Hornet!' he responded, but far from nastily, as he helped her into the saddle.

It took Marcus a few minutes only to satisfy himself that his ward was a very competent rider. She sat the hack gracefully and had good light hands.

'I wish I'd sorted you out something with a bit more spirit, child,' he remarked, casting her sluggish mount a frowning glance, 'but I thought it wisest to be cautious as you gave me the impression that you ride infrequently. Which I find very strange,' he went on matter-of-factly, 'considering I received a letter from my cousin requesting funds to purchase a horse for you, as riding was one of your favourite pastimes. And I have been paying stabling costs for almost a year.'

Sarah kept her gaze firmly fixed between her horse's ears, but instinctively knew her guardian was staring at her. Only honesty would serve, now. Ravenhurst was no fool, and had probably worked out for himself where her allowance had been going.

'As soon as I came to know you a little, I knew you would never have quibbled over furnishing me with a mount,' she said at length.

'Where has your allowance been going, Sarah? Gaming?'

'I think so.' She heard him muttering something under his breath, and found herself coming to Mrs Fairchild's defence. 'You mustn't think I have been ill-used, sir. Your cousin was always very kind to me.'

'Kind!' he ejaculated. 'I'll give her kind when I see her! Squandering your allowance on her own pleasures, whilst you went about in clothes fitted only for a servant. No wonder the confounded woman very nearly swooned when I turned up unexpectedly! She realised the game was up!'

Knowing that in his present mood it would be a waste of breath trying to make him view his cousin in a less derogatory light, Sarah encouraged him to vent all that pent-up condemnation on a different source by quite deliberately asking how Mrs Stanton had taken her daughter's elopement. It had the desired effect.

'And well may you ask, my girl!' The dark brows snapped together. 'What the devil do you mean by getting yourself involved in that disgraceful affair?'

'Clarissa has always been my closest friend, sir,' she answered, far from cowed by his staunch disapproval of her actions. 'And I'm very fond of James, too. I couldn't bear to see them made unhappy because of the selfish caprice of their respective fathers who, I might add, before a silly difference of opinion, actively encouraged their children's close friendship.'

She turned her head to look at him, and he could not mistake the flicker of combined sadness and regret in her eyes. 'Was Mrs Stanton very angry with me?'

He quickly discovered he was not proof against that look, and didn't hesitate to reassure her. 'No. In fact, I gained the distinct impression that she was more disturbed by your sudden flight than her daughter's.'

'I knew it!' Sarah exclaimed triumphantly, her aquamarine eyes sparkling again. 'I always thought that deep down Mrs Stanton was not happy with the state of affairs. She thinks a great deal of James, so I guessed she was far from opposed to the match.'

'Be that as it may, my girl!' he countered, his

disapproval returning. 'You ought not to have become involved. I well expect to receive a visit from your friend's father after my blood!'

'Oh, I shouldn't worry, if I were you,' she said dismissively. 'He's a blustering, bad-tempered individual at times but, believe me, you're more than a match for him, sir.' Sarah, the perfection of her forehead suddenly marred by a deep frown of concern, kept her eyes firmly fixed between her mount's ears, and so missed the look of almost comical outrage on her guardian's face. 'I think it most unlikely that Mr Stanton will seek you out. No, he's far more likely to go after Clarissa and James.'

A tiny sigh escaped her. 'I cannot help worrying about them, sir. James said it would take five or six days to reach the border. But, of course, he wasn't making allowances for a deterioration in the weather.'

Once again he found sympathy coming to the fore. 'Then you can stop worrying, child!' he ordered with a kind of rough gentleness. 'Before we left the inn yesterday, I learned from the magistrate that only the southern counties were affected by snow. No doubt your friends had a very tedious, but quite uneventful, journey to Scotland. And who knows, they might at this very moment be standing before that infamous anvil!'

He cast her a reassuring smile. 'If it will ease your mind, I shall try to discover the outcome when I collect my greys from Bath in a few days' time.'

He then changed the subject and, as they continued their ride, pointed out various features of interest on his uncle's vast estate. When the huge Restoration mansion came into view, he caused more than one amused chuckle to rise in Sarah's throat by his scathing condemnation of the imposing ancestral home. He stigmatised the building as a great draughty barn of a place.

It was his considered opinion that the addition of the two new wings during the previous century had ruined what little architectural beauty the house had ever possessed; and as if that were not bad enough, his great-grandfather, apparently terrified of a fire breaking out, had instigated the construction of a new kitchen area, which was only accessible through miles of corridor. Consequently, by the time meals arrived at the dining-room they were always cold.

Secretly, Sarah, too, thought it rather an unprepossessing structure with little to commend it, but was far too well-bred to comment. The park, on the other hand was very much to her taste. With the exception of a small area near the eastern boundary, the landscape was quite beautiful with its sweeping lawns, rippling streams and large clumps of majestic trees.

She frowned as they began to skirt the overgrown area. 'Why has this part been allowed to develop into a wilderness, sir?'

'A couple of centuries ago a woman accused of being a witch was dragged here by some of the villagers. Before she drowned, she was heard to put a curse on this place.'

He raised his eyes heavenwards. 'Complete nonsense, of course! Still, I suppose there's some justification for the superstition,' he added fair-mindedly. 'An ancestor met his death near this very spot, and my uncle came perilously close to drowning here himself when he was a youth. There's a good-sized lake hidden behind that wall of overgrown shrubs and brambles. If you like, we'll try to find a way through and I'll show it to you.'

Possessing an inquisitive rather than a fanciful nature, Sarah did not hesitate. After tethering their horses to the branch of a tree, they forged a way through the shrubbery, Sarah finding the brambles' wickedly clawing thorns more threatening than any supposed curse. When they did eventually arrive at the lakeside, she looked about her in dismay at the sheer neglect of what once must have been an idyllic spot.

Taking a hold of one slender gloved hand, Marcus led the way along the overgrown path round the water's edge. 'You can't deny, Sarah, it's an eerie place. Listen to that high-pitched wailing! The witch, I suspect.'

'That's the wind,' she scoffed.

'You think so? Well, you may be right. But what about those ghostly forms rising from the lake?'

'Mist. And you know it.' She detected the slight movement of broad shoulders shaking with suppressed laughter. 'You can stop trying to frighten me because you won't succeed! Tell me, instead, what that building is just ahead?'

'It's the old boat-house. Not used now, of course. Since my uncle's unfortunate experience, no one ever comes here.'

'Well, someone most certainly does,' Sarah countered as they arrived at the stone-built structure. A raised wooden platform had been constructed along the front wall, from which one gained access to a rather rickety-looking jetty that reached out some distance into the lake. 'And has been here quite recently, I should say,' she added, staring down at the clearly visible wet footprints.

Ravenhurst walked across the platform to the far side of the boat-house. 'Well, well, my dear! We evidently disturbed a trespasser. He's left his catch.'

Sarah looked down at the four large fish lying in the grass. 'A poacher?'

'More than likely. He must have seen or heard us approaching, and made himself scarce.' He scanned the dense area of shrubs to his right. 'No doubt he's watching our every move at this very moment.'

'Are you going to inform your uncle when he returns?' Sarah asked tentatively, but instinctively knew what his response would be even before he said,

'Certainly not! That lake must be teaming with fish. The Earl makes no use of them, and if some unfortunate wretch can provide himself with a decent meal, I shan't be the one to throw a rub in his way.' There was certainly more than just a hint of devilment in the smile he cast her. 'Come, let us away, so the poor fellow can collect his dinner.'

Their arrival back at the Dower House a short while later coincided with that of a very elegant travelling-carriage. Sarah watched with interest as a sparse man in his forties, dressed in a suit of severe black cloth, alighted. He then took a few rather mincing steps away from the equipage before bowing with studied elegance to Mr Ravenhurst.

'Ah, Quilp! In good time. Two pairs of my boots are in urgent need of your meticulous attention. You know your way.' Thus disposing of his valet, Marcus then acknowledged his stable lad who had driven the carriage to Somerset before turning his gaze on to his head groom who had not, even by the slight raising of his bushy, greying brows, betrayed the fact that he had recognised Sarah.

Ravenhurst's thin lips curled into a not unappreciative smile. 'I trust your journey passed without incident, Sutton. This young lady, whom you've never met before, is my ward, Miss Pennington.'

Although she had had little conversation with the groom during her stay at the Inn, only ever passing the time of day, Sarah flatly refused to partake in her guardian's rather childish and totally unnecessary game of pretence. She acknowledged the head groom with her friendly smile, asked him how he went on, and then returned to the house to change back into the dress she had been wearing earlier that morning.

When she returned downstairs, Clegg informed her that luncheon was not quite ready to be served, so she took herself off to the library and began writing a letter to Mrs Stanton.

She had felt untold relief to learn that her friend's mother bore her no ill-will. After apologising once again for the part she had played in Clarissa's elopement— which, in fact, had been woefully small—she began to relate what had befallen her since she had left Bath, which had been a mere five days, but which seemed like a lifetime ago.

She had just reached the part where Mr Ravenhurst had arrived at the inn when she was disturbed by a tapping sound, and turned her head to see the man himself standing on the other side of the window, beckoning to her with an imperious hand.

Rising from the desk, Sarah went across to open the windows, and Marcus, lifting one muscular, booted-leg over the sill, stepped into the room.

A frown of disapproval creased her brow. 'Why you cannot use the door like anyone—' Sarah caught herself up abruptly as his actions struck a chord of memory. 'Do that again!'

'Do what again?'

'Climb out of the window.'

He regarded her suspiciously. 'You're not going to close them by any chance, so that I have to walk round to the front door?'

'Of course not! Just do as I ask!'

He looked far from convinced, but obediently repeated the procedure. 'Satisfied, now?'

'That's it!' Excitement brought a sparkle to her eyes. 'That's what I found so odd on the night of Mr Nutley's death!'

Chapter Eight

Marcus regarded her in frowning silence for a moment. 'What precisely struck you as odd?'

'The way that intruder climbed out of the parlour window at the inn. I knew there was something peculiar about the action at the time, but it wasn't until I watched you just now that I realised precisely what had puzzled me. Here, let me show you.'

Brushing past, Sarah sat on the window-sill. Then, gathering the folds of her skirts beneath her, she swung both legs over the ledge together. 'That is how our intruder did it, just as any female would perform the feat.'

'Are you trying to tell me that you think, now, our mysterious cloaked figure might possibly have been a woman?' He helped her back inside, and then securely fastened the windows. 'The evidence on which to base such a judgement, if you'll forgive me saying so, child, seems rather flimsy.'

'Yes, perhaps it does,' she conceded. 'But the intruder's actions appeared so natural, just as though he— she was accustomed to wearing skirts. If my memory serves me correctly, that window at the inn was about the same distance from the ground as this one. The intruder was wearing breeches, so why didn't he simply step over the sill as you did? I could quite easily do so if I wore breeches.'

Marcus moved across to the small table on which several decanters stood and, at Sarah's shake of the head, poured out just one glass of wine. He sipped the rich dark liquid meditatively, then said, 'Assuming you're right, and I'm far from convinced myself, who are we looking at? Your actress friend, that middle-aged spinster and the farmer's wife.'

'I think we can safely rule out the farmer's wife,' Sarah responded with a twitching smile. 'She was, as you no doubt recall, a lady built on generous lines. Although that cloak concealed the intruder's identity, it couldn't possibly mask a person's size, at least not to that extent. Our intruder was much slimmer and rather taller, if my memory serves me correctly.'

'Could it have been the "Divine" Dorothea, then?'

Sarah gave the question due consideration as she resumed her seat at the desk. 'It's certainly possible, yet my instinct tells me otherwise.'

'What makes you so sure that it wasn't her?'

'Because Dottie is my height, and although I saw the intruder for a few brief moments only, I feel certain she was taller than I. And then there was that letter found on the murdered servant girl. It was rather a clumsy way of trying to incriminate Dottie in Nutley's death, don't you agree?'

Tossing the contents of his glass down his throat, Marcus came across to sit himself on the edge of the desk. 'Given what we now know—yes, I do. No doubt Stubbs will not fail to check out Dottie's story when he returns to London, but I for one do not doubt the truth of it.'

He was silent for a moment, absently swinging one well-muscled leg to and fro. 'Like Dottie, that servant girl was illiterate. Even supposing the girl did come across that letter, it would have meant nothing to her. But she certainly discovered something about someone, and evidently didn't hesitate in stooping to a little blackmail. And I think whoever murdered her planted Dottie's letter on the dead girl's body.'

'And you think the intruder and the person who murdered the servant girl are one and the same person? And that that person was someone staying at the inn, don't you, sir?'

'Yes, child, I do.' He stared down into her troubled eyes. 'Let us go through events step by step. I think you would agree that no one putting up at that inn did so by design. Taking that fact into account, it's highly unlikely that Nutley arranged to meet anyone there. Also, taking into account the state of the roads, it was impossible for our cloaked figure to have travelled very far.'

'But don't forget that it was possible to walk into the village,' she reminded him.

'True. And I'm sure it didn't take long for word to spread that the inn was filled with stranded travellers— easy pickings for someone willing to take a few risks, you might say. Very well, let's deal with that possibility first, and assume someone from the village did break in. His motive for doing so must have been robbery, wouldn't you say?' and he watched her nod in response. 'Yet nothing was stolen.'

'I know.' Sarah looked up at him intently. 'But Mr

Nutley's appearance would have put a stop to the burglar's intentions, surely?'

'You would certainly have thought so, wouldn't you? We still cannot be sure whether Nutley's death was an accident, or not. But let's assume for argument's sake that it was. There was a scuffle between him and the intruder. Nutley slipped, possibly knocking over the chair that we found upturned, hit his head on the settle and broke his neck. The noise woke you. How much time elapsed, after you had woken, before you entered the parlour?'

She shrugged. 'Perhaps five minutes, not much more.'

'And yet our villager, bent on a little petty theft, was still there.' The look he cast her was openly sceptical. 'Theft is one thing—being accused of murder is quite another. Had our intruder been some petty thief, I feel certain he would have departed, instanter!'

Sarah chewed these particulars over for a few moments and quickly came to the same conclusion. 'So why did our intruder remain, sir?'

'That's exactly the point! Why, my dear Sarah? Petty theft certainly wasn't the reason. Nutley had a purse in his pocket containing several sovereigns, there was a timepiece attached to his waistcoat and he was wearing a gold signet ring. All could have been quite easily filched in the time it took for you to get downstairs.'

'How very odd!' Sarah's brows drew together in a puzzled frown. 'What on earth was our cloaked figure doing, then, during that time?'

'I doubt foolishly trying to revive Nutley.' Marcus moved across to the decanters once more to refill his glass. 'Let us leave that for now and move on to yet another very interesting fact—the quite deliberate drugging of that rum punch. Nutley's intention, I feel fairly certain, was not to drug everyone. If that were the case, he would have tried harder to coax both you and me into accepting a glass. But he didn't. . . Why?'

Sarah gazed up into his intelligent dark eyes as he resumed his former position on the desk. 'I suppose it might have aroused suspicion had he done so.'

'Very true. . .or,' he continued after the briefest of pauses, 'it was of little importance to him whether we imbibed or not because his intended victim had already accepted a glass.'

He watched her lovely, expressive face closely and knew the instant enlightenment had dawned.

'Of course! Mr Stubbs!'

'Clever girl!' he remarked approvingly. 'Nutley was sharing a bedchamber with the Runner, and it's my belief that some time during that day he got wind of Stubbs's profession. But ask yourself this, Sarah—why should this knowledge bother him? Why should he want Stubbs drugged, dead to the world?'

Her puzzled frown returned. 'Well, we can be fairly certain that it wasn't because he had arranged to meet someone at the inn and didn't want Stubbs to witness that meeting. So, perhaps, he had something to hide? Something in his possession that he was terrified of Mr Stubbs discovering.'

'Precisely! And that is what I believe took Nutley back down to the parlour. I think he was endeavouring to hide something until he was able to continue his journey. Now, nothing incriminating was found on his person, nor amongst his possessions, and Stubbs and I searched that parlour thoroughly and discovered nothing out of the way.'

'So, you think our cloaked intruder took whatever it was Mr Nutley was endeavouring to hide?'

'I think he, or she, was searching for it, certainly, but without success, because you, my dear, inadvertently interrupted proceedings. Stubbs and I are positive that someone searched our rooms, possibly during the time we were interviewing you in the parlour. If our cloaked friend had found what Nutley had hidden, there would have been no need to search further.'

'You know, sir,' Sarah said after several moments' intense thought, 'the more I think about it, the more convinced I am that you are right, and that cloaked figure was amongst the guests staying at that inn. He or she must have heard Nutley leave his room that night, and followed him downstairs. Though, precisely who it was I cannot imagine. What is more, it seems he or she knew that Mr Nutley had something to hide. And if Nutley was involved in something underhanded, do you think this person might have been, well, an accomplice?'

He shrugged. 'It's possible, but we can only speculate on that, child. I'm just glad we're well out of it now.' He dismissed it from his mind, and gazed down at the letter she had been writing, one dark brow rising when he caught the name of the intended recipient. 'Ha! Guilty conscience, I see!'

She cast him a disapproving frown. 'You appear to have a propensity for reading other people's letters.'

'And those destined for myself!' he countered, his frown as pronounced as her own, as he recalled clearly the contents of the letter that he had found in her writing-case. 'How long did you intend keeping me in the dark as to your true identity?'

'I had every intention of informing you the day after

our arrival at the inn. But you were in such a disagreeable mood at breakfast. And then finding Mr Nutley that way. . . Oh, I don't know! The right moment just never seemed to arise.' She received not so much a growl in response to this as a grunt. 'Well, you could just as easily have informed me that you knew who I was,' she added in her defence.

'What? And risk your doing something bird-witted like loping off in the dead of night? Not a chance!'

She satisfied herself with casting him a look of impatience, and as Clegg entered the room a moment later to inform them that luncheon was about to be served, the topic of conversation ceased.

After they had all eaten, the Dowager was all eagerness to set off on their trip to Devizes. Mr Ravenhurst had mentioned that he might well accompany them on the shopping expedition, but Sarah, having by this time acquired a fair knowledge of his character, was not in the least surprised when he informed them quite bluntly that he had no intention of doing so, as he had one or two urgent letters he must write.

She was not very surprised, either, when he took it upon himself, in his usual high-handed manner, to organise their transport. Refusing point blank to permit his ward to travel even a short distance in what he stigmatised as her ladyship's antiquated bone-shaker of a berlin, which might easily become stuck in the inches of mud still lying on many of the minor roads after the recent thaw, he ordered his grandmother's team of handsome bays harnessed to his own well-sprung and far more comfortable carriage.

Not surprisingly, neither lady objected to these arrangements, and the short journey was achieved swiftly and without mishap.

Naturally, the small town could not offer those elegant establishments to be found in Bath, but Sarah was far from disappointed. For years she could only stare longingly at the pretty, frivolous bonnets and elegant gowns offered for sale; now, however, she could enter shops, confident in the knowledge that anything that happened to take her fancy would be hers for the asking.

She quickly discovered that the Dowager Countess of Styne was well known. No sooner had they entered the town's most fashionable shop, owned by a lady who had for a time worked under one of London's most famous modistes, than chairs were swiftly found for the distinguished customer and her young protégée. She quickly discovered, too, that her notion of an adequate wardrobe was certainly far removed from the Dowager's.

Lengths of silks, satins, muslins and velvets were brought out for inspection, whilst Sarah was pulled this way and that and her measurements taken with ruthless efficiency. Day dresses, walking dresses, pelisses and spencers were ordered to be made as quickly as possible and sent to Styne, and several lengths of material, including a very pretty turquoise silk, which the Dowager considered ideal for an evening gown, were parcelled up and placed in the carriage.

All Sarah's protestations fell on deaf ears. In the other shops the Dowager's reckless spending continued. A more than adequate supply of undergarments and nightwear was purchased before bonnets, shoes, gloves and many, many more 'absolute necessities', according to the Dowager, were chosen by her with blatant disregard for cost.

When they eventually arrived back at the Dower House, Sarah could only watch in silent dismay as the servants, having to make several journeys, collected the multitude of packages from the carriage and carried them up to her room.

Marcus emerged from the library to find his ward, a look of combined anxiety and guilt on her face, and the Dowager, a look of pleasurable satisfaction on hers, divesting themselves of cloaks and bonnets.

'What's the matter, child? Has my indomitable grandmother worn you out?'

'No such thing!' her ladyship put in before Sarah could open her mouth. 'She's been all of a twitter for most of the afternoon. Can't imagine why. Unless she's worried that you'll come the ugly, Marcus, at laying out blunt for a few little necessities.'

'A few little. . .?' Sarah placed a restraining hand on her guardian's arm as he made to follow the Dowager into the drawing-room. 'Sir, I couldn't stop her,' she told him, real perturbation sounding in her voice. 'I tried. Truly, I did! But she just wouldn't listen.'

'A family failing, I'm afraid,' he responded, casually pulling her arm through his and guiding her into the room his grandmother had entered. 'So don't waste your breath in trying, my child.'

Sarah knew that that was his rather tactful way of telling her that he simply wasn't interested in how much money had been squandered that afternoon. He was so wealthy, of course, that the day's expenditure represented a mere drop in the ocean, but Sarah could not reconcile her conscience with such wanton extravagance.

That night, dressed in one of her new nightgowns, she sat at the small table in her room, and poured out her thoughts in the letter she had begun earlier in the day to her friend's mother.

The words flowed so easily from her pen as her reflections centred on her guardian. What a surprisingly complex creature he had turned out to be! she wrote. He bore no resemblance whatsoever to the mean-spirited tyrant of her imaginings.

And just why his cousin Harriet Fairchild held him in such lively dread she could not imagine, because he was, for the most part, an agreeable man who could be quite touchingly thoughtful at times. The quill in her hand stilled suddenly, and she raised her eyes to stare blindly at the delicately patterned wallpaper.

Yes, why had she heard so many bad reports about Marcus Ravenhurst during her years in Bath? she wondered. Most of what she had been told was complete and utter nonsense. True, he could be very abrupt at times, and he certainly didn't suffer fools gladly, but he was far from the unfeeling monster she had been led to believe.

His appearance was against him, though, she mused. One glimpse of that heavy scowl would send the timid scurrying away even before he had opened his mouth, and she could quite understand why many a faint-hearted female might find his brusqueness a trifle off-putting. He could hardly be described as handsome, either, or of having a kindly face, but he did have a rather wonderful smile.

And there was no denying he was a fine figure of a man. Broad shouldered and muscular, he was ruggedly attractive and, therefore, must surely appeal to many members of her sex. Added to which he had many fine qualities. So, why then had he never married?

The thought, unbidden, came into her head, and she

absently brushed the feathers of her quill back and forth across her chin while pondering over this rather surprising circumstance. He had no title, it was true, but he was excessively wealthy. Could it be this fact alone that had kept him a bachelor? Was he wary of being coveted only for his great wealth?

If that was the case, she could quite understand why matrimony held no appeal for him. Why, it was despicable to marry someone merely for money! Yet, she was worldly-wise enough to know that both men and women did just that.

But supposing he did meet someone who loved him for himself; what sort of husband would he make? Her lips curled into a wicked little smile. Well, he would certainly wish to rule the roost. Which was only right and proper, she decided fair-mindedly. A man ought to make the decisions, and shoulder the responsibilities.

Sadly, though, given Mr Ravenhurst's temperament, if he eventually married some milk-and-water miss who hadn't the courage to stand up to him, he would be in grave danger of degenerating into nothing more than a rather unpleasant autocrat. On the other hand, though, if he married a girl of spirit, and one who, moreover, coveted the man and not his money, she felt sure he would be a devoted husband, attentive to his wife's every need.

She felt certain, too, that he was a man capable of deeply tender feelings who, when parted from his love, would no doubt write long and affectionate letters, letters intended for her eyes alone, which she would keep safely hidden away.

Instinctively, Sarah's fingers sought the little device which opened the secret compartment in her writing case, but nothing happened. She frowned as she set aside her quill. The spring was stiff, she knew, but it seemed almost as if something was jamming it, preventing the flap from opening. She tried again, but it took several more attempts before she eventually succeeded, and the flap reluctantly opened

'What on earth. . .?'

Very carefully she eased the tightly wedged object out of the compartment, and laid it across her hand. For several moments it was as much as she could do to stare down at it in astonished disbelief, then, throwing on her robe, she rushed from the room, almost colliding with Buddle in her headlong flight along the passageway.

Ravenhurst, comfortably established in bed, propped against a mound of pillows, hardly had time to raise his eyes from the book he was reading, and answer the imperious tattoo, before the door was thrown wide and Sarah charged into the room.

'Great heaven's, child!' He regarded her keenly. 'Whatever's the matter?'

'Oh, sir!' Breathless more from excitement than from her headlong dash along the passageway, Sarah plumped herself down on the bed, and almost threw her incredible find on to the coverlet in front of him. 'Just you look at that!'

Setting aside the book, he obeyed the command, casting only the most cursory glance at the necklace before raising enquiring eyes to hers. 'Well, and what of it?'

'But, sir, don't you see? It isn't mine!' she informed him in some agitation, slightly nettled by his lack of interest. 'I found it wedged in the secret compartment of my writing-case.'

At this his attitude changed abruptly. 'Did you, now?' Spreading the necklace out, he studied it more closely.

'I've seen you before,' he murmured. 'But where have I seen you?'

He looked back at Sarah, who was in the process of making herself more comfortable on his bed by tucking her slender feet beneath her. Her robe was unfastened, and the movement caused the material of her nightgown to pull taut, clearly revealing the tantalising outline of young, firm breasts.

He cleared his throat, made a mental note not to leave it very much longer before he made a trip to London to visit his mistress, and then forced himself to concentrate on the mystery in hand. 'So, your writing-case has a hidden compartment, has it? Have you no idea how long this gaud has been in there?'

'Well, no, not really,' she confessed. 'You see, I don't ever use it, so I—' She broke off, her eyes narrowing. 'No, wait a moment! The morning after we arrived at the inn, I was showing it to Mr Nutley, and the necklace certainly wasn't there then.'

He did not respond, and after a few moments she raised her eyes to find him regarding her rather quizzically, and the reason for the look was obvious.

'Oh, no! You don't think that this was what Mr Nutley was so afraid of a certain someone discovering in his possession, and so hid it in my case?'

'That is precisely what I think, child, because I've just recalled where I've seen this necklace before. . . The last time I set eyes on it, it was adorning the neck of Lady Felchett.'

He picked it up, studying the glinting jewels beneath the candle's glow. 'I don't know, though. I'm certainly no expert, but it looks to me—' He checked on what he had been about to say when he noticed Sarah staring in unblushing fascination at his naked torso. 'Something seems to be puzzling you, child?'

'Yes, it's that.' She didn't hesitate to respond, pointing rather rudely at the triangular mat of dark hair covering his chest. 'Are all men similarly cursed with all that hair on their bodies?'

'Cursed with. . .? You really are the most outrageous little baggage, Sarah!' he scolded, slightly affronted by this slur on his manliness but, far from cowed, she dissolved into laughter.

'I'm sorry,' she apologised, wiping her streaming eyes with the back of her hand, 'but it came as rather a shock. You see, I've never seen a man without his clothes on before.'

'Good God! I sincerely trust not!'

A further gurgle escaped her. 'You know very well what I mean. I shouldn't have been surprised, though,' she admitted. 'I did notice when you came to my bedchamber, that time at the inn, that you had hairs at the base of your throat, but I didn't realise just how far they spread.'

She watched as he, with all the modesty of an embarrassed virgin, pulled the bedcovers further up his chest, and chuckled again. 'Do you never wear a nightshirt, sir? Not that I suppose there's much need,' she went on, not giving him the opportunity to answer. 'With all that on your person you must be warm enough.'

'God in heaven!' He clapped a hand over his eyes. 'What will the outrageous chit say next? And kindly move yourself—you're sitting on my feet!'

Sarah altered her position. 'I think it might be best if we concentrate on the diamond necklace,' she suggested with what he considered the most provocative feminine smile he had ever witnessed. 'What do you intend doing with it? Are you going to return it to Lord Felchett?'

He scratched the side of his head, ruffling his dark hair into disarray. 'No. I suppose I'll need to pay a visit to Bristol, and see if I cannot locate Stubbs,' he responded without much enthusiasm. 'I intended making a return trip to Bath in a few days, anyway. So I shall go to Bristol first, and then go on to Bath afterwards.'

He could clearly read the unspoken question in her eyes. 'Yes, Sarah, I fully intend to pay a visit on my swindling cousin. And I shall also call upon Mrs Stanton while I'm there, and discover if she has heard anything from your runaways.'

Sarah brightened at this. 'Oh, would you give her my letter, sir? I've nearly finished it. I'll return to my room and do so now.'

She had only just slipped her feet back on to the floor when the door was thrown wide, and the Dowager came purposefully into the room. 'What is the meaning of this?' she demanded in outraged tones. 'Sarah, return to your room at once!'

'Yes, you run along now, child,' Marcus urged gently before she had time to open her mouth and explain the reason for her presence in his bedchamber. 'Finish your letter, and then give it to one of the servants to bring along to me. I intend leaving early in the morning, so I'll bid you farewell now.'

The Dowager bade her a curt good-night, and then waited for the door to close behind Sarah before moving towards the bed where her far from penitent grandson regarded her with a wickedly mocking gleam in his eyes.

'What do you mean by permitting that child to visit

you in your bedchamber, Marcus? Have you such scant regard for her reputation?'

'Oh, for heaven's sake!' he responded in combined exasperation and amusement. 'What the devil did you think I was proposing to do. . .ravish the girl?'

She could not prevent a twitching smile at this. 'No, I did not. You have faults enough, but despoiling innocent damsels isn't one of them. But Sarah is an exceedingly pretty young woman, and—'

'Yes, I had noticed.'

'And you are a man.'

'I wouldn't be at all surprised if Sarah hasn't come to that conclusion, too.'

'Marcus!' The Dowager rapped her cane on the floor. 'This is no time for flippancy! Who will believe her innocent if she continues to visit you in your bed-chamber?'

He regarded her for a moment in brooding silence. 'Yes, you're right, of course,' he admitted, rather reluctantly it seemed to her. 'I'll have a word with Sarah when I get back. But in the meantime,' he went on, giving her back look for look, 'I won't have you scolding the child. The last thing in the world I want is for her to be afraid or embarrassed to come to me.'

She assured him that she had absolutely no intention of doing so and, satisfied, he turned his attention once more to the necklace, requesting her to take a look at it, and explaining how it came to be in his possession.

'I don't care for it very much,' the Dowager remarked when she had learned all. 'The setting is rather heavy. Quite ugly, in fact! No doubt the Felchetts will be relieved to have it restored to them, though. Which is more than the Nutleys will experience when they learn about the goings-on. One cannot but sympathise, Marcus. It is one thing to discover your offspring is dead, and quite another to learn he was nothing more than a common thief.'

'Nutley was a nincompoop, ma'am,' her grandson responded, betraying his scant regard for the deceased. 'I should be very surprised if his was the brain behind the robbery.' And that is precisely what concerns me, he added silently.

The following morning Marcus was up early, and went out to the stableyard even before his ward had left her room. He had sent a message for Jeb's bays to be harnessed to his curricle and for his young stable lad to accompany him, and everything was in readiness for his departure.

Sutton cast a rather petulant look up at his subordinate, who was already seated in the carriage, keeping the bays well under control, before slanting a rather hopeful glance in his master's direction. 'Will you be collecting the greys, sir? Cause ifen you are, I could quite easily go wi' young Ben 'ere, and save you the bother.'

Marcus could not prevent a smile as he climbed up on to the seat beside the young groom and took the reins from him. He knew Sutton must be feeling peeved at not being the one to accompany him, but this time he had far more important work for his head groom.

'I have business in Bristol first, Sutton. Then I shall go on to Bath. I don't know just how long I'll be away, but it's important you remain here. I need you to watch over my ward whilst I'm gone.'

Sutton's ears pricked up at this, and he looked up at his master in some alarm. 'Lord bless me! She ain't likely to lope off again, is she, sir?'

This drew another smile from his master, but it seemed much softer this time. 'No, Sutton, rest easy. Now having come to know my ward, I can safely promise you that she wouldn't do that. That isn't my Sarah's way. But I want you to accompany her whenever she ventures out of doors. Never let her go off on her own, whether on foot or horseback. I don't care what excuses you need to make, so long as you never let her out of your sight.'

There was no semblance of a smile, now, and his eyes grew flint-like as he stared down at the ground. 'Guard her with your life, Sutton. . .I would not be best pleased if aught ever happened to my Sarah.'

Chapter Nine

It was difficult to believe that within the space of less than two weeks there could be such a marked change in the weather. But so it was. February with its biting-cold winds and snowstorms was well and truly a thing of the past. March had arrived, bringing with it pleasant days of mild sunshine and almost cloudless skies, though the nights continued to be cold and there was always a light covering of hoar-frost by morning.

Spring seemed to have arrived, surprisingly, quite early. Everywhere the light greenish hues of new growth were to be seen, and Sarah, having always been an avid walker, ventured out of doors much more often. Her strolls around the Dowager's garden, however, soon began to pall. Like Ravenhurst, she found the overgrown grounds rather depressing, and decided to venture further afield.

The previous day she had walked across the Earl's vast estate and had spent a very pleasant afternoon exploring the home wood; and today she had decided to inspect the pretty village that she had passed through on the day her guardian had brought her to the Dower House.

She had almost reached the main driveway leading to the big house when she became aware of the sound of heavy footsteps, and turned to see Sutton striding purposefully in her direction. Since Mr Ravenhurst's departure, six days before, Sutton had ridden out with her each morning, and she most certainly didn't object to his company.

The groom made a cheerful companion, and his rather dry sense of humour never failed to amuse her. Apart from this, he knew the county well, and had shown her some of the more pleasant rides, and had escorted her to several places of interest round about.

She had been rather surprised, though, suddenly to come across him in the home wood the day before. Her eyes narrowed suspiciously. Yes, that encounter might well have been purely accidental. But for it to happen twice in as many days was just too much of a coincidence!

'Well, well, Sutton,' she greeted him as he reached her side. 'What a surprise! I expect, like me, you decided on the spur of the moment to enjoy this rather pleasant afternoon sunshine and go out for a walk.'

'Aye, that's it, ma'am!' He made a sound suspiciously like a sigh of relief. 'There ain't much for me to do back at the stables with the master away.'

'No, quite. You'll no doubt be pleased to return to Ravenhurst and your own domain.' They reached the main driveway, and Sarah's lips curled into a wicked little smile. 'Where were you thinking of walking? Up to the big house?'

As this seemed the most obvious goal, Sutton did not hesitate. 'Aye, that's right, ma'am.'

'In that case, I'm afraid we must part company. My destination lies in quite another direction.' The expression on his face was so ludicrous that Sarah dissolved into laughter. 'Oh, Sutton! You must consider me the veriest dunderhead! How long did you suppose it would take me to work out your little ploy?'

The suspicion of a blush showed beneath the weathered skin, and he looked so uncomfortably guilty, like a child caught in some mischievous prank, that Sarah took pity on him.

'Oh, come along with me. I don't mind in the least if you accompany me to the village. Though just why your master should have asked you to keep an eye on me I can't imagine.' She cast him a rather thoughtful glance. 'Unless, of course, he suspected that I might try to leave in his absence.'

'Oh, no, miss. It weren't 'cause he were afraid of owt like that,' he hurriedly assured her. 'And that I do know. But he did ask me to keep me eye on you, right enough,' he freely admitted.

Did he, now? Sarah thought, eyes narrowing again, and it didn't take many moments before she had worked out the possible motive behind the request.

'Sutton, was anything else discovered about those unfortunate happenings before you left the inn?'

'What inn would that be, Miss Pennington?'

'Don't prevaricate!' she snapped. 'I have no intention of indulging in one of your master's foolish games of pretence.'

A spark of respect glinted in the groom's grey eyes. He had swiftly come to the conclusion that his master's ward was a sweet-natured filly, but she certainly didn't lack spirit. Anyone who could stand up to Mr Ravenhurst the way she did must have considerable pluck, and Sutton admired her for that. Added to which his master was clearly very fond of her. And that in itself was good enough for him!

'No, nothing, miss. 'Cepting I did overhear someone complaining that someone had been in their room, going through their things, like.'

'Who was complaining?'

'Can't be sure, but I reckon it were that gangling wench that put me in mind of a school-ma'am. They were in the parlour at the time. . .her and the magistrate, I think it were. Only just caught a snippet as I passed the door. The magistrate arranged for Nutley's body to be sent back to Oxfordshire. But apart from that,' he shrugged, 'nothing much else 'appened. We were all allowed to leave not long after you and the master went.'

'And did Mr Stubbs resume his journey with the other passengers?'

'Aye, miss, that he did. Though whether he went as far as Bristol, I couldn't say. I left the stage at Chippenham as I 'ad to go and collect the master's carriage and old mincing bree—Mr Ravenhurst's valet,' he amended quickly.

Sarah could not prevent a smile at this. It had not taken her very long to discover that the head groom and valet had scant regard for each other. She had heard Quilp sniff rather pointedly at mention of the groom's name; and Sutton's rather vulgar response to any mention of the valet was to spit on the ground.

It had not taken Sarah very long, either, to discover that Sutton, in particular, was touchingly devoted to his master. Ravenhurst could do no wrong in the head groom's eyes. There wasn't a better master in the land, according to Sutton, nor a more idyllic spot to be found anywhere than the Ravenhurst estate.

His master's word was law, and Sutton had not hesitated to carry out Ravenhurst's orders to the letter, though Sarah suspected that time hung heavily on the groom's hands as he had been only too eager to ride out with her in the mornings. But Ravenhurst had not commanded him to go with her whenever she ventured forth in order to keep the groom gainfully employed, nor to provide her with some genial company.

Oh, no, her guardian had done so because he feared that the mysterious cloaked figure would, by a simple process of elimination, work out who must have the diamond necklace.

By the time she had arrived back at the Dower House, after having toured the quaint little village that lay just beyond the estate's boundary wall, Sarah had still been unable to work out who Mr Nutley's possible accomplice might have been.

If, as Sutton had suggested, Miss Grimshaw had suspected that someone had been going through her belongings, and if the cloaked figure had, indeed, been a female, there was only one possible candidate. Sarah shook her head in disbelief. If Dottie Hogg turned out to be the malefactor, then she was the most accomplished actress alive. And that was something Miss Dorothea de Vine most certainly was not!

On entering the hall, Sarah was informed by the butler that the Countess of Styne, accompanied by her eldest daughter, had called, and that she was to go straight up to the Dowager's private sitting-room. Sarah had learned from Buddle the day before that the family had returned from Kent, and she was eager to make their acquaintance.

Delaying only for the time it took to remove her cloak and bonnet and to tidy her hair, Sarah entered the room to discover a rather colourless female in her mid-forties, and a rather pretty girl, with large brown eyes and a riot of dusky locks, sitting side by side on the sofa, and the Dowager in her favourite armchair, making not the least attempt to stifle a yawn.

'Ah! Sarah, my dear. Come, let me introduce you to my visitors,' the Dowager said, brightening perceptively.

After the introductions were made, Sarah seated herself in the chair on the opposite side of the hearth and politely thanked the Countess for the use of her horse.

'Not at all, my dear. I ride so infrequently these days that my mare gets little enough exercise. You are most welcome to make use of her whenever you wish.' The kind offer was accompanied by a warm smile. 'It is rather a pity that Sophia is not fond of that form of exercise, otherwise I am sure she would have been delighted to accompany you on your rides. Unfortunately, she sustained a bad fall some years ago, and is disinclined to get back in the saddle again.'

'Very understandable, ma'am,' Sarah responded, ignoring the Dowager's unladylike snort of disapproval, and bestowing a smile on poor Sophia, who had grown quite pink with embarrassment at her grandmother's all-too-evident derision. 'It would be unkind to force her to sit a horse if she was disinclined. Perhaps she may overcome her fears, given time.'

Her sympathetic understanding earned her a warm look of approval from the kind-hearted Countess. 'Mama-in-law has been telling me that you are to spend a few weeks here, and then go to London in the spring. I have been endeavouring to persuade her to stay with us in the town house for the duration of the Season. You and my daughter would be company for each other.'

Sarah steadfastly refused to look in the Dowager's direction. 'That is most kind of you, ma'am. But I believe my guardian is wishful for us to stay at his house in Berkeley Square.'

'Perhaps he can be persuaded to change his mind.'

'I shouldn't bank on that, Hetta, if I were you,' the Dowager put in bluntly. 'You know Ravenhurst.'

'Yes, yes, I do.' The Countess responded, casting a sympathetic look in Sarah's direction. 'He's grown so very like his dear papa. . .well, in looks, at any rate,' she amended.

Sarah regarded her with interest. 'Does he resemble his father, ma'am? I remember dear Godmama very well, but I cannot bring to mind my guardian's father.' She shrugged. 'But then I was very young when I paid those visits to Ravenhurst.'

'Yes, Marcus resembles his father,' the Dowager confirmed. 'Warren Ravenhurst could never be described as a handsome man, either. But, like his son, he had a presence. Eyes instinctively turned in his direction. Just as they do when Marcus enters a room.'

'Yes, that is certainly true,' the Countess agreed, flashing Sarah an unmistakable look of concern this time. 'Your guardian, though, does have a rather more forceful nature than his father had.'

'He certainly does have that, ma'am, but one grows accustomed. Added to which I don't let it worry me. If he tries to become too high-handed, I merely take him down a peg or two by giving him a scold.'

The Dowager's eyes glinted with unholy amusement as both visitors gaped in amazement, just as if they had suddenly discovered that Sarah had descended from another planet.

'Your sympathy is quite misplaced, Hetta. I'm pleased to say that Sarah isn't afraid of Marcus in the least. It is so very refreshing!' She looked approvingly at her grandson's ward. 'It is Sophia's birthday next week, and the family is celebrating the occasion with a party. Remind me to have a word with Buddle. I want your new evening gown finished in good time.'

The following afternoon Sarah had to forgo her walk as Buddle, having worked hard on it for many hours, brought the gown along to Sarah's room for the first fitting. The dress needed only a few minor alterations, the abigail decided before kneeling on the carpet to pin up the hem.

From her position Sarah was unable to catch sight of her reflection in the full-length mirror, but thought the turquoise silk had made up quite beautifully, although she did consider the square neckline had been cut indecently low, but refrained from comment. She soon grew tired of looking down at Buddle's bowed head and turned her own to stare out of the window, her eyes narrowing as she caught sight of a fair-haired young man busily raking up dead leaves.

'Who's that outside in the garden, Buddle? I cannot see his face clearly, but I can tell that it certainly isn't Wilkins.'

'It's probably the new lad who came round the other morning looking for work. Wilkins could do with the help. He isn't getting any younger. The lad will be here only a few weeks, though. He's hoping to find work in London for the Season, so Clegg tells me.' Buddle's brows snapped together suddenly. 'Will you keep still, miss! How am I supposed to get this hem straight with you fidgeting away?'

Sarah looked down again at the abigail's bent head, and her lips curled into a fond smile. For all her snappishness and impatience the woman really was a dear. 'Do you know, Buddle, you're a wonderful abigail. You arrange hair beautifully, and you're an excellent seamstress. Pity you're such a scold. . .and a tale-bearer,' she added meaningfully.

Not once since the night she had been discovered in her guardian's bedchamber had mention been made of her presence there, a circumstance which she considered most strange. Although she had sought him out in all innocence, and nothing improper had occurred, she was fully aware that she had committed a scandalous breach of conduct by being alone with a man, guardian or not, in such intimate surroundings.

She was very well aware, also, who had alerted the Dowager to the possible dangers, and raised a quizzical brow as Buddle lifted guilty eyes to meet hers.

'Now, Miss Sarah, don't you go holding that against old Buddle. What was I supposed to do? I knew there was no harm in it, even before I learned about you finding that necklace an' all. But others might have viewed things different. You were lucky I spied you. Had it been one of the other servants seeing you slip into Master Marcus's room that way, I shudder to think of the gossip.'

Sarah had never supposed that Buddle's actions had been prompted by anything other than the purest of motives, but could not resist the temptation to tease her further.

'I've learned from her ladyship that you began life with this family as nurserymaid; have learned, too, which among those many chicks placed in your capable hands was your undoubted favourite.'

One finely arched brow rose again. 'Whose reputation were you trying to protect, Buddle—his or mine? I can only imagine,' she went on, suddenly finding the fingernails on her right hand of immense interest, 'that you must have feared I had gone to that room with the intention of compromising your favourite nursling.'

Buddle rose to her feet instantly, and was halfway through voicing a staunch denial when she noticed the mischievous twinkle in blue-green eyes. 'Why, you little monkey!' she scolded, just as though Sarah had been one of her former nursery charges. 'You never thought nothing of the sort!'

'No, I never did,' Sarah confessed, not in the least shamefaced. 'But I have frequently wondered why the Dowager didn't take me roundly to task. Do you know, Buddle, she has never said a word.'

'Ah! Well, I know why,' she responded, forgetting to be cross. 'Master Marcus told her in no uncertain terms that she wasn't to do so.'

'Did he, really? Well, was that not kind of him!' Sarah frowned suddenly. 'Unless, of course, he wishes to have that privilege himself, and intends to scold me when he returns. . . Yes, that sounds much more likely, much more like him,' she decided finally, and drew a surprising gurgle of laughter from the maid.

'I knew it! Knew the instant I set eyes on you that hidden behind that sweet face was the mind of a wicked minx.' Buddle's disapproving shake of the head might have looked convincing had her thin lips not twitched slightly. 'I know what signs to look for, you see.'

Sarah's eyes glinted in response. 'Oh, I knew it would be fruitless trying to fool you. You're quite right, of course. I am utterly depraved. Quite beyond the pale, in fact!'

'Well, I wouldn't go as far as to say that,' Buddle's lips twitched again as she resumed her former kneeling position. 'But it will be no bad thing when Master Marcus returns and takes you in hand again.'

Sarah became serious, and raised troubled eyes to gaze sightlessly across the room. 'Yes, I wonder what can be keeping him? It's been a week since he left.'

'Aye, miss. But Master Marcus has always been one for keeping his own counsel. Mayhap he hasn't been able to locate that Bow Street Runner, or maybe other errands have kept him busy. Either way, there's no need for you to fret none. Master Marcus is quite capable of taking care of himself.'

Sarah wasn't so much worried as just eager for news. No, she amended silently, she was eager for his return. The simple truth of the matter was that she was missing their bantering exchanges; missing his caustic remarks and heavy dark-browed scowls. . . She was, quite simply, missing him. Which was really quite silly when one came to think about it, she reflected. After all, she had known him for such a short time, and yet it seemed as if she had known him all her life. How very strange that was!

As the days passed and still no word reached them of his possible return, Sarah's discontentment increased, but she was careful not to show it. She found some relief in her continued daily rides with Sutton, and although she enjoyed the groom's company, he was no substitute for Ravenhurst.

She also derived much pleasure in the evenings when she would sit with the Dowager, either reading aloud to her or playing cards; and she, at least, looked forward to the regular afternoon visits made by the Countess and her eldest daughter, both of whom she considered friendly and charming; but no matter how much satisfaction she attained from these varied interludes, she began to feel increasingly that there was something fundamentally missing from her life.

As the second week drew to a close and there was still no word from Ravenhurst, Sarah had resigned herself to attending Sophia's birthday celebration without the comfort of his escort.

As Buddle had warned her that she wished to create a more elaborate hairstyle for the occasion, Sarah repaired to her room in good time, and sat obediently still on the chair before the dressing-table mirror, watching in fascination as the experienced abigail's artistic fingers busily worked away. Buddle piled the golden-brown hair high on Sarah's head so that it cascaded down in a shower of long ringlets, and then intricately weaved a turquoise ribbon through the silken locks.

When at last she was permitted to stand before the full-length mirror to see the finished results, Sarah stared at her reflection with scant enthusiasm. The dress was lovely, and Buddle had added a flounce, decorating it with tiny rosebuds fashioned from the same turquoise silk.

Her arms were covered in the first pair of long evening gloves she had ever owned, and the Dowager had insisted that she wear a lovely string of pearls and matching earrings, which had once belonged to Sarah's godmother. Never had she been so elegantly attired. She ought she knew to feel overjoyed. But the simple fact remained that she felt anything but.

'What is it, miss?' Buddle's shrewd dark eyes had not missed the forlorn expression. 'What is it that doesn't please you?'

'Oh, nothing, nothing! Everything is just perfect!' she hurriedly assured her. 'The dress is beautiful, and I simply love the way you have arranged my hair.'

There was a moment's silence, then, 'Come, on, miss. You can tell old Buddle. What is it that you're not happy about?'

Sarah's forced smile faded. 'I'm not happy about Mr Ravenhurst's continued absence,' she admitted at last. 'I cannot help thinking something must have happened to him.'

Buddle stared deeply into the blue-green eyes for an endless moment. 'You'll do,' she surprised Sarah by remarking softly. 'Yes, you'll do very nicely, I think.

'Now, come along, miss,' she went on in her usual no-nonsense manner, 'otherwise you'll be late. Let's get this shawl round you, and you'll need make do with your old cloak for the carriage drive as your new one hasn't arrived. And, miss,' she added, arresting Sarah's progress to the door, 'don't you go worrying your pretty head over Master Marcus no more. He'll turn up safe and sound. You see if he don't.'

A little of Buddle's optimism must have rubbed off on her, for as Sarah entered her guardian's elegant carriage, awaiting them at the side entrance, she experienced a tinge of excitement at the prospect of attending Sophia's seventeenth birthday celebration which, according to the Dowager, was not likely to be a small affair.

Although she rarely had a good word to say about her eldest son, her ladyship had had to own that the Earl was far from miserly on these occasions. She had mentioned earlier in the day that musicians had been hired for the evening, and that she wouldn't be in the least surprised to discover half the county had been invited.

Sarah was unable to confirm whether this was true or not, but as they neared the mansion, only a matter of a few minutes later, she could see a long line of carriages waiting to deposit their passengers at the front entrance.

The early March evening was dry, with a starlit, cloudless sky, but there was that inevitable frosty nip in the air. None the less, with their legs covered with a fur-lined rug, and with hot bricks at their feet, the Dowager and Sarah remained comfortably warm until the carriage reached the front entrance and it was their turn to alight.

This was not Sarah's first visit to the ancestral home. She had been invited to dine twice since the family's return from Kent. The Earl, a rotund little man in his late forties, had made her feel most welcome, and the evenings had passed very pleasantly, though she had found herself unable to mask a chuckle on the first occasion when the meal had arrived at the table far from warm, and she had been reminded of her guardian's scathing condemnations.

He had been right, too, about the large, high-ceilinged rooms being draughty; but she had no fault to find with the furnishings, which managed to combine both elegance and comfort.

The ballroom, however, was not so very comfortable. Many of its windows were ill-fitting, and the large fireplace had an unfortunate tendency to billow out smoke at regular intervals. Therefore, the Countess, very wisely, had decided not to hold the party in there, but had thrown open two connecting ground-floor rooms for the occasion.

Sophia, dressed in a very pretty gown of white sarsenet, adorned with the most delicate pink rosebuds round the sleeves and neckline, stood shyly beside her parents at the entrance to the first salon. After receiving the warmest of greetings from the kindly host and hostess, Sarah complimented Sophia on her lovely gown before following the Dowager into the room where chairs had been placed all along the walls.

They had only just seated themselves when a tall, rather handsome young man, sporting a dazzling waistcoat embroidered with bright crimson poppies, approached them. He bore too strong a resemblance to his younger brothers and sisters for Sarah not to know, instantly, who he was, even before he said,

'Grandmama! What a pleasure it is to see you looking so well!'

'Bah! Jackanapes!' was the Dowager's rather charming response, and her grandson's finely chiselled lips twitched as he winked rather cheekily in Sarah's direction.

'Now, now, ma'am, you know you don't mean that. You like me, really, you know you do. Not as well as you like Cousin Marcus, but I come a close second.'

Her ladyship gave vent to one of her unladylike snorts, but there was a decidedly appreciative gleam in her eyes as she said, 'If you have not already guessed, Sarah, this impertinent young chub is the Honourable Bertram Stapleton, the Earl's son and heir. Bertram, this is Ravenhurst's ward, Miss Sarah Pennington.'

His bow was a study in elegance. 'Would you do me the honour, Miss Pennington, of standing up with me for the next set of country dances?'

Because she had frequently practised with her friend Clarissa, Sarah knew the steps to most country dances, and did not hesitate to accept the invitation.

'I cannot tell you, sir,' she remarked as they made their

way towards the wide open doors leading to the salon
where people were already forming sets for the next
dance, 'how refreshing it is to discover someone who
isn't afraid of the Dowager. The other members of your
family seem almost terrified of her. Poor Sophia never
dares to open her mouth when in the Dowager's presence,
and even your father appears to be somewhat in awe
of her.'

'Yes, madness, ain't it?' He raised his eyes heavenwards. 'The only way to deal with the old lady is to stand
up to her, give as good as you get. Cousin Marcus told
me that years ago.'

Sarah decided she liked Sophia's elder brother. He
seemed a friendly young man with pleasant, easy-going
manners, and she found herself saying, 'Yes, and he's
another many seem in awe of.'

He slanted a quizzical glance. 'Are you?'

'It would be a little unpleasant if I were, considering
I am his ward. But, no,' she admitted. 'No, I'm not in
the least afraid of him.'

'Pleased to hear it! Marcus is a great gun. Pulled me
out of a scrape or two, I can tell you.' His glance down
at her this time was almost apologetic. 'It wasn't until I
arrived yesterday that I was aware of your existence, Miss
Pennington. I cannot recall my cousin ever mentioning
that he had a ward.'

Far from offended, Sarah admired his honesty. 'I suspect, sir, that that was because he had forgotten himself.'
Her eyes danced with wicked amusement. 'How very
glad I am, now, that I took it upon myself to leave Bath,
and put him to the trouble of scouring the country in
search of me. I can safely promise you that he won't
forget my existence again in a hurry.'

The Dowager, following their progress into the other room, saw her grandson suddenly throw back his head and roar with laughter. She was not in the least surprised that Sarah had captured his interest so soon. She was a lovely girl whose rather wicked sense of humour would appeal to Bertram. Her grandson was, the Dowager secretly thought, a charming rascal, both handsome and good-natured, but rather too young yet to pose any real threat.

She continued to watch them, a satisfied smile curling her lips, as Sarah performed the dance's intricate steps with effortless grace. As the evening wore on her charge returned to her side from time to time, but Sarah was in great demand. Many of the young men, and some not so young, requested her as a partner, and so she spent much of the time on the dance floor, leaving the Dowager quite happily conversing with her numerous acquaintances.

The evening was almost half over when she became aware of a large dark shape looming at her side, and broke off her conversation with her daughter-in-law to turn her head.

'Ha! So, you've returned at last, have you? And high time, too!'

Chapter Ten

Marcus gazed down at his grandmother in his usual lazy affectionate way. 'The warmth of your greeting, ma'am, never ceases to affect me deeply.'

'Ha! When has there ever been need for wordy sentiment between you and me, Marcus?' Her tone was indifferent, but the look in her eyes as she cast them over his tall figure, immaculately attired in satin knee-smalls and a long-tailed coat of black cloth, was anything but apathetic. His bearing was always impressive, but in full evening garb he looked magnificent. 'How long have you been back?'

'Only long enough for me to freshen up, change and come here.' He turned to his aunt, who was gazing up at him with the customary mixture of admiration and awe which he always managed to instil in her. 'I hope you will overlook my late arrival, ma'am, and my arrogant presumption that I might descend upon you without invitation.'

'Oh, no, no! Not at all,' she hurriedly assured him, slightly breathless in her confusion. She had grown accustomed over the years to a man whose conversation was

191

frequently blunt to the point of rudeness, and never in her wildest imaginings had she believed him capable of such courteous charm. 'You are always most welcome, Ravenhurst. You should know that.'

'Your graciousness, madam, is only just matched by your excellent taste in dress,' he responded, which had the effect of sending her quite pink with pleasure, and even caused his grandmother to blink several times. 'As always, your appearance is faultless.'

'Well, you've certainly made her day,' the Dowager remarked a few minutes later when her daughter-in-law, still with a suspicion of a gratified glow in her cheeks, moved away to mingle with her other guests.

'I have never rated my aunt's intelligence very high. But you will need to go a very long way to find a woman with better dress sense. She is always immaculately groomed. I believe in giving credit where it's due, ma'am.' His eyes scanned the salon. 'Where's my ward?'

'She's in the other room, dancing. The poor child must be quite exhausted. She's hardly sat down all evening. Which is something I wish you would do, Marcus. I am getting a crick in my neck looking up at you all the time.'

He obeyed automatically, seating himself in the chair his aunt had just vacated, while his dark eyes continued to scrutinise the dancers in the other room. 'Is that her?' he enquired, suddenly frowning. 'The one in the bluish-coloured dress?'

'Of course it is!' The Dowager cast him an impatient glance. 'Don't tell me you've forgotten what the poor child looks like already?'

'Of course I haven't forgotten! But her hair has been arranged differently. And what the devil do you mean by letting her wear such an indecent gown?'

'Indecent?' she echoed, rather taken aback by the unjustified criticism. 'It's nothing of the sort! It is cut no lower than most of the other gowns the young ladies are wearing. Besides, Sarah has nothing of which to be ashamed. She has a charming figure. Quite delightful, in fact!'

'I can see that!' he retorted. 'And so can every other man in the room!'

The Dowager refused to comment further, for it had suddenly dawned on her what lay at the root of his ill-humoured remarks. She smiled to herself as she watched the dancers leave the floor, and knew by the undisguised delight that suddenly sprang into a pair of aquarmarine-coloured eyes the instant Sarah had caught sight of her guardian.

'Oh, sir! It is so very good to see you again!' Almost running the last few steps towards him, she held her hands outstretched and, standing up, he took them eagerly in his own.

'And it is good to see you again, my child. I do not need to ask if you are well. Your delightful colour informs me clearly enough.'

He then dispensed with the services of the young man who had kindly restored Sarah to the Dowager Countess by casting him a slight smile, and then turned his attention back to his ward.

Having nearly attained the age of two-and-thirty, he was certainly no stranger to feminine charms. He had seen many beauties over the years, many lovelier than Sarah, but he had never glimpsed a figure to better hers. Slender yet shapely, she was perfectly proportioned. He allowed his gaze to wander over the slim waist and hips before raising his eyes to dwell for an appreciative moment on the delightful swell of the firm young breasts.

Sarah had received numerous compliments on her appearance that night, and countless admiring glances from the many gentlemen present, but Ravenhurst's swift appraisal had felt more like a soft caress, causing a pleasurable tingling sensation to feather its way over her skin, and bringing added colour to her cheeks.

When, however, he did finally raise his eyes to meet hers, she was unable to tell whether he approved of her appearance or not, nor was she able to account for the strangely disturbing intensity in their dark fathomless depths.

'Why not ask your ward to dance?'

The Dowager's suggestion broke the mesmeric hold of that ardent gaze, and Sarah looked down at her, and then rather shyly back at her guardian in hopeful expectation, but he disappointed her by saying in his usual blunt way,

'Because I never dance, as you very well know. I leave all that prancing about to the young nincompoops. And talking of which,' he added, noticing someone heading in their direction, 'who's this tailor's dummy about to descend on us?'

Sarah glanced round. 'You know very well who it is. And don't you dare to say anything rude to him, sir!' she ordered in an undertone. 'He thinks very highly of you, and he has been very kind to me this evening.'

'By all that's wonderful!' Bertram gave his cousin an affectionate slap on the back. 'So you made it after all, Marcus!'

'As you see. But what the duece are you doing here?'

'Came down for m'sister's birthday. What do you think?'

'Came down?' One dark brow rose suspiciously. 'Or sent down?'

'Now, now, cuz! You know I don't get into scrapes any longer. Well, none that I'm admitting to, at any rate.' He noticed those dark, intelligent eyes move fleetingly to the bright red poppies adorning his waistcoat, and puffed his chest out rather proudly. 'What do you think of it, Marcus? Wonderful, ain't it?'

'Believe me, young man, I should take the greatest delight in telling you exactly what I think of it,' he responded with feeling. 'Unfortunately, though, I have been forbidden.'

'Do not take any notice, Bertram,' Sarah hurriedly intervened before the young man was foolish enough to prompt further. 'The musicians are striking up, and I have promised you this dance.'

She whisked him on to the dance floor with unseemly haste, and soon afterwards noticed her guardian escorting the Dowager into the room set out for cards, where most of the older people present had sought refuge well away from the the younger and more boisterous guests.

She was impatient to discover what had been decided with regard to the diamond necklace, but as she had promised to take supper with Bertram, and as Ravenhurst spent the remainder of the evening in conversation with many of the other people present, most of whom were known to him, she was unable to broach the subject until the evening had drawn to a close and they had climbed into the carriage awaiting to take them the short distance back to the Dower House.

She looked across at him eagerly. 'Now that we're alone, sir,' she said, with sublime disregard for the lady seated beside her, 'you must tell me what happened in Bristol. I'm simply bursting with curiosity.'

'Bursting. . .? Bursting! What sort of language is that for a young lady, may I ask!' the Dowager admonished crossly. 'Why, if such a word had ever fallen from my lips when I was your age, I would have been soundly whipped.'

Marcus caught the mischievous twinkle in the lovely blue-green eyes before Sarah cast a look of mock censure at the Dowager. 'Now, ma'am, that is a shocking untruth,' she admonished, mimicking her ladyship's disapproving tone to a nicety. 'And well you know it! No one would ever have dared to do such a thing to you.'

The Dowager gave a shout of laughter before wrapping Sarah across the knuckles with her fan, and then turning to her grandson, whose dark eyes were alight with amusement. 'You see how incorrigible the chit is, Ravenhurst. You have been away far too long.'

'Yes, far, far too long,' Sarah agreed. 'What happened in Bristol, sir?'

Leaning back against the plush velvet squabs, he regarded her indulgently. 'Not very much, child. It took me several days to locate Stubbs's whereabouts, and only did so because I had the great good fortune to run in to your friend Captain Carter.'

'Oh, is he still in Bristol, sir?'

'Not now, no. The delay on the road caused him to miss his boat. He has departed for the Peninsula now, however. But whilst he was kicking his heels in the city, he offered his services to the Runner. Stubbs, as I believe I mentioned once before, was sent to Bristol for the sole purpose of keeping watch on certain premises owned by a man suspected of dealing in stolen goods.

'However, being a conscientious individual, Stubbs

wanted to check the information given to him by our stranded fellow-travellers. You will no doubt be pleased to learn that he never for one moment suspected Carter of being responsible for either Nutley's death or the servant girl's, and didn't hesitate, therefore, to make use of him. He set him to keep watch on those premises I mentioned, whilst he went about verifying the information he had been given by the other stagecoach passengers.'

'And did all the stories turn out to be true?' she prompted eagerly when he fell silent.

'All but one, yes. You'll no doubt also be relieved to hear that the "Divine" Dorothea does have a mother living in Bristol. She is residing with her at present. A couple of days after they had arrived, Stubbs followed her when she left her mother's house, and saw her enter a theatre, presumably looking for work.

'The clerk's story also turned out to be authentic. He lives and works in the city. But I'm afraid of the Grimshaw woman there is no sign. Her sister's address turned out to be a church, of all things!'

Sarah frowned, remembering clearly what Sutton had disclosed. If Miss Grimshaw had, indeed, suspected that her belongings had been searched, then she was hardly likely to turn out to be the cloaked intruder. But why had she deliberately given Mr Stubbs false information? There seemed no good reason for having done so unless, of course, she had something to hide.

'How very odd!' she murmured.

'Quite!' he agreed laconically. 'Well, as you have probably gathered, all this was discovered before I turned up with the Felchett diamonds. Which really did start things moving. Stubbs wanted to return here with me, but felt he couldn't leave his post. So he sent an express to

London, and whilst he was awaiting reinforcements, I went on to Bath, leaving the—er—diamonds in his safe-keeping.'

He refrained from mentioning that he hadn't remained long in that city, and had taken the opportunity to travel to London to pay a much-needed visit to his mistress. The night of unbridled passion had certainly assuaged his bodily needs, but that was all. His heart and mind had been quite otherwise, and he had left the house the following morning feeling strangely hollow inside, and experiencing not the least desire to spend a further night in the arms of his skilful light o' love.

'Did you call in to see your cousin?'

Sarah's tentatively spoken enquiry drew him out of his reverie. 'I had a word or two, certainly.'

She eyed him gravely. 'Yes, I can imagine.'

'Sarah, surely you didn't expect Marcus to permit all his cousin's underhandedness to go unpunished?' the Dowager put in in her grandson's defence. 'Why, the deceitful, conniving wretch has been fleecing him for years!'

Sarah wasn't in the least surprised to discover that the Dowager was in full possession of the facts, although she herself had never breathed a word. She did consider any actions her guardian had taken completely justified in the circumstances, but the fact remained that she could not help feeling sorry for Mrs Fairchild, for the woman had been neither cruel nor even mildly unkind to the little orphaned girl placed in her charge.

'Yes, you're both right, of course,' she conceded at last. 'It's just that. . .'

'I did not turn her out on to the streets, Sarah, if that is what concerns you,' he assured her, much to her intense relief. 'But I have made it abundantly clear that, if she chooses to remain in that house, she will pay me rent, and at the going rate. If she falls behind with her payments, then I have left her in no doubt whatsoever that she will be evicted. And I shall suffer no qualms in doing so, either.

'But rest easy, child,' he added, casting her a rather crooked smile. 'I know for a fact that she was left adequate funds by her husband to live quite comfortably. If, however, she wishes to indulge in her particular vice, then I'm afraid she will need to find another source of income to cover the expenses, for she will get not a penny more from me.'

Silently, she was forced to admit that he had been really most lenient, and looked at him approvingly before asking him if he had also found the time to call on Mrs Stanton.

'Certainly. And you will be overjoyed to learn, no doubt, that the runaways were successful in their endeavours, and that Mrs Clarissa Fenshaw, as she is now, has been restored to the bosom of her family, for the time being at least.' He smiled at her exuberant expression. 'I have brought letters from both Clarissa and her mother, which will no doubt explain events far better than I ever could.'

'I must say, Sarah,' the Dowager remarked after listening quietly to her grandson's tidings in increasing dismay, 'you're a dear sweet girl, but it would appear you have a propensity for becoming involved with the most unsavoury characters—runaway couples, jewel thieves. . .and murderers, no less! I should imagine you find the peace and quiet at the Dower House quite a refreshing change.'

No sooner had she spoken than the carriage pulled up

in the stableyard. Without waiting for the groom, Ravenhurst jumped out, and had only just let down the steps when the elderly butler, carrying a lantern, emerged from the house.

'Oh, Master Marcus, sir!' Clegg, looking decidedly distraught, hurried across to the carriage. 'Thank heaven's you've returned! I was on the point of sending a message up to the big house to bring you back.'

'Why? What's happened?'

'We've had a break-in, sir. And poor Mr Quilp has been attacked. We've laid him on the sofa in the drawing-room, and I've already sent for the doctor.'

'Attend to your mistress!' Ravenhurst commanded, and then went striding into the house without another word

'Well, well! It would seem I spoke too soon, child,' her ladyship remarked as she stepped down from the carriage. 'It would appear that the gods have ordained that you won't be experiencing peace and quiet whilst you reside with me. How very enlivening!'

Clegg, raising the lantern aloft, saw them safely across the few feet of yard and into the house. They paused briefly by the drawing-room door, saw that not only Ravenhurst but Buddle, too, was attending the injured Quilp, who was now, thankfully, sitting up on the sofa, holding a cloth to his head.

As neither of them felt they could be of any help, and might possibly be in the way, they went straight upstairs to the Dowager's private sitting-room where a fire still burned welcomingly on the hearth. At her ladyship's request, Sarah poured out two glasses of Madeira, and then sat herself in the chair opposite and stared down into the glowing flames.

It would be comforting to think that the break-in had

been perpetrated by some opportunist thief, but Sarah could not delude herself. Foolishly, she had believed that, once the diamond necklace had been handed over to the authorities, the unfortunate affair would be at an end. How wrong could anyone be! Thankfully, though, her guardian had not been so simple-minded, and that was precisely why he had taken the precaution of ordering Sutton to watch over her in his absence.

She closed her eyes, recalling vividly the look in Ravenhurst's when Clegg had given him the unfortunate tidings. There had been such a strange mixture of anger and foreboding in their dark depths. Two people had died and another had been injured because of that wretched necklace! But why? Robbery, as Ravenhurst had pointed out, was one thing; murder quite another.

What on earth was so significant about that particular diamond necklace? she wondered. Surely there was more to it than just a simple case of robbery and greed? More importantly, how many more people would suffer before the mystery was finally solved?

A heartfelt sigh escaped her as she raised her eyes to gaze across at the Dowager. 'It would seem, ma'am, that I have, unwittingly, brought trouble to your house. It might have been better had I never come here.'

'Nonsense, child!' her ladyship responded, realising at once what had prompted the suggestion. 'Who is to say it wasn't some local rascal who, learning that there was to be a party at the mansion, thought to try his luck at a few houses in the vicinity.

'Not that I have much here worth stealing, you under-stand,' she went on matter-of-factly. 'There's my jewellery, of course, and a bit of silver. But not much else. I must ask Clegg to check and see just what is

missing.' She sipped her wine, and a contented smile
hovered about her mouth as she savoured its taste. 'I must
say I prefer this to the champagne served earlier. Never
could stomach the stuff myself. Weak and insipid, I
call it!'

It was quite evident that the Dowager did not wish to
discuss further what had occurred in their absence, and
so Sarah followed her lead.

'It was a lovely party, ma'am, didn't you think so?'

'Yes, most enjoyable. Although I've never held my
daughter-in-law in high esteem, I have to own she is a
very gracious hostess.' A wicked cackle of amusement
escaped her. 'Ravenhurst sent her quite pink with pleasure
this evening. You are a very good influence on him,
my dear.'

Sarah was not given the opportunity to enquire what
she meant, for the door opened and the man himself
entered the room to inform them that the doctor had
arrived, and to assure them that Quilp, thankfully, was
not too badly hurt. He then went on to warn them that they
would shortly be disturbed by the sounds of hammering as
he had ordered the broken window in the library boarded
up until a new piece of glass could be installed.

'Thank you, Marcus, for seeing to everything. You are
always to be relied upon.' The Dowager finished the
contents of her glass and rose to her feet. 'Well, it has
been a long evening and I'm rather tired, so I shall bid
you both good-night. No doubt Clegg will present me with
an inventory of exactly what is missing in the morning.'

Sarah watched her guardian close the door behind his
grandmother, and then walk across to the table on which
the decanters stood. He lacked none of his natural athletic
grace, and yet she detected a suppressed tension in those

fluid movements as he seated himself opposite in the Dowager's favourite chair.

'Nothing has been taken from the house, has it, sir?'

He looked at her for a moment above the rim of his glass before tossing the contents down his throat in one large swallow. 'No,' he said at length.

'No, I didn't think so.'

'Don't jump to conclusions, child. One cannot rule out the possibility that it was some local bent on a little petty theft. It is not an infrequent occurrence, after all.' He placed his empty glass down on to the table before looking directly across at her again. 'And do not forget the intruder was disturbed only a matter of minutes after he had gained unlawful entry. Which would hardly have given him time to relieve my grandmother of any of her belongings, now would it?'

Sarah chewed these remarks over in silence for several moments, and had to own that his suggestions were not unreasonable, but she remained sceptical and asked him to explain exactly what had occurred.

All the servants with the exception of the valet, it transpired, had congregated in the kitchen to enjoy a late supper. Quilp, having a fastidious nature, had insisted upon tidying his master's bedchamber before joining them. He had been descending the stairs when he had thought he detected the sound of breaking glass and, suspecting the footman of dropping a decanter whilst helping himself to its contents, had gone into the library to investigate.

The only light in the room had come from the fire which, apparently, had still been burning quite brightly in the grate. Even so, he had seen no one. The next instant, he had been struck from behind.

'Apart from the table, which had been overturned,' he went on to inform her after a thoughtful pause, 'no doubt by Quilp himself when he fell, and the broken window, everything seems to be in order.'

'So it might well have been an opportunist thief, but, personally, I do not think so.' She held his eyes with her own. 'And neither do you.'

He did not attempt to deny it, and said, taking her completely by surprise, 'We'll discuss this evening's incident, and our views on the matter, with Stubbs in the morning.'

'Mr Stubbs?' She was startled. 'Did you bring him back with you?'

'Yes. I made a return trip to Bristol to collect him. He's putting up at the village inn. I deposited him there earlier before I came here.'

'Then you both must think that an attempt will be made to retrieve the necklace, if this evening's fiasco was not, indeed, the first attempt to do so.'

His mouth set in a grim, straight line. 'One person has already been murdered, possibly two. And tonight there might easily have been a third fatality. . . Yes, child, I do think that this night's occurrence was perpetrated by our mysterious cloaked figure,' he admitted at last. 'Furthermore, I fear that whoever it is will not stop now.'

'But why, sir? Why?' she demanded urgently. 'What is so important about that particular necklace that someone is prepared to commit murder just to get their hands on it?'

'I have asked myself that very same question,' he admitted. 'And with perhaps more reason than you have had for doing so,' he finished rather cryptically.

Chapter Eleven

A hundred years before all the people inhabiting that tiny village nestling in the hollow just beyond the estate's boundary wall had had some connection with Styne. There was not a family living there that did not have at least one member working on the vast estate, either in the house or gardens; in the stables, or on the land itself. Generations had lived and died there without so much as travelling the merest five miles from home.

Over the years the tiny community had thrived, attracting outsiders. A blacksmith from Devizes had purchased some land off the previous Earl and had built his forge on the outskirts of the village, serving the community itself and people from miles around; and the inevitable inn had been erected where the men could relax and enjoy a tankard of ale after a hard day's toil.

The improvement in the roads during the second half of the previous century had inevitably brought changes. Where once everyone had known everyone else, now, many strangers came into their midst, either putting up at the inn, or merely passing through the village on their travels. It was quite a common sight to see sporting carriages of all descriptions bowling along the main street.

Consequently, when Sarah and Mr Ravenhurst, seated side by side in his curricle, entered the peaceful community, they aroused little interest, attracting no more than a fleeting glance from an elderly woman busily working in her front garden, and from the group of children playing happily together in the road.

Like most of the other buildings, the inn had whitewashed cob walls and a charming low thatched roof. At this time of the morning there were few, if any, customers. Marcus brought his curricle to a halt in the stable yard, and the sound of wheels on cobble stones so early in the day brought the innkeeper's inquisitive son out of a side door to investigate. He took immediate charge of the equipage, allowing the Dowager's grandson, whom he recognised instantly, to alight.

Sarah, who was looking perfectly charming in one of her new outfits, a pale blue walking dress and matching pelisse, and a very becoming bonnet lined with blue silk and with a matching silk ribbon tied in a coquettish bow beneath her chin, gratefully accepted her guardian's helping hand to alight. It never crossed her mind to demur when he tucked her arm through his, even though she was acutely aware of the latent rippling strength beneath the faultless sleeve of his blue superfine coat.

The instant she entered the inn the sweet smell of lavender, mixed with tobacco and spirits, assailed her nostrils, reminding her vividly of The Traveller's Rest. Here, too, the landlady seemed an industrious person, for already the wooden tables had been polished to a looking-glass shine and the floors swept clean.

As soon as her eyes had grown accustomed to the dimness, Sarah could see that the inn was deserted except for one customer, sitting at the table in the corner, casting his grey eyes over a copy of the *Morning Post*.

After ordering two tankards of ale, and a glass of wine for Sarah, Marcus wasted no time in apprising Mr Stubbs with details of the previous night's incident. The Runner listened intently, but from time to time would cast his eyes in Sarah's direction, a look in their shrewd depths that was hard to interpret.

'Well, sir, it would appear that it has happened rather sooner than either of us had expected,' Mr Stubbs remarked after learning all. 'The wretch certainly didn't waste much time. It would be a grave mistake to underestimate her.'

'Her?' Sarah echoed. 'Oh! Did Mr Ravenhurst inform you that I had come to the conclusion that the intruder that night at The Traveller's Rest was a female?'

'He did, Miss Pennington. And may I say it was an excellent piece of deduction. However, I already knew we were looking for both a man and a woman in connection with a series of robberies that took place last year.'

'Really?' Sarah's eyes began to twinkle as a rather amusing thought struck her. 'Did you never suspect that I might be that woman? After all, I did discover Mr Nutley's body.'

'In my line of work, one needs to question the authenticity of everyone. But one also, in time, becomes a fairly shrewd judge of character. And Mr Ravenhurst was sensible enough not to waste any time in apprising me of your true identity, and the reason why he had found himself at that inn.'

Sarah cast her guardian a reproachful glance, and he reciprocated with a rather mocking one.

'Yes, I don't doubt you would have preferred I

remained silent. Knowing you as I do, I feel certain you would have derived a deal of wicked amusement had you been carted back to Bow Street by Mr Stubbs.'

'Oh, I wouldn't go as far as to say that. But I would certainly have enjoyed putting you to the trouble of journeying to the capital in order to rescue me.'

Sarah could not prevent a chuckle at the look of exasperation on her guardian's face, but then became serious again as a thought struck her. 'You said you were looking for both a man and a woman in connection with certain robberies, Mr Stubbs. Did you know all along that Mr Nutley was the thief? Were you following him?'

'Oh, no, miss. It were pure coincidence we were both passengers on that particular stage coach.' Leaning back in his chair, he regarded her for a moment in silence, then said, 'Do you recall that morning when we were all in the parlour, Nutley included, and Mr Ravenhurst here mentions, quite innocent-like, that several items of jewellery had gone missing in recent months, and wondered whether it were the work of the same person or persons?'

'Yes, yes, I do, Mr Stubbs. I remember it quite clearly.'

'Well, he weren't far wrong. We at Bow Street had suspected for some time that at least two people were involved in the thefts. In each case a large party had been held at the house. Sometimes the jewellery wasn't discovered missing until days later. But in every case a recently employed maidservant would take exception to being questioned, and would soon afterwards leave in high dudgeon.

'During a London Season, miss, most of the large houses employ extra help. Most get staff from reputable agencies, but not always. And folk are so careless. You wouldn't believe it! Often they don't even bother to check references.

'It were the same in the case of the Felchett diamonds. Local girls, at least they were thought to be all local, had been hired for the occasion. The following day, after the diamonds had been discovered missing, one of the women took umbrage at being questioned, and upped and left.'

'But surely she was searched before being allowed to leave?'

'Yes, miss, she were. But the family assured us that nothing was discovered on her, nor amongst her belongings. Each robbery were the same.'

Sarah drew her brows together in profound thought. 'So, unless the searches were not thorough enough, the stolen items must have been handed over to someone else.'

'Precisely, Sarah!' Marcus concurred. 'Not another servant, however, but someone above suspicion. . . One of the guests attending the party, perhaps?'

'And was Mr Nutley among the guests at these parties?'

'He certainly was, miss,' Stubbs answered. 'But there were a dozen or more names that kept cropping up. Mr Ravenhurst were at three of 'em.'

'But what about the maidservant?' she enquired, resisting the temptation to goad her guardian on this very interesting circumstance. 'Surely you managed to get an accurate description of her?'

'Lord bless you, miss!' The Runner looked genuinely amused. 'In two cases she has black hair. In the others, seemingly, fair or brown. She were a Londoner, a Northerner or a West Country lass. She were described as a 'andsome wench—sometimes quite plain. The only things that never varied were height and build. She were taller than average for a woman, and of slim build.'

Sarah fell silent, digesting what she had learned. The woman was evidently an expert at disguise. An actress, perhaps. . .? Yes, she might well have been just that at one time, and had evidently been putting her considerable talents to a more profitable use during the past twelve months. And Dottie Hogg was an actress, of course. But Dottie was not tall, nor did she have a particularly slim build.

No, only one person putting up at that inn fitted that description. An image of the middle-aged spinster appeared before her mind's eye. That greying hair could have been a wig, and the dark circles round the eyes and the sallow complexion might easily have been effected by artificial means. She recalled, too, the way Miss Grimshaw had run with such agility down those stairs, just as though she had been years younger.

And how very cunning the woman had been, too! She had quite deliberately kept herself to herself as much as possible, and had remained in her room for fear, perhaps, that someone discerning enough just might penetrate the disguise.

'I think you've perhaps worked out for yourself who Nutley's accomplice must have been,' Mr Stubbs remarked after watching her expressive face closely. 'But, as I mentioned a while back, I didn't take a seat on that stage coach in order to follow Nutley. One of those stolen items of jewellery had turned up in Bristol, and I were being sent to that city to keep watch on a certain pawn-broker's shop that we at Bow Street had been getting some rather disturbing reports about.'

He paused to take a large swallow from his tankard. 'Nutley told me he were travelling to the West Country to visit an aunt, and until his death, and the subsequent events, I had no reason to disbelieve him, nor to think he was involved in the robberies.'

'But after his death, did you begin to suspect Miss Grimshaw, or whatever her real name is, of being his accomplice?'

'Oh, aye, miss, I suspected her right enough, but I couldn't go arresting her just 'cause she 'appens to be quite a tall wench.'

'One cannot go about accusing people and carting them off to Bow Street without good reason, Sarah,' Marcus put in gently, amused by the look of frustration on her face. 'Citizens do have their rights. If Stubbs had been able to discover her in possession of the necklace, then that might have been a different matter, but he knew it would avail him nothing to search either her, or her room.

'Remember what I told you,' he reminded her. 'Both Stubbs and I were convinced someone had searched our rooms. It was obvious that Grimshaw couldn't have been in possession of the diamonds.'

She looked at her guardian intently. 'And did you suspect her all along?'

'No, I didn't. Our friend, here, kept his own counsel. I had made it clear right from the start that the only person I was concerned about was you. I really did not want to become involved, Sarah, in something that was, after all, none of my affair. But your discovering that confounded necklace has changed all that. When I eventually succeeded in locating Stubbs's whereabouts in Bristol, I did, then, insist upon knowing all the details.'

His expression was suddenly very grim. 'And there's little point in trying to delude ourselves. We all feel fairly sure that she'll come after that necklace again. The trouble is, if I passed the confounded woman in the street, I'm certain I shouldn't recognise her. The only time I saw her was on the evening she arrived at the inn, and that bonnet she was wearing at the time hid most of her face.'

'And the only occasion I got a close look at her was when I interviewed her.' There was a faint rasping sound as the Runner stroked his chin thoughtfully. 'The dratted wench is so good at changing her appearance, though. I still can't be certain that even I'll recognise her again.'

'You might not be able to, Mr Stubbs. But I'm fairly confident that I should.' Both men looked at her sharply. 'You see, I spoke to her twice. On the second occasion she came to my room. I recall thinking at the time that there was more behind that visit of hers than mere solicitude. I realise, now, that she had sought me out for the sole purpose of ascertaining whether I had recognised her the night before. I had not and, therefore, didn't hesitate to admit to it.

'If my memory serves me correctly, I believe I also gave her the impression that I thought the cloaked intruder was a man. Which, of course, is precisely what I did think at the time.'

'Then that, Miss Pennington, is what saved you.' The Runner looked gravely across the table at her. 'I had thought for some months that we were dealing merely with a pair of harmless thieves. One of them was most certainly just that, but the other is a very different proposition. She has murdered once...and I think she wouldn't hesitate to do so again.'

He moved his head slightly to stare directly into a pair of dark brown eyes betraying deep concern. 'Well, sir, it's up to you. As you know I was hoping for more time, but in the circumstances I think it might be best if we do what you suggested.'

'Which is?' Sarah prompted when both men remained silent.

'Remove you to Ravenhurst, where I can better protect you,' her guardian answered softly, 'and the necklace will, of course, be returned to its rightful owner.'

'No!' Both men were startled by the vehemence in her voice. 'I will not hide away like some frightened child for weeks, possibly months.'

Marcus's sigh was audible. 'Sarah, you don't understand the peril you're in.'

'On the contrary, I understand perfectly.' Sarah began to twist the strings of her reticule absently round the fingers of her left hand. 'Naturally, if you are concerned for your grandmother's safety,' she went on after a moment's thought, 'then I shall go. But don't ask me to do so for my own sake.'

She looked across at the Runner again. 'Returning that necklace to its rightful owner might well put an end to the affair. On the other hand, though, it might not. Added to which, don't you think we owe it to that servant girl, and possibly Nutley, too, to bring this woman to justice?'

There was more than a hint of respect in both men's eyes, but in Marcus's it was compounded with grave concern and something else, too—something so deeply disturbing in its intensity that Sarah was startled by it.

'Well, sir?' Stubbs prompted, drawing those unsettling dark eyes on to him. 'What do you say?'

Sarah waited with bated breath, knowing full well that, if her guardian insisted that she be removed to Ravenhurst, she would be unable to prevent it, and almost sighed with relief when he said,

'I say, as no doubt Captain Brin Carter would phrase it, we stand and fight.'

A faint smile of understanding touched the corners of the Runner's mouth. From the first moment he had set eyes on Mr Ravenhurst at The Traveller's Rest, he had respected his no-nonsense attitude, and had quickly grown to respect his judgment, too. Unlike Sarah, he had interpreted that look in those dark eyes and knew just how much that decision must have cost him to make.

He gave nothing away, however, as he said in his usual businesslike manner, 'Very well, sir. Firstly, we must try and discover if there have been any strangers about in recent days. I've already had a word with the landlord, and he assures me that no one, apart from myself, has put up at this inn in the past three weeks.

'I'll wander down to the smithy later, and hire a horse. I don't want to spread my profession abroad, but it might be worthwhile having a chat with the blacksmith. It's a fair bet he'd notice anyone not local hanging about the place.'

'And I shall not delay in paying a visit on my uncle, and discover if he has hired any new staff of late.'

Sarah gave a visible start. 'Good gracious! I'd forgotten about that. Your grandmother hired someone to help Wilkins in the garden.'

'Did she, now? Right, I'll look into that first.' Marcus tossed the contents of his tankard down his throat, and rose to his feet. 'I'll get back to you today, Stubbs, if I learn anything of significance.'

Throughout the short journey back to the Dower House, Ravenhurst maintained a flow of inconsequential chatter that masked quite beautifully the almost unbearable anxiety he was experiencing over his ward's safety.

Even now, the temptation to spirit her away to Ravenhurst, where he could place complete reliance on his trusted servants to watch over her every minute of the day, remained a highly tempting solution to his immediate problems. But deep down he knew that Sarah had been right. Even supposing the necklace was returned to Lord Felchett without delay, there was no guarantee that that would bring an end to the affair.

The Grimshaw woman had already committed murder, therefore, it was not beyond the realms of possibility that she might try to extract some petty form of revenge for having been thwarted. A sigh escaped him. How could he expect Sarah to live for weeks, possibly months, forever looking over her shoulder, watching, waiting for that harridan to strike? Of course he could not. It was unthinkable! Inhuman! Yes, he reiterated silently, Sarah had been right: the woman had to be caught and brought to justice.

As soon as they had arrived back at the Dower House, he suggested that Sarah change into her riding habit and meet him again in the stableyard in half an hour, and they could ride over to see his uncle together. He then wasted no time in going in search of his grandmother's newest employee. There was not a soul to be seen in the garden, which he noticed was beginning to look much tidier, but he did eventually run the old gardener to earth, busily at work in the potting shed.

'Why, Mr Ravenhurst, sir!' Wilkins grinned broadly as Marcus entered the gardener's private domain. 'Ain't often I sees you about the grounds.'

Marcus would never have dreamt of hurting the old man's feelings by informing him that he avoided entering whenever possible what was probably the worst maintained and most depressing garden he had ever had the misfortune to see. Wilkins had worked loyally for the family all his life; and it was hardly his fault that the Dowager stubbornly refused to have some of the trees chopped down, which would not only make his job much easier, but would instantly make the grounds much pleasanter.

So, he merely made some light response, and then wasted no time in asking where the young assistant was to be found.

'Wish I knew, sir. Sent the lad up to the big 'ouse first thing this morning with the barrow to pick up a few bits and pieces, and ain't set eyes on 'im since.' He raised his hat to run a grimy hand over his balding pate. 'Eh, sir, you don't think he'd owt to do with the break-in last night, do 'ee? Heard all about it when I arrived this morning.'

'That's what I am endeavouring to find out.' He looked at the gardener sharply. 'What do you know about the lad, Wilkins? Where's he from?'

'Over Devizes way, I reckon he said. Came strolling into the garden a week or so back, asking if there be any work going up at the big 'ouse. Told 'im I reckoned not, as the family were away at the time. We got to talking, and 'ee seemed a nice enough young fellow, so I tells 'im I'd ask if 'er ladyship would take 'im on for a few weeks as I could do with the 'elp.

'Seemingly, that were all 'ee wanted as 'ee were 'oping to work as a footman or the like in Lunnon. Which would suit 'im better, I'm thinking.' He shook his head. 'Never seen 'ands blister up so easy. Only got to pick up a shovel an' the poor lad's suffering.'

Marcus's eyes narrowed. 'So, he hasn't done much hard manual work?'

'Ha! Wouldn't o' said so, sir. Got 'ands as soft as a woman's, so the lad 'as.'

'Has he, now. . .? How very interesting!' The sinister smile that curled his thin-lipped mouth sent a frisson of fear to scud its way down the length of the old man's slightly twisted spine. 'Where does he bed down for the night?'

'Wi' me, sir, in the cottage. Lad didn't 'ave nowhere else to stay.' Wilkins cast his mistress's grim-faced grandson a sidelong glance. 'The lad's a good worker, sir,' he added in his underling's defence. 'Look' ow much better the garden be looking. And he be right 'andy in the cottage. Cleaned it up right fine!'

But Marcus's expression did not alter. 'What did you do after finishing work yesterday?'

'Went back to the cottage, 'ad a bite to eat and then wandered down to the inn.'

'Did the lad go with you?'

'Aye, sir. That he did, but he didn't stay long. Said he weren't feeling too good. Didn't even finish is ale, now I come to think on it.'

'What time did you leave the inn?'

'About nine, or thereabouts. The lad were fast asleep when I got back. And he were still there, tucked up in bed, as snug as yer like, when I gets up this morning.'

Marcus realised, even if the old gardener did not, that this proved nothing. The lad, if indeed he was a lad, could quite easily have waited until Wilkins was asleep, slipped back here and returned to the cottage without the old man being any the wiser.

If anything, his expression was grimmer than ever as

he returned to the Dower House to change his clothes, but when he met Sarah in the stableyard a short time later, he looked for all the world as though he hadn't a care, his face a perfect mask of sublime unconcern.

For her part Sarah, too, was doing her level best to put a brave face on it all. From that moment at the inn, earlier, when Mr Ravenhurst had freely admitted that he hadn't wanted to become involved, she had suffered pangs of conscience. And the simple truth of the matter was that he would not be involved at all but for her.

Common sense told her that she could not be held responsible for the actions of others, but at the same time she was very well aware that, had she remained in Bath with her guardian's cousin, the lives of those residing at the Dower House would not now be in peril.

Her depressing thoughts were for a moment set aside when she entered the stableyard, and was surprised to discover only the big bay that Mr Ravenhurst had commandeered from his uncle's stable saddled and tethered to the post.

'Oh! Did her ladyship request the return of her mare?'

'No. But I asked Sutton to take her back. I have something rather more suitable for a lady of your ability to ride.' Ravenhurst nodded to his groom, who disappeared into the stable, and emerged again moments later leading a lovely dapple-grey mare. 'I thought it time you had your own mount,' he told her, smiling at the look of combined astonishment and delight on her face.

'Oh, thank you,' she said huskily, the lump that had suddenly lodged itself in her throat making speech difficult. 'She's beautiful!' Sarah introduced herself to the mare very gently, talking softly while stroking the sleek neck. 'Where did you find her?'

'When I discovered your flight from Bath, I called in at The King's Head to hire a fresh team of horses. The landlord there used to work for my family. I noticed this lovely lady in one of the stalls. Jeb mentioned that the owner was wishful to sell her, so when I returned there last week, I made an offer for her, and brought her back with me yesterday. Now,' he went on, leading the mare to the mounting block, 'let's put her through her paces.'

Sarah quickly discovered that the horse was a gentle-mannered creature, but thankfully far from sluggish. She was delighted with her, and for a short while she managed to forget that fearful cloud under which she now lived, but cruel reality returned all too quickly as her guardian, after an extended canter across the park, headed towards the mansion, and she recalled the reason behind their visit.

As they rode into the stableyard, they discovered Bertram in the process of mounting his horse.

'Hello there!' he greeted cheerfully. 'I was just about to ride over to see you all.' His pleasant smile faded. 'Heard all about the break-in. Do you know what was stolen?'

'Nothing, thankfully.' Marcus dismounted, and handed the reins over to a waiting groom. 'As you intend paying a call, perhaps you would be good enough to escort my ward back?' He turned to Sarah. 'There's no reason for you to remain, my dear. Tell Clegg that I won't be home for luncheon. I'll eat with Stubbs at the inn.'

Sarah did not object, for Bertram was an amusing rascal, and the journey back to the Dower House was very pleasant and over far too quickly as far as she was concerned. They learned from Clegg that the Dowager was in her private sitting-room and, after passing on her guardian's message, Sarah went straight up to the room, without changing her clothes, to discover the Dowager seated at the escritoire, engrossed in writing a letter.

'I have brought you a visitor, ma'am,' she informed her brightly. 'And I apologise for coming to you without first changing out of my habit.'

'Do not trouble yourself over that, my dear. I do not object to the smell of the stables.' Placing down the pen, the Dowager turned to see who it was Sarah had with her. 'Oh, it's only you, Bertram.'

By his cheerful expression it was apparent that he was completely undaunted by his grandmother's total lack of warmth. 'Yes, it is I. And a bottle of Madeira purloined from my father's cellar. Thought you might like it.'

Her ladyship's attitude changed abruptly. 'My boy, you rise further in my estimation each time I see you! Open it up, and let's sample a glass!'

Although the day was dry and bright, and quite warm for the time of year, the Dowager always had a good fire burning in the grate, even on the warmest summer's day. She settled herself in the chair by the hearth, and bestowed a rare smile of approval on her grandson as she sampled the wine.

'I'm not sorry you came now, my boy,' she remarked handsomely. 'Though I'm sure it wasn't just to bring me a bottle of wine.'

'No. I've come to take my leave of you, ma'am. I'm returning to Oxford this afternoon.'

She shook her head. 'My poor old brain must be going soft, for I feel sure your mama told me you were staying until the end of next week.'

'And so I was, until I learned that she's invited her eldest brother to stay. Uncle Horace will be arriving late this afternoon. And I fully intend to be well away from the place before he gets here.'

The Dowager's wicked cackle echoed round the room. 'Can't say I blame you, Bertram! Who wants to sit down to a sermon each mealtime?'

'Is your uncle a cleric?'

'Not just a cleric, Sarah, my dear. A bishop, no less!' He rolled his eyes in a very disrespectful way. 'And the most prosy old bore who ever drew breath! I'll probably come down again at the end of the month when I'm certain he'll have left. Will you still be here then, Sarah?'

'No, she won't,' the Dowager put in before Sarah could reply. 'I'm taking her to London, and we need to arrive before the Season begins, so that we have plenty of time to add substantially to her wardrobe,' she added with a meaningful glance at her future charge.

'Is Cousin Marcus escorting you?' There was more than just a hint of devilment in Bertram's wickedly glinting eyes. 'I shouldn't worry too much about finding Sarah a suitable husband, ma'am, if I were you. You'll have no trouble there. Why, I might even marry her myself! I think we'd suit admirably,' he remarked handsomely, and earned himself a flashing look of annoyance from his grandmother, but he was not deterred.

'I think your time will be better employed in finding Marcus a suitable wife. He ain't getting any younger, you know. And he ain't every woman's idea of a suitable spouse, rich as he is.'

'I shall take leave to inform you, you impertinent young jackanapes, that your cousin is not on the look out for a suitable wife, because he has already found himself the ideal mate,' the Dowager retorted in defence of her favourite grandchild. Then, realising she had been goaded into a foolish indiscretion, added, 'It so happens he—er—informed me a few weeks ago that he was considering offering for Bamford's eldest gel.'

Bertram was highly delighted with the unexpected news; Sarah was anything but. It felt almost as if an iron band had been clasped about her, and was slowly tightening, causing the most excruciating pain in a certain region beneath her ribcage.

Throughout the remainder of Bertram's visit and, later, when she sat down to luncheon with just the Dowager for company, she was able to maintain a reasonable flow of light-hearted conversation, but it was an effort. She felt anything but light-hearted, and as soon as she was able, she sought the solitude of her bedchamber.

She couldn't deny that the Dowager's disclosure had come as a bitter blow, both painful and totally unexpected. But why should this be? she wondered, sitting herself on the edge of the bed, and trying desperately to make some sense out of her wildly conflicting and surprisingly agonising thoughts. Her guardian would very soon attain the age of two-and-thirty. It really was high time he was thinking seriously about settling down.

He was a very wealthy man, and it was only natural that he would want his own offspring, children begot from a legal union, to inherit the Ravenhurst fortune. And there was no doubt in her mind that he would make a wonderful father, strict when necessary, but loving and devoted too. No matter what the world at large said of him, she knew that behind that hard, cynical exterior lay a deeply caring and very considerate man. But he was also, she reminded herself, extremely astute.

No, she reflected sombrely. He would never contemplate marriage without very serious consideration. The

woman he had chosen must, therefore, have complied
with all his ideals. She was no doubt a female of unim-
peachable birth, a lady of grace and charm whose faultless
manners and good breeding made her the perfect mistress
for that lovely house at Ravenhurst. Sarah closed her eyes
against the painful image of that oh, so faultless and, no
doubt, very beautiful woman.

She ought, she knew, to feel overjoyed that her surprisingly kind and thoughtful guardian had at long last found
the woman with whom he wished to spend the rest of his
life. But the simple fact was that she hated the mere
thought of his marrying.

A heartfelt sigh escaped her. She was, of course, simply
suffering the reactions of an over-indulged child who had
learned that its pampered existence would soon be coming
to an end. Not since before her mother's sad demise had
she experienced that comfortable feeling that comes from
knowing there is someone close by who really cares about
one's well-being.

For a brief time she had sampled the joys of a certain
someone's undivided attention, and she was honest
enough to admit that she resented bitterly the prospect of
that certain someone bestowing his thoughtful consider-
ations on another. Yes, that was why she felt so miserably
depressed, so hollow inside, she decided, trying desperately hard to convince herself that there couldn't possibly
be any more to it than that.

Well, this childishness must stop! she told herself brac-
ingly, rising from the bed, and going across to the door.
She had always prided herself on being a level-headed
young woman. And she must continue to behave like one!

The Dowager, she knew, had retired after luncheon to
the small downstairs parlour where the sun's rays did

manage to penetrate the wall of trees and filter into that west-facing room. She would join her there, and they could discuss plans for their removal to the capital, and talk about the heady delights awaiting them in the forthcoming London Season.

Sarah was halfway down the stairs when the front door opened, and her guardian stepped into the hall. She stopped dead in her tracks, as though held by some intangible force, and watched him place his hat and gloves on to the table. As if sensing he was being watched, he looked up suddenly, and that wonderful smile reached his eyes.

His reaction at seeing her seemed so natural, so wonderfully spontaneous, that Sarah could only stare back down at him in wonder, in disbelief, almost, as the true state of her feelings hit her with such frightening clarity that it was as much as she could do to stop herself from gasping.

Then, without giving him the opportunity to address her, she swung round on her heels, and fled back up the stairs to her room, unable to believe, not wanting to believe the state of her own heart. It was all too new, all too frighteningly incredible to be true!

For a few moments she remained with her back firmly pressed against the door, trying desperately to listen for the sound of his footsteps above the deafening pounding in her ears. When she considered enough time had elapsed for him to have reached his bedchamber, she flew across to her wardrobe to collect her cloak. Thankfully, she saw no one lurking in the hall as she crept back down the stairs, and she hurried across to the front door and let herself quietly out of the house.

Both the small parlour and her guardian's bedchamber

were situated at the rear of the building. If her guardian
was not still in his room, then the chances were he would
have joined his grandmother downstairs. Which would
be a blessing if he had. The last thing in the world she
wanted was for a pair of sharp, dark eyes to catch sight
of her.

So, Sarah hurried along the path at the front of the
house that led to the large and rather overgrown shrubbery, and hid herself behind the dense foliage of a large
clump of rhododendrons.

After a few minutes, when she saw no one coming
along the path in pursuit, and felt fairly confident that
she had not been spotted from the house, she began to
relax a little: her breathing became slightly less erratic,
and the all-too-betraying flush of colour that had mounted
her cheeks from the moment she had made that startling
discovery slowly began to fade. But she still felt unequal
to facing him.

No, not yet, she told herself as she forged her way
further into the dense area of shrubs. It was too soon, and
he, the astute devil, would know instantly that there was
something wrong. A shudder ran through her. She
couldn't bear his knowing the state of her feelings, for if
he for one moment suspected, it would lead to constraint,
embarrassment, even, and the camaraderie that had
existed between them right from that first night at The
Traveller's Rest would be gone forever.

But when had it happened? More importantly, how had
it happened? Even now she found it difficult to accept
the simple truth that she loved him, and yet it had to be
true, otherwise why should she feel the most intense dislike for this unknown female whom he had chosen for
his future wife? Added to which, she couldn't deny that

she was consumed with jealousy, virulent and agonisingly painful. And where there was no love, of course, there could be no jealousy.

Her lips trembled into a wry smile. How on earth could she have allowed herself to do such a foolish thing as to fall in love with that overbearing and frequently irritating man? After all, when had there ever been aught of the ardent lover in him throughout his dealings with her? True, he had kissed her once, but that had been merely to punish her. Why, he behaved towards her more like some strict uncle, forever scolding, than a gentleman wishing to fix his interests.

And therein lay the crux of the matter. His only interest in her was that of a concerned guardian, nothing more, nothing less. He liked her well enough. She did not doubt, either, that he found her attractive. She was definitely to his taste. . .as he was to hers. . . But his heart, unlike hers, belonged to another.

A sudden sound behind her brought her out of her despondent thoughts with a start, and she swung round, praying that her guardian had not, after all, seen her go out into the garden, and chosen to follow her. She just couldn't bring herself to face him yet. It was too soon-far, far too soon. She needed more time to get her emotions under control, to come to terms with the almost unbelievable state of her own heart.

Her eyes scanned the length of the overgrown path, and for a few moments she saw nothing at all, but then she detected the movement of foliage, and watched in horrified silence as a shadowy figure stepped out on to the path.

'Oh, my God!' she croaked, from a rapidly constricting throat. 'It's you!'

Chapter Twelve

'It is, indeed, Mrs Armstrong.' A far from unpleasant smile curled the attractive mouth. 'Or should I say, Miss Pennington.'

Quite surprisingly, Sarah suddenly felt very calm, mistress of her emotions once more, as she looked the woman over from head to foot. It was quite remarkable—there was no denying that it really was the most marvellous disguise. Anyone, Mr Stubbs, her guardian included, would never have suspected for a moment that the person standing before her now wasn't, indeed, a youth.

With short-cropped fair hair, and with her slender figure clad in workman's rough clothes, the woman bore little resemblance to that dithering middle-aged spinster who had resided for a time at The Traveller's Rest. Only those ice-blue eyes, so cold and calculating, remained the same. And Sarah hadn't forgotten those eyes.

For a moment or two she allowed her gaze to waver as she glanced fleetingly at the lethally formed piece of metal clasped in the slender fingers. 'Is there really any necessity for that?'

'I sincerely trust not, Miss Pennington.' The educated

voice, too, was far from unpleasant. 'Believe me, I have no desire to harm you, but I most certainly shall if you do not do exactly as I say.' She gestured with the pistol. 'Now, we shall leave this deplorable wilderness that I have been forced to work in these past days. And no more talking for the present, if you please.'

It took Sarah a moment only to come to the conclusion that little would be gained by crying out for help. Even supposing someone did happen to hear, she felt fairly certain she would be lying on the ground with a piece of lead shot in her long before any help arrived. So, she decided, for the time being at least, it was in her own best interests to do exactly as she was told.

Without a word, and yet so very conscious of that pistol pointing directly at her back, she turned and ventured deeper into the shrubbery. It was far from easy trying to forge a way through the tangled mat of branches, which snared at her hair, dislodging most of the pins, but eventually, looking very dishevelled, she came out on the far side where a rough wooden fence separated the Dowager's garden from the parkland.

Ordered to climb the fence, and then to keep as far as possible to those clumps of trees dotting the landscape, she continued to lead the way across the open stretch of land towards the wood.

Her young eyes, ever watchful, scanned the rich green acres in the hope of seeing one of his lordship's many estate workers, but, sadly, she detected no other human soul. Only sheep and cows, feeding on the lush pasture-land, turned inquisitive eyes in their direction, but soon lost interest and lowered their heads again to continue grazing.

Once they had entered the relative privacy of the wood,

Sarah sensed the woman behind her relax slightly, though her abductor still made no attempt to speak, except to tell her in which direction to walk.

Keeping well away from the main tracks, where the gamekeeper might well be found patrolling, they headed in an easterly direction, but it was not until they had reached that part of the estate that had been left to deteriorate into a wilderness that Sarah had some inclination of where their destination might possibly be.

She had long since realised, of course, that she was being used as a means to attain the Felchett diamonds. Just how her abductor intended going about this, however, defeated her completely, for she suspected that the necklace, by this time, had been taken to London, and was probably safely locked away in a drawer somewhere at Bow Street.

All things considered, it might be wisest in the circumstances, she decided, her eyes narrowing assessingly, as the stonebuilt boat-house came into view, to allow this woman to believe that the necklace was still at hand.

'Be kind enough, Miss Pennington, to remove that wooden bar from across the door and place it against the wall,' her abductor said politely, stepping back a pace to enable Sarah to carry out this feat, which was no easy task as the wood happened to be a stout piece of oak and far from light.

She then gestured to Sarah to go inside and, without giving her the chance to take stock of the dim and musty-smelling interior, ordered her to sit on a pile of empty, evil-smelling sacks, and then promptly bound her hands with a strong piece of cord before tethering her like an animal to a stout metal ring fixed into the wall above Sarah's head.

'I apologise for all this melodrama,' the woman remarked with a wry smile. 'I think there's little chance you'll escape when I leave and secure the door. The bars at the window are pretty stout as well. But one cannot be too careful. I hope you are not so very uncomfortable?'

'Not at all,' Sarah responded with equal politeness as she studied her abductor, who had seated herself on a wooden box placed a few feet away. She made a strikingly handsome youth, and was, no doubt, an exceedingly pretty woman when dressed appropriately. She was not in her flush of youth. Nearing thirty, Sarah judged. Her features were regular, although there was a rather aristocratic line to her nose, and her hair was a soft, pretty shade of blonde.

'You are taking stock of your abductor, Miss Pennington,' she remarked after watching Sarah closely for a few moments. 'No doubt so that you will be able to give a detailed description to your friend from Bow Street.'

Sarah was unable to prevent a smile at this. 'With your undoubted talents I rather think that would be a complete waste of time.' She held the woman's gaze steadily. 'But may I be permitted to know your real name?'

One slender shoulder rose in an indifferent shrug. 'I don't see why not. It is Grant, Miss Pennington. Miss Isabella Grant.'

Sarah sighed as she looked down at the musty-smelling sacks beneath her. The woman had committed murder, and yet, now, having come face to face with her again, she could not find it within herself to hate her, or dislike her, even.

'What do you intend doing with me, Miss Grant?' she asked, raising her head to stare into those calculating blue eyes once again. Then, after a moment's deliberation, added, 'I think you ought to know that I am no longer in possession of the diamonds.'

'I don't doubt that for a moment.' A glimmer of something resembling respect added a sparkle to those ice-blue eyes. 'I was far from certain that you had the necklace, of course, even though I had managed to search everyone's room but yours back at that inn.

'But as soon as I saw Stubbs last night, I knew for sure that at one time it must have been amongst your possessions. Unlike me, you are an upstanding citizen. Upon discovering the necklace, you handed it over to your guardian who, in turn, wasted no time in making contact with the Runner.'

Sarah digested this in silence before a thought struck her. 'But how on earth did you know where to find me? And how did you know Mr Ravenhurst was my guardian?'

'As soon as I discovered you and Ravenhurst had left the inn, I made an excuse to see the magistrate. Stubbs wasn't with him at the time, but he had conveniently left all his notes on the table. The magistrate left me alone for a few minutes, and that was all it took for me to glean the necessary information. Ravenhurst very obligingly had even informed Stubbs where he intended taking you.'

She frowned suddenly. 'Now, may I ask you a question? Out of pure interest, where did you find the necklace?'

'It was in the secret compartment of my writing-case,' Sarah did not hesitate to tell her. 'I presume Mr Nutley must have placed it there.'

For a moment her blue eyes seemed to take on a faraway look, then she smiled. 'Of course! The case was on the table in the parlour. Well, well, well! I should never have credited Nutley with such ingenuity. He truly was a halfwitted buffoon, you know, Miss Pennington. I should never have become involved with him, but—' she shrugged again '—for a time our liaison proved worthwhile.

'But that is neither here nor there. As I was saying— I saw Stubbs last night at the village inn. He didn't see me, or didn't recognise me, one or the other. Pity your guardian brought him back. It forced my hand, somewhat.'

'So, it was you who broke into the Dower House last night.' Sarah looked across at her gravely. 'Do not underestimate Mr Stubbs or my guardian. They are not fools.'

'I realise that, Miss Pennington. It was foolish of me to have broken in last night in the slim hope that Ravenhurst had retained possession of the necklace, but as you know I was foiled in the attempt, and have only succeeded in alerting Stubbs and your guardian to the fact that I am, indeed, in the locale.' She waved her hand airily as though this fact was only of minor importance. 'But the trinket I covet far outweighs any possible danger. . .I must have that necklace!'

There was no mistaking the determination in the voice, and Sarah experienced a strange sense of satisfaction knowing that she had not been merely fanciful when she had suspected as much. That particular necklace meant everything to this woman, much, much more than just its material value. She was consumed with curiosity and was unable to curb it. 'Why, Miss Grant. . .Isabella? Why does that particular necklace mean so much to you?'

'Oh, it's a long story, my dear,' she responded, her mouth twisting into a bitter smile, but the enquiring look remained fixed in Sarah's eyes, and after a moment's indecision Isabella relented. 'Well, and why shouldn't I tell you? It can do no harm, after all, and it will help to pass the time. I don't intend leaving here until it begins to grow dark.'

She rose to her feet and went over to the window to stare out between the iron bars at the rippling grey water beyond. 'I have never learnt to swim, Sarah, have you?'

'No, I haven't.'

'Then we have something in common. . . But that is all, I suspect.' Thrusting hands into her pockets, and standing with feet slightly apart, she looked every inch the swaggering youth. 'You see before you the result of my poor mother's one foolish indiscretion, her one night of all-consuming passion. She was the only child of a country parson. Like you, she was sweet-natured, virtuous and very lovely.

'My grandfather lived close to a large estate, not unlike this one. He and his daughter were frequent guests at the house. On one occasion when they were invited to dine there, my mother met a young man of noble birth who was staying with the family. He charmed her and, foolishly believing him to be in love with her, she gave herself to him.'

Her bitter laugh was mirthless. 'The following day she discovered he had left without even so much as a note of farewell. Once my grandfather learned of my mother's unfortunate condition, he sent her to stay with his sister in Bristol. My mother died giving birth to me.'

Sarah, her eyes now filled with compassion, looked up at Isabella, who continued to stare resolutely out of the grimy window at the fading light. There had been no bitterness in her voice as she had related her mother's sad story. If anything, she had sounded quite matter-of-fact about it all, but then, Sarah reminded herself, it must be difficult to feel any sense of loss at all for someone you have never known. Isabella began to speak again, and she forced herself to listen.

'Needless to say, I did not enjoy a happy childhood. My great-aunt was a self-righteous, narrow-minded creature who never allowed me to forget for one moment my mother's shame. But she did educate me, and well enough for me to obtain a position as governess with a well-to-do family residing on the outskirts of Bristol. Before I had been with them a month, I was violated by the master of the house.'

Sarah's gasp of anguish seemed to hang in the air for endless moments.

'Yes, Sarah. I was raped. I doubt you have any real notion of what that means. . . And I hope to God you are never forced to find out!'

Isabella's sudden shout of laughter was a hollow sound that echoed round the cold stone walls. 'My grandfather never wanted anything to do with me. I was an embarrassment, you see—a blot on his stainless reputation. My father was and still is, for that matter, a womanising wastrel, who cares for nothing and for no one. . . And my first employer initiated me so tenderly into the gentle art of lovemaking. It is little wonder, is it not, that I have scant regard for the male sex?'

'No, it isn't any wonder,' Sarah agreed sombrely when Isabella fell silent. 'What did you do? You didn't stay with the family, surely?'

'Oh, no, my dear. I sought refuge again with my oh, so very loving aunt. Needless to say, she didn't believe my side of the story. She happened to be a friend of the family, and was firmly convinced I had encouraged her friend's husband to be unfaithful to his wife. She refused to take me back, so I joined a band of travelling actors.

'From childhood I had always been fascinated by the theatre. The world of make-believe is far more pleasant than cruel reality. And I was a good actress, a natural, even though I do say so myself, but being fairly tall, I was always given male roles to play. Which suited me very well. I think I should have been a boy. My life, I'm sure, would certainly have been less. . .traumatic.'

Sarah felt her sympathy coming to the fore once again, but concentrated her thoughts on the matter in hand by asking Isabella what made her turn to a life of crime.

'The theatre is not all joy, I assure you. But I shan't sully innocent ears by relating some of the more lurid aspects of an actress's life. Suffice it to say that, after eight years of travelling from place to place, I had had my fill. Besides—' she shrugged '—I was becoming a little too old to continue playing youths of sixteen and seventeen. So, I began to wonder how else I could make use of my undoubted talents.'

'How did you meet Mr Nutley?'

'I met him when our little company was giving a private performance at a large house in London. We talked for a while, and it became obvious that he was tired of trying to exist on the paltry allowance his father made him. He seemed an ideal choice at the time. He was invited everywhere, and he was certainly more than willing to make some easy money.'

Drawing her fair brows together in a deep frown, she shook her head. 'But it was foolish of me to have taken him as a partner. He was greedy, you see, and impatient to get his hands on the money.'

'So you started robbing the wealthy?' Sarah prompted when once again Isabella fell silent.

'Yes. I attained a position as a maid in different households. Sometimes I would work a week, maybe two, and then on the evening when a large party was being held, and the staff were fully occupied, I would steal the various items, and give them to Nutley that night, or the following day when he would call to thank his hostess for the pleasant evening.

'A week or so later I would take our ill-gotten gains to Bristol, hand them over to a certain gentleman I know, and deposit the money I received in the bank, to be shared between Nutley and myself at some later date. But as I mentioned before, he was eager to get his hands on the money. I warned him that if he started throwing brass about, people would wonder where it had come from and get suspicious. But he wouldn't listen.

'So, I made a bargain with him. If he helped me steal the Felchett diamonds, he could have all the money in that account of ours. He agreed, but insisted on retaining the diamonds and accompanying me to Bristol.'

'Did—did you kill him?' Sarah asked tentatively, and almost found herself sighing with relief when Isabella, a moment later, shook her head.

'No, I didn't kill him. We managed to get a few moments alone together at that inn, and he told me that he suspected Stubbs of being a Bow Street Runner. I asked him to hand the diamonds over to me, but he wouldn't. He said he would hide them somewhere safe until we were able to continue the journey to Bristol, and so I gave him that little concoction he put into the punch. But as I have already told you, he was a fool. I could never trust him to do anything right.'

Again she shook her head as though at some private thought. 'The close confines of that inn posed problems, though. I didn't want anyone to see me wandering about at that time of night, so I dressed in masculine attire and waited. I heard Nutley leave his room, and after a few minutes followed him down the stairs, but I waited too long, Miss Pennington. He flatly refused to tell me where he had hidden the necklace.

'I became angry, and took a step towards him. I must have startled him. He stepped back, fell over the chair, and hit his head on the settle. It was whilst I was searching for the necklace that you came down. I heard you in the coffee-room, and had only just enough time to open the windows before you came into the parlour. I went straight round to the back of the inn, climbed on to the lean-to roof, and managed to open my bedroom window and get back inside.'

'And the servant girl, Isabella. . .did you kill her?'

Isabella turned her head and looked down at her. 'Yes, I did,' she admitted, her voice emotionless, but Sarah could not mistake the flicker of regret in the blue eyes. 'It was never my intention to do so. . .it was never my intention to harm anyone. But the nosy little strumpet had been poking about my room. I believe I told you that, when we met for the first time at the head of the stairs, remember?

'She had opened the box where I keep my make-up and wigs, and knew I wasn't quite what I seemed. As soon as she had learned that Nutley had died, she came to me. Threatened to tell the Runner what she had seen in my room. The walls in that inn were paper-thin, and I was afraid our conversation might be overheard, so I managed to persuade her to meet me that night.'

Everything slotted so neatly into place, and Sarah might have believed Isabella nothing more than a victim of circumstance except for one or two rather damning facts. 'You said you never meant to harm anyone,' she reminded her. 'But you had one of the kitchen knives with you, Isabella, when you went to meet Rose. And you also planted a letter belonging to Dottie on the dead girl in a rather callous bid to implicate her.'

Isabella made not the least attempt to deny it. 'I saw the knife lying on the table when I returned my tray to the kitchen that evening. Truly, I meant only to frighten her, but I realised as soon as we met outside that I could never trust the conniving little harpy. Sooner or later she would have talked, no matter how much I paid her.

'And as for the letter. . .' There was a touch of malice in her smile this time. 'I went along the passageway, intending to search Dottie's room, as a matter of fact, when I saw that letter beneath the door.' She gave a shout of laughter. 'If my memory serves me correctly she was—er—rather occupied with the dashing Captain at the time. But then, she always was a flighty piece.'

This struck a cord of memory and Sarah, thrusting aside the embarrassingly vivid memory of that bedroom scene, said, 'Dottie mentioned once that she thought she recognised you. You did know her, then?'

'Oh, yes. We worked together some years ago in Bristol. Then I went off touring with the company. Can't recall what she did. She certainly didn't come with us.' Isabella moved away from the window, and was silent while she busied herself with lighting a candle set on one of the crates.

Then she turned to look at Sarah again. 'I'm afraid I must leave you now as I have certain arrangements to make. Wilkins assures me that no one ever comes here, and I must confess I have been here on several occasions and have never caught sight of a soul. You'll be safe enough for now, but I shall need to make arrangements so that I can hide you somewhere else early in the morning.'

She frowned heavily. 'That confounded Runner turning up out of the blue has caused me a great deal of trouble! It had never been my intention to abduct you, Sarah. But,' she shrugged, 'one must learn to be adaptable.'

'What makes you so sure the necklace is still here? All this might be a complete waste of time,' Sarah suggested, but Isabella shook her head.

'If your guardian hasn't retained possession of it, then you can be sure that Stubbs has it. He no doubt thought to use it in an attempt to draw me out into the open.' She picked up the candle and placed it on the crate nearest to Sarah. 'I'll return as soon as I can with some food, but I'm afraid it won't be for some little time, so I'll leave you the candle.'

'Isabella,' Sarah said softly, arresting the woman's progress to the door, 'don't do this. You'll be caught. They will hang you.'

The woman's laughter held a note of recklessness. 'Well, as my dear aunt was so fond of telling me, I was born to be hanged. But not in this country, my dear. I have a fancy to try my luck in the New World.'

'Then go, Isabella!' she urged. 'Go now while you still have the chance! The necklace cannot be that important to you.'

There suddenly seemed fire in those ice-blue eyes. 'Oh, but it is, Sarah,' she countered, her voice throbbing with emotion. 'It means everything to me. . . Had Lord Felchett been an honourable man, had he married my mother, those diamonds would eventually have been mine. They are mine by right!'

As soon as he had changed his clothes, Marcus took himself off to the library, and began to compose a long letter to his secretary. It had never been his intention to stay away from Ravenhurst for this length of time. Even had he stuck to his original plan and gone to the Bamfords, he would have remained with them for a week at most.

But, of course, Sarah had changed all that. And he certainly had no intention of leaving her now. In a week or two he would escort her to London. But would she be any safer there? He paused in the act of dipping his quill into the standish, his dark brows snapping together. No, confound it, she wouldn't! There could be no peace of mind until that Grimshaw woman had been caught and placed safely behind bars.

Thoughts of his ward continued to break his concentration, and it was quite some time before he had completed his task. After sealing the letter with a wafer, he left the library and went across the hall to the parlour, and was surprised to discover his grandmother the sole occupant of the room.

'Where's Sarah?'

The Dowager glanced up from her embroidery. 'I've no idea. I haven't seen her since luncheon. I thought she was with you.'

'Perhaps she's still in her room, then.' He sat himself down, and absently began to tap the arm of the sofa with his fingertips. 'When I came back earlier, she gave me a most peculiar look, and then shot up the stairs. It really was most odd. She looked at me just as though I were a complete stranger.'

'You do tend to have that effect on people, Marcus. I expect you said something beastly and upset the poor child.'

He cast her a glance of exasperation. 'I'll have you know I never so much as opened my mouth. Still—' he shrugged '—I expect it's nothing. Women do tend to take queer turns at times, as you know.'

'No, I'm afraid I don't know, Marcus. You'll need to explain yourself.'

'You know very well what I mean!' he retorted. 'Females tend to behave oddly at a—er—certain time each month.'

The Dowager placed her embroidery on her lap, and looked directly across at him. 'If that is your rather indelicate way of trying to ascertain whether Sarah is suffering from her monthly, then I can tell you with absolute certainty that she is not. That was over days ago. But if the poor child seems not quite herself. . .well, it's hardly surprising in the circumstances, now is it?'

Before going to see Stubbs that morning, he had taken the Dowager into his confidence, admitting freely that he suspected the break-in the previous night had been perpetrated by none other than Nutley's accomplice, after the Felchett diamonds. Her ladyship had betrayed not the least sign of surprise, nor dismay. Her only comment, in fact, had been to agree wholeheartedly with him when he had suggested that Sarah be removed to Ravenhurst for her own safety.

A ghost of a smile hovered about his mouth. 'By the by, Sarah refuses to leave. I tried to persuade her, but she won't run away.'

'A pity, but I cannot say I'm surprised, Marcus. It's in the child's blood, after all. Her father was a courageous man, and her mother was most certainly no shrinking violet.'

They were interrupted by Clegg, who entered to light the candles. When he had completed his task, the Dowager requested him to ask Buddle to go up to Sarah's room and check that all was well. Five minutes later the maid came in, her expression grave.

'Miss Sarah isn't there, my lady, and her cloak's missing from the wardrobe.' She cast anxious eyes across at her mistress's grandson. 'I know on fine days she's in the habit of going out for a walk with Sutton, so I checked. But he hasn't seen her, not since this morning.'

'It's probably nothing, Marcus,' the Dowager suggested, but not very convincingly. 'Sarah may have wanted to be by herself, that is all.' Out of the corner of her eye she caught sight of her butler hovering, uncertainly, behind Buddle. 'Yes, Clegg. What is it this time?'

He came forward, a note in his hand. 'I have just found this pushed under the door. It's for you, sir.'

The Dowager watched her grandson pale visibly as he cast his eyes over the single sheet, and nodded dismissal to her servants before saying, 'That woman has Sarah, hasn't she?' He did not respond, but then he really didn't need to, for his grim expression was answer enough. 'We must get every able-bodied man on the estate out searching for her,' she suggested in some urgency, but surprisingly he shook his head.

'No, we can't do that. Here, read it for yourself.'

Although the Dowager's eyesight was not good, the letter was written in a neat hand, and after a few moments she was able to focus sufficiently to read:

I have your ward, Ravenhurst. She is unharmed and shall remain so providing you make no attempt to locate her whereabouts. You know what I want in exchange for her safe return. I shall contact you again tomorrow with further instructions.

The Dowager looked across at her grandson, who had gone over to stare sightlessly out of the window. 'Do— do you think she will harm her?'

'She has committed murder once, I'm sure she's quite capable of doing so again.'

'Oh, Marcus, no!' The Dowager had been reared to consider any display of the weaker emotions quite vulgar. Not since the death of Ravenhurst's mother had tears been seen in her grey eyes, but they were clearly visible now. 'You must hand over the necklace,' she urged him. 'You have no choice.'

'I fully intend to.' His voice was impassive, but the look of cold fury in his eyes as he turned away from the window almost made her gasp. 'And if she has harmed so much as one hair on my little Sarah's head, I will kill that woman with my bare hands.' He went across to the door, but turned back to add, 'I must contact Stubbs and tell him what has occurred. For the time being, ma'am, I should be obliged if you keep your own counsel.'

Half an hour later Marcus, his expression as grim and as darkly threatening as a thunder cloud, rode into the inn yard. He was suffering agony over Sarah's well-being; but resentment at his inability to do anything positive to aid her only fuelled his rage. Throughout his adult life he had always been resolute, making decisions swiftly when necessary, no matter how unpalatable they had happened to be; and yet here he was, still, frustratingly in two minds.

If he sent men out searching for his ward, as his grandmother had suggested, he might well be placing Sarah in yet more danger. On the other hand, though, once that woman had the necklace in her possession, Sarah would be of no further use to her, would be a liability, in fact. Could he really trust a woman who had killed before to keep her word, and not harm Sarah? It was a risk he was not prepared to take.

And yet, where did he begin searching? Sarah might be anywhere: here in this very village, or miles away by now. He ground his teeth in vexation. The situation seemed hopeless!

As he entered the inn he suffered a further setback when the landlord informed him that Stubbs had ridden out of the village on a hired horse that afternoon, and had not as yet returned.

'Did he say where he was going?'

'No, sir, that he didn't.' The landlord scratched his head. 'I mind that he mentioned he'd be back for supper, though. So p'raps he won't be too long.'

'Very well. I'll have a tankard of ale whilst I'm waiting.'

Marcus sat himself at a corner table, his mind deep in sombre thought. He was vaguely aware that the tap was becoming crowded with locals, refreshing themselves after a hard day's toil, but it wasn't until the room suddenly echoed with hoots of raucous laughter that he ceased his contemplation of the logs burning brightly on the hearth, and gazed about the inn. Unfortunately, his sharp eyes caught no sign of Stubbs. It appeared he was in for a long wait.

Tossing the dregs of the tankard down his throat, he went across to the counter for a refill. 'What's all the commotion about?' he asked, after noting the amused expressions on several faces.

'Oh, it be only old Saul 'ere, spinning one of 'is yarns,' the landlord answered.'

'I tell 'ee I seen it!' vowed a near-toothless individual in a rough homespun jacket, and battered, misshapen black hat. 'Seen it wi' me own eyes, I did. And 'eard it too. Oh, m'lord,' he said, fixing his myopic gaze on Ravenhurst, 'the scream it were fearful, so it were. Like the cry of something un'uman.'

'Pay 'im no mind, sir,' the landlord advised. 'He always be in 'ere telling some tale. Reckons he saw the old witch up at the boat-house on your uncle's land.'

The hand raising the tankard to Marcus's lips checked in mid-air, and his eyes narrowed fractionally. 'So, you heard someone scream. When was this?' He caught the warning glance the landlord cast in the old man's direction. 'Come on, man! I'm not interested in what you were doing on my uncle's land. But I want to know if you genuinely saw or heard someone near that boat-house.'

'It were 'bout an hour ago, sir,' the old man said after a moment's indecision. He stared fixedly down into his empty tankard. 'Sometimes I takes a short cut across 'is lordship's land. Weren't doing no 'arm.'

'And you're certain you heard a woman scream?'

'It were the witch, sir! 'Orrible wailing it were. And I saw 'er ghostly shadow through the window. All bent and twisted she were. Weren't 'uman!'

Marcus was far from convinced. The old man looked just the type to say anything to gain a bit of attention, but on the other hand the boat-house would be an ideal place to hide someone. No one local, he cast a shrewd glance in the old man's direction, except perhaps someone engaged in an unlawful pursuit, would ever venture there.

Demanding pen and paper, he returned to his table. The landlord's writing materials left much to be desired. The single sheet he brought was decidedly grubby and dog-eared, the ink bore a strong resemblance to thick mud and the quill was in urgent need of sharpening. Nevertheless, Marcus managed to pen a note which was reasonably legible. He then folded the letter carefully and tucked the note he had received from Sarah's abductor inside before taking it over to the counter.

'It is imperative that you give this to Mr Stubbs the instant he returns, understand?' He handed the folded sheet over to the landlord, watched him place it for safety upon a shelf, and then turned to the old man who was regarding him rather suspiciously. Taking a handful of coins from his pocket, he tossed them down on the counter. 'Buy yourself another drink. And if I should discover this witch of yours, you shall be rewarded with the finest supper, fish or otherwise, money can buy!'

The old man watched Ravenhurst leave, not quite knowing what to make of him. If the Earl's nephew chose to go on a witch-hunt, that was his business. At least, he mused, he would be getting a decent supper at the end of it. Because he had seen her. As large as life, all bent double and swaying from side to side, and with hair all wild and tangled. . . Of a certainty he'd seen her!

Chapter Thirteen

The flame flickered yet again, casting weird shapes across the cold greystone walls. The candle would soon gutter, and then the only light would come from that, Sarah thought, staring up between the bars at the window at that bright crescent shape in the cloudless late evening sky. She shivered, but with her hands confined she was unable to draw her grey cloak more tightly about her.

As soon as the sun had gone down the temperature had dropped like a stone, and yet she tried desperately not to think of the comforting warmth of the Dowager's sitting-room, or of the pheasant pie that was to have been served for dinner that evening. She doubted very much if that delicacy had been sampled by anyone. Hidden beneath the Dowager's prickly exterior was a sweet old lady who would have had little, if any, appetite. And her guardian. . .?

Sarah blinked back the threatening tears. Poor Ravenhurst must be out of his mind with worry. Right from that very first evening when they had dined together at The Traveller's Rest, he had taken such good care of her, attentive to her every need. Dear God! What a fool she had been to go out into the garden alone! But she had done so, and it was entirely her own fault that she was now suffering the consequences of her own folly.

She gave herself a mental shake. Despondency certainly wouldn't aid her cause. Perhaps she ought to try again to free herself from her bonds? she thought, but then dismissed the idea. Her wrists still felt raw after her last attempt. And what a complete waste of effort that had turned out to be! She had succeeded in getting to her feet, but try as she might she could not pull the metal ring from the wall, and had screamed out in frustration.

The memory of her fruitless efforts drew a reluctant smile from her. She would scream her head off if she thought there was the remotest possibility of someone hearing her, but she doubted a search would be instigated until morning. By which time, of course, there was every chance she would have been removed from Styne.

The depressing realisation had just filtered across her mind when she thought she detected a sound outside, and turned her eyes towards the door. Yes—yes, there it was again! It was definitely a footstep. Isabella, no doubt, returning with some food. Well, that was something, at least! She was absolutely famished!

She heard the heavy piece of oak being removed from its confining metal brackets, and then the creaking sound of the rusty hinges as the door swung open. The inevitable pistol barrel came into view first. Isabella, evidently, was remaining cautious, no doubt fearing that her prisoner just might have released herself from her bonds, and was lurking, ready to attack.

Some hope! Sarah mused, glancing heavenwards. Then she realised that the dark shape filling the aperture was too large to be that of a woman. It couldn't possibly be. . .? Her heart seemed to turn a somersault. Yes, yes, it was!

A strange little sound somewhere between a sob and a squeal of joy escaped her, and then she heard that beloved deep masculine voice.

'Ah! So the witch does exist, after all. And, I might add, looking every inch the evil crone with her hair all wild and tangled.'

'Oh, sir!' Sarah was too deliriously happy to see him to pay any heed to his insults. Nor could she prevent an errant tear from escaping as she watched his approach. 'How on earth did you know I was here?'

'I hadn't a clue where to start looking for you, my darling.' Placing his pistol down on the wooden crate nearby, Marcus knelt down in front of her and began to undo the cord. 'It was whilst I was waiting at the inn for Stubbs to put in an appearance that I learned from our poacher friend that he had seen and heard someone, or— er—something, in the boat-house. He was firmly convinced it was the witch.

'And I must say,' he added, casting a wry glance at her grime-streaked face, and tussled brown locks, 'you do resemble one.'

'And you wouldn't be looking at your best, either, if you had done battle with your grandmother's shrubbery!' she retorted, her spirit returning, but couldn't prevent a tender little smile as she distinctly heard the half-smothered oath as he grappled with a particularly stubborn knot. 'You are like a knight of old, sir, riding *ventre à terre* to rescue the damsel in distress.'

'Loath though I am to disillusion you, my child, but I left my fiery steed back at the inn, and walked. As I was ordered not to go searching for you, I thought I'd be less likely to be seen if I came to the exceedingly foolish damsel's rescue on foot.'

As Sarah had cursed herself more than once for going out alone into the garden, she did not waste her breath trying to account for her actions. The criticism was entirely justified, after all. Instead, she asked him when he had heard from Isabella.

'Is that her name?' He untied the last knot, and was silent for a moment as he examined her sore wrists. 'I received a note from her shortly before we were due to dine. Which reminds me. I haven't eaten, and I'm slightly peckish.'

'You're not the only one! Oh, do let's hurry, sir,' she urged. 'Isabella said she would return.'

'Has returned,' a rather smugly sounding voice corrected.

A gasp rose in her throat, but everything happened so quickly that Sarah hardly had time to move. She saw Ravenhurst reach for his pistol, saw the sudden flash of light from the doorway before the deafening report echoed round the stone building and her guardian slumped down on to his knees, gripping his left arm just above the elbow. Then Isabella, with lightning speed, had his pistol in her hand and was levelling it at his head.

'No!' Sarah screamed. Scrambling to her feet, she placed herself between the pistol and her guardian without a thought for her own safety. 'You'll not shoot him again, Isabella. That I swear!'

'Get out of the way, Sarah!' Ravenhurst ordered in a far-from-gentle way, but she ignored him, and took a step towards Isabella to avoid his outstretched hand.

'I mean it, Isabella. You'll need to shoot me first.'

Ice-blue eyes looked deeply into Sarah's. 'Yes, I really

do believe you mean that. Well, well, well! What have
we here?' She sounded genuinely amused. 'You're a
lucky man, Ravenhurst. But a rather foolish one, too, for
I did warn you not to go searching for her.'

The look he cast her, as he rose slowly to his feet,
betrayed his utter contempt. His arm throbbed painfully,
and already he could feel the stickiness of blood oozing
between the fingers of his right hand as he held the
wounded portion of flesh. 'You'll need me to get the
diamonds.'

'Stay just where you are!' Isabella commanded, levelling the pistol threateningly as he made to take a step
round Sarah. 'Although I would dislike very much to hurt
your ward, I would think nothing of putting a period to
your existence. You don't imagine for a moment that I
would foolishly trust you. I'm not so gullible.

'You will get the necklace when I have Sarah safely
hidden in some other place. She will be returned to you,
unharmed, when you have handed over the necklace.
Now—' she slowly backed away from them '—stay perfectly still, both of you.'

Sarah didn't need telling twice, and she prayed that the
man standing beside her wouldn't foolishly make another
sudden move, for the pistol clasped in those slender
fingers was still levelled in his direction. Hardly daring
to breathe, Sarah watched her bend to pick up something
lying by the wall, and caught it deftly as it was hurled
in her direction.

Then Isabella disappeared into the night, the door was
slammed shut, and she almost sighed with relief when
she heard the scraping sound of the wooden bar being
fitted firmly into place.

'If I do not end by flaying your rear, my girl, it will

be no thanks to you!' Marcus ground out when the sound
of Isabella's footsteps had died away. 'You have the crass
stupidity to go out walking by yourself and, not satisfied
with that lunacy, you then place yourself in front of a
maniac brandishing a loaded pistol!'

Totally unmoved by the threat, and the scathing condemnation of her actions, Sarah set the small sack which
Isabella had hurled at her on the wooden crate, and then
persuaded her still seething guardian to remove his cloak
so that she could take a look at his injured arm.

Tossing the cloak on top of the crate, he sat himself
upon it. He felt more than one stab of pain as Sarah eased
him gently out of his jacket, but he was gratified to note,
as she rolled up his shirt sleeve, that she did not flinch
at the sight of blood.

'I was fairly confident that she would not attempt to
shoot me,' Sarah remarked after inspecting the wound,
which thankfully was little more than a deep scratch, 'but
quite certain that she would not hesitate to shoot you
again. She doesn't like men, you see.'

'No, I don't see!' he snapped, far from appeased; then
promptly forgot his anger as Sarah, unexpectedly, raised
the hem of her dress and tore a strip off her underskirt,
and he was afforded a tantalising glimpse of a neat ankle.

Sarah delved into the sack, wondering if it contained
anything that might help clean her guardian's wound, and
drew out a small flask. 'I wonder what's in this?'

He took it from her, deftly flicked off the lid and raised
the flask to one thin nostril. 'Brandy,' he informed her,
only to have the flask snatched from his fingers moments
later as he was about to place it to his lips.

'In that case I'll have it. James Fenshaw told me that
soldiers in Spain use this to clean wounds when they can

get hold of it. At least,' she amended, pouring it liberally over his upper arm, 'I think he said brandy.'

'Here, don't waste it all, woman!' he ordered, snatching the flask back and taking a large swallow before she could reach for it again. 'Ahh, that's better! It'll do more good inside than out.'

He took no heed whatsoever of the disapproving look she cast him, and so Sarah concentrated on making a pad with her clean handkerchief, and wrapping the wound up deftly with the piece of material torn from her petticoats.

'Does that feel any easier?' she asked, rolling down his shirt sleeve, and helping him back into his jacket.

'Much. You make a capital little nurse, my darling,' he informed her, using the endearment for the second time, she noticed, and was glad the dimness concealed the pleasurable glow that rose in her cheeks.

Being a level-headed young woman, however, she tried not to read too much into those sweet words, and went back over to the small sack to see what other goodies it contained. Luckily, Isabella had had the forethought to bring more candles, together with a bottle of wine, a wholesome loaf of bread and a good wedge of cheese, and Sarah quickly lit a fresh candle from the remnants of the old before it finally went out.

Holding the new candle aloft, she gazed about their makeshift prison, and noticed something lying near the door. 'How thoughtful of Isabella!' she exclaimed, bending to pick up the item. 'She's brought us a blanket.'

His jaw dropping perceptively, Marcus gazed across at her as though she had taken leave of her senses. 'Thoughtful. . .? Thoughtful! I'll give her thoughtful when I get my hands on her!'

The look in his dark eyes boded ill for their captor as

he stalked across to the door. It was securely fastened by
the wooden bar and did not so much as creak when he
put his full weight behind it. He then went over to the
window, but here again the metal bars were solidly in
place, and he knew that it would be a complete waste of
time and energy trying to prise one loose. It looked as
though their only chance of escape lay firmly in the hands
of the Runner.

He threw himself down on the pile of sacks, and sniffed
suddenly, his threatening expression being replaced by
one of distaste. 'Phew! What is that revolting stench?'

'I expect it's those sacks you can smell. One gets accustomed to it after a while.'

'Does one?' He looked far from convinced. 'Well, I'll
take your word for that. What else did the darling creature
see fit to provide us with?'

Sarah collected the food and wine and joined him on
the pile of old sacking. While she busied herself breaking
two goodly chunks off the loaf and dividing the wedge
of cheese, Marcus picked up the wine, drew the cork out
with his teeth and spat it on the dirt floor before offering
her the bottle first. Sarah found that she was thirsty and
swallowed the rich red liquid with gusto.

'Here, steady on, child!' He snatched the bottle from
her. 'I don't want you tipsy. And have a thought for
your bodily functions, for heaven's sake! There aren't too
many places to hide in here when the time comes for you
to relieve yourself.'

Sarah paused in the act of biting into her chunk of
bread. 'Must you be so vulgar! I was just beginning to
enjoy this candlelit supper, and now you've gone and
ruined it.' She betrayed more than just peevishness in the

look she cast him. 'Though I suppose it's hardly a new experience for you.'

'And what, precisely, is that supposed to mean?' he enquired, after taking a drink himself and wiping the back of his hand across his mouth.

Flatly refusing to admit that she had felt a twinge of jealousy at the thought of the many times he must have enjoyed an intimate meal with only his mistress for company, Sarah merely shrugged and began to eat the wholesome fare, but after a while broke the silence that had grown between them by saying, 'Isabella wouldn't have hurt me, you know. It's only men she dislikes.'

'Yes, so you've mentioned before.'

'And it's quite understandable really.'

She then went on to relate the woman's rather sorry life history, but the look on his face informed her clearly enough that he was far from sympathetic, even before he said, 'Others have suffered equally, Sarah, and have not resorted to murder.'

'I know,' she agreed softly, brushing the crumbs from her skirt, 'but I cannot help wishing, now, that I'd never given you that necklace. For all I care, Isabella is welcome to the wretched thing!'

'My sentiments exactly!' he astounded her by divulging. 'If I hadn't given it to Stubbs, I would have willingly handed it over to her already.'

'She won't rest until she has it, sir. She considers it hers by right. She told me she is Lord Felchett's illegitimate child.'

This ignited a spark of interest, and his brows rose. 'Is she, by gad? Well, I can't in all honesty say I saw any resemblance, but then, I was hardly looking for it.' He reached for his cloak and the blanket, and began to spread them over their legs. 'Let's hope Stubbs doesn't delay too long bringing it here.'

'Is it still in his possession then, sir?' Sarah was astounded, even though she recalled Isabella saying that this was possibly the case. 'I thought he wouldn't have hesitated in returning such a valuable item to Bow Street.'

The look in his eyes was decidedly guarded. 'Stubbs suspected that she would make an attempt to get her hands on it again, and so retained possession of it to——er——flush her out, as it were. Now, let's try and get some sleep. With any luck it won't be too long before Stubbs comes to our rescue.'

Sarah made to move a little way away, but was pulled roughly back against him, her head forced down on to his broad chest and firmly held there.

He felt her slender body stiffen, and could well imagine that that lovely face of hers had already stained to an embarrassed shade of deep crimson. Undoubtedly, this was the first time she had ever lain stretched out beside a man, and the knowledge brought a gleam of satisfaction to brighten his eyes.

'We'll keep each other warm this way,' he remarked in an attempt to assure her she had nothing to fear. 'We've little enough coverings, and it's beginning to get damned chilly.' As though to add credence to his words he shivered. 'There'll be a frost before morning.'

Sarah dared not move, hardly dared even to breathe. The latent strength in that hard muscular frame both frightened and aroused, causing her pulse rate to soar and awakening that strangely disturbing yearning deep within.

If the feel of his fully clad body could have such a devastating effect on her, how would she react if that image she had had of them lying together naked, their limbs seductively entwined, ever became a reality? She was powerless to prevent a little shiver of sensual pleasure running through her at the mere thought.

Misunderstanding completely the reason for the convulsive movement, Marcus removed his hand from her head, and pulled the blanket further up about her shoulders. The simple action brought her back down to earth with a jolt, and she did not know whether she felt reassured, or utterly disenchanted: perhaps a little of both.

No matter what her own private fantasies might be, her practical guardian was holding her this way for one reason only, and although it was grossly improper, it did make sense to give each other warmth if they could. So, she wriggled into a more comfortable position, moulding her slender body close to his, and was ordered in no uncertain terms to stop fidgeting. She could not forbear a smile; scolding was, after all, so much a part of his nature.

For a while she lay there listening to the steady pounding of his heart but, lulled by the steady rise and fall of his chest, and the comforting stroking of her hair, it wasn't long before her eyelids grew too heavy to keep open.

By the sudden deepening of her breathing Marcus knew the instant she had fallen asleep, but continued absently to caress the soft golden-brown locks. It had been a mistake to force her so close to him; he realised that now. He could clearly feel the soft roundness of her breasts through the thin material of his shirt and the warmth of her slender legs nestling against his own, and experienced that inevitable stirring deep in his loins.

He was a virile man, and not accustomed to curbing his very natural male desires. A string of experienced mistresses over the years had satisfied his needs whenever the mood had taken him; but he had never felt for one of them, nor indeed any other human soul, the tender emotions he experienced for this young woman.

Without conscious thought he raised his other hand to trace the sweet curve of her jaw, and Sarah stirred slightly, murmuring in her sleep. Yes, he could quite easily raise that lovely face and awaken her with softly coaxing kisses. He was experienced enough as a lover not to frighten her with urgent passion, but to arouse her with gentle caresses until she willingly gave herself to him.

Yes, it would be so delightfully easy, so intoxicatingly pleasurable to do so, too, but he knew he must not. Certainly not at the time, but soon afterwards she might regret what had taken place between them; might possibly become resentful, especially when the inevitable happened and they were forced to marry. And that, he reminded himself, far from concerned at this very real possibility, might well prove to be the outcome of this night's escapade if Stubbs didn't hurry and put in an appearance.

Sarah was the first to wake the following morning. For a few moments she was a little disconcerted to discover her head not resting on the accustomed softness of a comfortable pillow, but on what felt something very like a hard stone wall. Then memory returned, and she carefully raised herself so as not to disturb her guardian, who appeared to be resting, still, in the arms of Morpheus.

Her lips curled into a tender little smile. How different he looked when asleep, and yet the high-bridged aristocratic nose was just the same, as was that square determined chin; but the deep clefts on either side of his mouth seemed less pronounced, as were the tiny lines at the corners of his eyes.

Suddenly his eyes were open, staring fixedly up at her. 'Ah! So you're awake at last. You sleep as one dead, Sarah. I was beginning to get cramp.'

Not the most loverlike words from a man who had held her in his arms all night, she thought wryly. But how typical of him! She edged away a little, and turned her head to stare at the early morning light filtering through the grimy window.

'Mr Stubbs never turned up, then?' she remarked absently.

'Oh, he popped in for half an hour or so, but the sound of your snoring soon sent him away again.'

The fulminating glance she cast him before scrambling to her feet brought a deep rumble of masculine laughter to echo round the cold greystone walls.

'I am not an aggressive person by nature, sir, but there have been many occasions when I have experienced an almost overwhelming desire to box your ears soundly. Never more so than now!'

Raising his good arm, he rested his head on his hand, and gazed up at her with the most wickedly masculine smile she had ever seen. 'In that case I shall take leave to inform you, young woman, that you are a very disrespectful ward.'

'And I shall take leave to inform you,' she countered, 'that from the beginning of our acquaintanceship, I have never considered myself your ward. Nor have I ever looked upon you as a guardian, for that matter.'

'No? How very interesting!' The look he cast her was openly challenging. 'How do you look upon me, Sarah?'

As my love. . .my life, her heart answered. She turned

away lest he should glimpse the truth mirrored in her eyes, and said, in quite a remarkable interpretation of a frosty middle-aged spinster, 'I look upon you as possibly the most irritating man I have ever had the misfortune to encounter.'

He chuckled at this. 'Never mind, my darling. You'll grow accustomed to my little foibles in time.'

He made to rise, checking perceptively at a noise outside. Sarah, who had heard it too, looked back at him, but remained silent at the warning look in his eyes. She turned her attention to the door. Could it possibly be Mr Stubbs at last? Her hopes plummeted when the door opened, and she glimpsed that, now, all-too-familiar pistol clasped in slender fingers before Isabella came slowly forward.

'I trust you passed a not-too-uncomfortable night?' The smile she cast Ravenhurst was not pleasant, enmity clearly visible in her eyes. 'Sarah, if you would be good enough to come over here to me, we shall be on our way.'

'Enough of this tomfoolery!' Marcus ground out before Sarah had taken more than a pace or two towards the door. 'Take me, and let Sarah get you the diamonds.'

'Thank you for the offer,' Isabella responded, her eyes never wavering from his face for a second as she gestured Sarah to approach, 'but I think I'll stick to my original choice. Not only am I certain that Sarah would never willingly harm me, as you most assuredly would given half the chance, but I rather think that her company is more to my taste.'

Sarah noted the look of disgust flit across his features, and hurried forward before he could even think of trying to overpower Isabella. Her wrist was snatched, and the pistol was placed to her temple, and yet, strangely, she experienced no fear whatsoever for her own safety, only for the man's standing several feet away.

'Don't even think of moving, Ravenhurst,' she warned, pulling Sarah back and out of the door.

Once outside, Isabella released her hold to toss a folded piece of paper down on the boat-house floor, and then slammed the door closed in what seemed almost a triumphant gesture while signalling to Sarah to pick up the wooden bar.

She did not hesitate. The last thing in the world she wanted was for Ravenhurst to come charging out, and receive another bullet. He might not be so lucky next time. She bent, about to pick up the heavy piece of oak when she saw a sudden movement out of the corner of her eye.

Mr Stubbs seemed to appear from nowhere. The next instant he was cursing loudly as he grappled with Isabella for the weapon. Although they were both of a similar height, the Runner was far stronger; but Isabella, with a strength generated by stubborn determination, fought like a wildcat to retain a hold on the pistol. They swayed this way and that, almost toppling over at one point, then retrieving their balance.

Had Sarah not been witnessing it with her own eyes, she would never have believed it possible for a mere woman to put up such resistance. Two pairs of arms rose in the air, and then swung in a wide arc down again. There was a sudden deafening report, the boat-house door flew open and Ravenhurst came hurtling out, almost knocking into her as she watched Mr Stubbs fall to the ground, his face contorted in agony as he gripped his leg.

With lightning speed, Isabella ran part of the way along the jetty and drew out a second pistol from her jacket pocket to hold Ravenhurst once again at bay. She either did not notice, or was simply unconcerned that Sarah had gone to the Runner's aid.

Ripping yet a further strip off her already depleted undergarment, Sarah attempted to staunch the flow of blood pouring from the badly injured knee. She was vaguely aware that a conversation of sorts was taking place between Ravenhurst and Isabella, but so concerned was she over Mr Stubbs's welfare that she took little heed of just what was being said.

The remnant of petticoat was soon sodden, and blood oozed between her fingers. She raised deeply troubled eyes to Mr Stubbs's face, and saw him make a gesture with his own.

The silent message was discernible enough. Altering her position slightly in an attempt to hide her actions from the ever-alert Isabella, Sarah felt in the pocket of the Runner's jacket. Her fingers came into contact with cold metal, and something else, too.

Very slowly, she eased both pistol and necklace out, handing the pistol to the Runner before rising slowly to her feet. Ignoring his gesture for her to step aside, she turned and walked slowly towards the jetty, coming to a halt beside her tall guardian.

'Here, Isabella, this is what you want.' She held out the necklace in the hand coated in the Runner's blood, and felt heartily sickened by the unmistakable flash of triumphant delight in the woman's eyes. 'Here, then, take it! More than enough blood has been spilled already over the wretched thing,' and with that she hurled the necklace away from her in a gesture of revulsion, as though to handle it further would infect her with the same malignant obsession.

The sparkling stones, glinting with all the colours of the rainbow, seemed to hang suspended in the frosty morning air for such a long time. Isabella leaned against the wooden rail, her arm and fingers stretching out in a frenzied attempt to grasp the precious trophy.

There was the sudden sound of splintering wood, followed by a terrified, high-pitched scream as Isabella tumbled over the edge. And the last thing Sarah saw as she rushed forward were Isabella's fingers, still clasping the necklace, disappear beneath the murky grey waters.

'Oh, my God!' She turned imploring eyes up to Ravenhurst. 'She cannot swim, sir...she cannot swim!'

He seemed to hesitate, but only for a moment. His cloak and jacket were tossed on to the jetty, quickly followed by his boots; then he dived into the lake. Sarah waited, her heart pounding against her ribcage, her eyes frantically scanning the surface of the water for what seemed an interminable length of time, but what was possibly no more than two or three minutes. Then she saw bubbles rising to the surface, and Ravenhurst's head, blessedly, appear above the water.

His fingers blue with cold, he held on to the jetty with difficulty. 'God, it's freezing down there,' he gasped, trying desperately to catch his breath, 'and as black as pitch. I can't see a blasted thing!'

He took a deep breath, and looked as though he was about to submerge again, but Sarah, kneeling down, reached out and held on to his arm firmly, as though her very life depended upon it.

'No, sir! Please don't try again! It's hopeless, and maybe it's better this way... Perhaps it was the only way.'

Then she promptly dissolved into tears.

Chapter Fourteen

Setting aside the book, which had failed completely to capture her interest, Sarah went across to the window and stared down into the garden. It was set to be yet another dry, bright day. Everywhere looked quite normal, quite tranquil. It just didn't seem right somehow. Surely there ought to be something, anything, to betray the tragic happenings of a few hours earlier?

Isabella's triumphant expression as she had reached out and grasped that most coveted of objects flashed once again before Sarah's mind's eye, as it had so many times that morning. She shook her head in disbelief. Three people had been injured, and three others had died, including Isabella herself... And all because of that cursed gaud! Was it really worth all that carnage?

She gave an almost imperceptible shake of her head. Of course, it was not...at least, not to her. But to Isabella, of course, it had meant everything. To her, no price would have been too high...and she had paid the ultimate price: her own life.

Sarah closed her eyes, trying desperately to blot out the memory, but it would not leave her; perhaps it never would. But she remembered other things too: the way Ravenhurst had clambered on to the jetty, and had taken her in his arms, comforting her until all tears had been spent. Then, gentle understanding thrust aside by the domineering aspect of his character, he had insisted on being the one to summon help, leaving Sarah to do what she could for Mr Stubbs.

It had seemed to take no time at all before several of the Earl's men had arrived, bearing a stretcher. Sutton, appearing with her mare, had escorted her back; and no sooner had she set foot inside the Dower House than Buddle, at her most dictatorial, had whisked her upstairs, where a hip-bath, already brought up from the nether regions, had been awaiting her.

It had been bliss to soak in that rose-scented water and rid herself of the unpleasant odour off those evil-smelling sacks, which had clung to her like a second skin. Some time later Buddle had returned, bearing a breakfast tray, and had informed her that the doctor had arrived and that Mr Stubbs had had the bullet removed from his knee and was now resting comfortably in the guest bedchamber.

That at least was something, Sarah supposed, releasing her breath in a tiny sigh. But how long would poor Mr Stubbs be laid up? And, more importantly, would he ever be able to return to Bow Street if the injury left him a cripple? She shook her head in disbelief. Who would have believed it possible that putting up at such an innocuous-looking place as The Traveller's Rest would have resulted in such very grave consequences for so many people?

She felt even she would never be the same person again. When she had left Bath, believing the life of a governess would eventually be her lot, she had experienced at least some hopes for the future, but she experienced no such pleasurable expectations now. She had met Ravenhurst again and, incredible though it was, had fallen in love with him.

But it would not be too long now, a wickedly taunting voice reminded her, before she would see the only man she had ever loved, the only man she could ever love, married to someone else. . . No, her life most certainly would never be the same again.

The bedchamber door opening broke into her deeply depressing reverie. She did not need to turn her head to see who had entered: the loud tut-tutting reverberating off the walls informed her clearly enough.

'I don't know, Miss Sarah. You haven't eaten a morsel of that food I brought you.'

'I wasn't hungry.'

Buddle drew her disapproving gaze away from the untouched tray, and fixed it on Sarah's slender back. Her eyes softened at once. 'Come over here, miss, and let me see to your hair.'

Like an automaton, Sarah moved across to the dressing table, and sat herself down on the chair. Buddle piled the silky brown locks high on Sarah's head, her expert fingers working quickly, but from time to time her eyes would stray to the mirror to look at the reflection of the forlorn little face.

'It probably won't make you feel any better, miss, but his lordship's men managed to fish the body out of the lake. All twisted among the weeds it were, with the diamond necklace still clutched in the fingers. But at least she'll be buried proper, now. And she won't be placed in a pauper's grave, neither. Master Marcus has seen to all that. She's to be buried in the churchyard, and no one any the wiser. They'll just think the poor woman drowned in the lake.'

'That was kind of him to arrange that.'

There was a further long silence, then Buddle said, 'And poor Mr Stubbs is still sleeping like a baby. Mind, the doctor gave him that much laudanum he'll probably sleep the day through.'

'It might not be a bad thing if he does.'

'No doubt you'll be taking luncheon with the others, miss. Her ladyship and Master Marcus are in the downstairs parlour now, if you would care to join them.'

'No. I think I'll remain up here. I'm not very good company at the moment.'

Buddle's eyes narrowed as she pinned an errant curl into place. There was more behind all this apathy than reaction to the events of yesterday evening and this morning; Buddle felt certain of it. Time for a little harmless deception, she decided, casting her eyes ceilingwards in a brief request to the Almighty for forgiveness.

'Well, that's a pity, because I was hoping you'd take a look at Master Marcus. I passed him in the hall a while back, and it might have been my imagination, but he looked a little flushed to me.'

Sarah's eyes rose from their contemplation of the lacy covering on the dressing table and met those of Buddle's in the mirror. 'Didn't the doctor take a look at his arm?'

'Oh, yes, he did that, miss. Said the wound was good and clean, and put a fresh dressing on it, but. . .' Buddle shook her head, looking genuinely perturbed. 'I've known many a light wound turn very nasty, the patient becomes feverish, and then. . .'

Sarah was on her feet in an instant. 'I'll go down and take a look at him.' As she went over to the door, she missed the satisfied smile curling a pair of thin lips. 'And if I think it's necessary, we'll summon the doctor back at once.'

Sarah entered the parlour a minute or two later to find the Dowager sitting in the chair by the fire, busily plying her needle, and her guardian lounging on the sofa, appearing perfectly composed. He looked up as she entered, and rose at once. They moved slowly towards each other, each scrutinising the other's face.

'You are looking a little pale, child,' he remarked, grasping her hand and guiding her over to the other chair by the fire. 'Perhaps you should return to your room and try to rest.'

And you are looking. . .fine, she thought, deciding Buddle must have been imagining things after all.

'If the roses have faded from her cheeks, Marcus, it's hardly surprising after what she has been through.' A hint of respect gleamed in the Dowager's grey eyes. 'I saw you so briefly this morning, child. I'm afraid Buddle is the most wickedly overbearing creature alive, hauling you upstairs that way. But if it's any consolation, she only ever bullies people she likes.'

Sarah couldn't prevent a slight smile at this intelligence, and turned to look across at her guardian, who had seated himself on the sofa again, and who looked back at her with such a depth of warmth in his dark eyes that if she had been pale earlier, she felt very certain that that was no longer the case.

'It—it was very kind of you to arrange Isabella's funeral, sir,' she remarked shyly.

'I didn't do it for her, Sarah. I did it for you. I knew you would fret if she was placed in a pauper's grave. Very few know of the circumstances surrounding her

death, and it shall remain so. As far as the local inhabitants
are concerned, a woman merely drowned in the lake.'
His lips twisted into a wry smile. 'Yet another fatality to
substantiate that wretched curse.'

'And it is certainly more than the woman deserves,'
the Dowager remarked. 'Yes, I know of her life history,
child. Marcus has just been telling me all about it,' she
went on as she received an unmistakable look of reproach
from a pair of blue-green eyes. 'But it doesn't alter the
fact that she was a murderess, and perhaps it is only
justice after all that she died for what is little more than
a piece of trumpery.'

Sarah caught the frowning glance her guardian cast in
his grandmother's direction, and looked at him sharply.
'What does her ladyship mean, sir?'

He appeared slightly discomforted, but responded
promptly enough with, 'The necklace was quite a remarkable imitation of the original. When you brought it along
to my room, I was not perfectly satisfied that it was
genuine, so when I went to Bristol I had a reputable
jeweller take a look at it, and he confirmed it was paste.'

'I do not perfectly understand you, sir.' Sarah drew her
brows together, genuinely puzzled. 'Are you trying to say
that at some point after it was stolen someone switched
the genuine article with a forgery? If so, where in
heaven's name is the real necklace?'

'No, child, I'm not suggesting that at all.' He couldn't
prevent a smile at her continued bewilderment. 'It's my
belief that, some time in the past, Felchett himself had a
copy made and sold the original to pay off his mounting
debts. He's always been a gamester, always been heavily
in debt, but whilst his wife was seen wearing that valuable

necklace, he managed to fool his creditors into believing that he still had funds.

'That, I would imagine, was the reason behind his anger when a stir was caused over the necklace's disappearance. Any expert would have seen at once that it was a forgery. And he certainly didn't want any scandal attached to his name, especially not having just arranged his son's very advantageous marriage to a wealthy Cit's daughter.'

Somehow, the knowledge that the necklace was nothing but a worthless imitation seemed to make everything so very much worse: the loss of life; poor Mr Stubbs lying upstairs, his career as a Runner probably at an end. Sarah looked gravely across at her guardian, her eyes mirroring her concern. 'What will happen to Mr Stubbs, sir, if he doesn't make a full recovery?'

'It's too early to tell whether he will or not, but there's no denying his knee is badly damaged. In a week or two when he's stronger, I'll arrange for him to be taken to London to see my private physician.' He cast her a reassuring smile. 'Don't worry, child, I have no intention of abandoning him to his fate. He came to our aid. Rather later than I had hoped, but that was hardly his fault.'

The look of concern in Sarah's eyes was replaced by one of interest. Evidently, much had passed between Mr Stubbs and her guardian before the injured man had succumbed to the effects of the laudanum. She was curious to hear the Runner's side of the story, and didn't hesitate to ask.

'When I had luncheon with Stubbs yesterday, I informed him of the disappearance of my grandmother's under-gardener, and of my suspicions that he might not be a youth. Stubbs guessed that, if the gardener was the woman he was seeking, she would have put up at an inn not too far away.

'After I had left him, he hired a horse, and began visiting the villages round about. At a place about five miles from here, he struck lucky. The landlord of the inn had let a room to a lady, and had been paid to keep it until her return. Once the landlord discovered Stubbs was a Runner, he didn't hesitate to show him the room, and sure enough, tucked away at the bottom of the wardrobe was the damning evidence—a box containing wigs and make-up.'

'I wonder if she was proposing to take me there?'

'As to that, child, we'll never know. The note she threw on the boat-house floor merely informed me where to leave the necklace for her collection. However, to continue: Stubbs informed the local magistrate, and a round-the-clock watch was arranged to be placed on the inn. It was getting late by this time, so Stubbs dined there, and then set off on his journey back here.'

His lips twitched. 'Unfortunately his mount decided to cast a shoe, and poor Stubbs was forced to walk the best part of the way back. It was very late by the time he arrived at the village. Our landlord, roused from his bed by Stubbs's thunderous knocking, completely forgot about the letter I had written.

'Fortunately, the landlady, an early riser, was up before daybreak, spotted the note on the shelf and, thankfully, didn't waste any time in taking it up to Stubbs. And it was while he was making his way through the home wood that he had the great good fortune to spot Isabella and followed. . . The rest you know.'

'Well, that is all very interesting, I'm sure,' the Dowager remarked, breaking the short silence that followed her grandson's disclosures. 'But we have far more important matters to discuss. . . Your marriage for a start.'

A spasm of pain ran through her, and Sarah lowered her eyes, thereby missing the angry glance Marcus shot at his grandmother.

'Yes, it's all very well you looking at me like that,' the Dowager continued, completely unruffled by her grandson's scowling disapproval. 'But you know yourself that Sarah cannot possibly remain unmarried now.'

The surprising mention of her name brought Sarah's head up sharply. She glanced from her guardian's angry countenance to her ladyship's smugly satisfied one. 'W-what are you talking about, ma'am?' she asked, taken aback somewhat. 'I am not going to be married.'

'My dear child, you cannot possibly spend all night alone with a man and remain single. Why, it's unthinkable!'

'B-but I didn't spend all night alone with a man. I spent it with my guardian.'

The Dowager gave a cackle of wicked laughter at the look of outrage on her grandson's face, but Sarah, not quite realising just what she had said, rose to her feet in some confusion, and continued to look at them both in dismay. 'But nothing improper occurred, ma'am, I assure you.'

'I do not need your assurances over that, child,' the Dowager responded, still smiling wickedly. 'I am certain Marcus behaved like a perfect gentleman. But no matter what you may think, he is very much a man, and a marriage between you must be arranged without delay.'

'No!'

Sarah's staunch refusal echoed round the small room with devastating clarity, bringing Marcus to his feet. He

cast a brief glance at the determined set of her lovely
features and then turned to his grandmother in no little
annoyance.

'Would you kindly leave us, ma'am?' His tone was
clipped, making it abundantly obvious that he was more
than just a little nettled over her interference. 'Kindly
allow me to do my proposing in my own way.'

'Oh, very well, Marcus.' Setting her embroidery aside,
the Dowager begrudgingly rose to her feet. 'But for
heaven's sake don't be afraid to put it to the touch!
You've been shilly-shallying long enough.'

Annoyed though he was, Marcus was powerless to
prevent a grudging smile of admiration from curling his
lips as he watched the door close behind his grandmother.
She had probably known from the day he had brought
Sarah to this house that his feelings for his ward went
rather deeper than those of just an attentive guardian.

His smile turned rueful. Not that he had ever seen
himself in that light. Right from that very first night at
The Traveller's Rest he had been attracted to Sarah, and
not only physically: her wit and intelligence had appealed
to him too. Never before had he experienced such an
overwhelming desire to protect; to cherish.

Discovering her true identity had certainly been a setback—no, much more than that, a bitter blow; but he had
taken comfort in the knowledge that the constraints placed
upon him as her guardian were, blessedly, for a limited
period only.

He had been fully prepared to indulge her with a
London Season; he had owed her that much, at least, for
all those joyless years she had endured in Bath. He might
possibly have derived much pleasure himself from squir-
ing her through the social whirl; and would certainly have

attained much satisfaction from keeping all would-be suitors at bay.

In June, once she had attained her majority, of course, his guardianship would, thankfully, be at an end. Freed of encumbrance, he would then have been in a position to further his own interests, and woo her in earnest. Sadly, though, that delightful prospect had now been denied him; the events of yesterday had effectively destroyed all his well-meaning intentions and carefully made plans.

A deep sigh of regret escaped him. The Dowager had meant well, but she had probably quite unwittingly done more harm than good. Sarah, he felt sure, was still brooding over the events of the morning. It was hardly the most appropriate time to declare himself. . .but what choice had he now?

He turned to look at her. She was staring fixedly down at the brightly patterned carpet, as though to look at him were abhorrent to her. But he knew this wasn't so. She liked him well enough. . . But was liking enough?

'I'm sorry it had to happen this way,' he said softly, his voice sounding diffident, totally unlike his own, even to his own ears, 'but you must realise that we have little—'

'I realise nothing, sir!' she cut in sharply. He was right: her emotions were raw, and this on top of the battering they had received during the past twenty-four hours was almost more than she could bear.

She stormed over to the window, fighting to control the hot tears of biting anger that threatened at what she deemed a most unflattering proposal. She was being offered the one thing in the world she most desired, and yet she was being offered nothing at all.

If he loved her—yes—then it would be perfect, utter

bliss to accept; but he was offering her the protection of his name no doubt out of some misguided sense of chivalry and obligation. . . And for what? What had he done after all? Nothing! Well, she wouldn't permit it to happen!

'I believe the acknowledged mode is to thank the gentleman for his kind offer, but unfortunately I find myself unable to accept.' In a desperate attempt to appear politely composed, she had tried to keep her voice level, unemotional, but had only succeeded in sounding haughty, disdainful almost, and his eyes narrowed. 'After all, there is no need for such drastic measures. We have done nothing of which we need be ashamed. Nothing improper occurred between us.'

'I don't need reminding about that, my girl!' he ground out, both hurt and annoyed by what he took for indifference on her part. 'But I damned well wish it had, then you wouldn't be standing there now spouting out this flummery at me!'

Astonished by his vehemence, Sarah swung round and regarded that beloved scowling countenance uncertainly for a moment before an almost hysterical gurgle of laughter rose in her throat. 'Why, Mr Ravenhurst! I could almost believe you wish to marry me.'

'But of course I wish to marry you, you foolish creature! Why the devil else would I be asking you?'

For a few moments it was as much as Sarah could do to gape across at him, while trying desperately to suppress the surge of exhilaration coursing through her. He had sounded so convincing, as though he genuinely meant it. . . But how could that be? What of this other woman he wished to marry? Surely he was not prepared to thrust her aside without so much as a second thought like some worn out shoe?

No, he wouldn't do that; she felt certain of it. His disposition was far from fickle. He was not the kind of man to transfer his affections from one woman to another with callous disregard for anyone's feelings but his own. So, could the Dowager have been mistaken? Might it just be possible that his affections were not already engaged?

She watched him move with less than his usual athletic grace over to the decanters and reach for the brandy. She wanted nothing more than to believe that he truly wished her to be his wife and was not merely offering her the protection of his name, and yet a nagging doubt remained.

'It is kind of you to say that, sir,' she responded, managing to keep the hard lump which was trying desperately to lodge itself in her throat at bay. 'But I understood from the Dowager that you were as good as betrothed already to a certain lady whose name I'm afraid I cannot recall.'

The hand raising the glass to his lips checked for a moment as he turned his head to look at her, his expression unreadable, then he tossed the contents down his throat in one large swallow. 'So, she told you that, did she? Confound the woman!'

Sarah was not quite certain at whom this curse was directed, but she suspected it was at the poor Dowager. She watched him reach for the decanter again, his hand not quite steady. 'You do not deny it?' she prompted when he remained silent.

'No, it's true enough.' The contents of the second glass went the way of the first: down his throat in one swallow. 'There was a time when I foolishly considered marrying Celia Bamford. Thankfully, though, I never got round to asking her. You saw to that.'

Sarah felt as though she were on a see-saw, one moment her hopes plummeting, only to soar the next.

'How—how did I manage to do that?'

'It was while I was journeying to her parents' home in Somerset that I suddenly took it into my head to pay a call on you. I'll admit, I wasn't best pleased at the time to discover you'd absconded.' Sarah watched in fascination as a tender little smile curled his lips. 'But since, I've blessed you every waking moment. Your actions stopped me from making the biggest mistake I could ever have possibly made.'

Placing his glass back down on the tray, he turned to face her squarely. 'Look, Sarah, you and I get along very well. . . Come, couldn't you stomach me as a husband?' His voice, now, was like a caress: gentle; coaxing. 'I'd never hurt you, you know that. You could have anything you wanted—carriages, jewels, fine dresses. . . Anything you asked for would be yours. But I would want children, Sarah. I would try to be patient, give you time to come to. . .'

He caught the tiny sound like that of a suppressed sob, and saw the tears glinting on her lashes. He took an uncertain step towards her, wanting desperately to take her in his arms, and to assure her that everything would turn out fine, but checked himself. He didn't doubt the depths of his own feelings, only hers.

'Oh, confound it!' he cursed. 'I'm no damned good at this sort of thing. If you cannot bear the thought of me as a husband, then say so. I can't. . .won't have it forced upon you!'

Sinking her small white teeth into her bottom lip in an attempt to stop it trembling, Sarah watched him stalk across the room to stare down at the brightly burning coals on the hearth. Her spirits had soared to such dizzy heights, she felt as if she were floating on a cloud of pure happiness. He loved her. Against all the odds he loved her. . .and more. He loved her so much that he would not force her into marriage.

Once again she found herself having to do battle with that stubborn lump before she could manage in a voice barely more than whisper, 'I think I ought to make it perfectly clear right from the start, sir, that you cannot buy me. I want neither carriages, nor jewels. . .I only want. . .you.'

For a moment it seemed as though he had not heard, then very slowly he turned his head, and what he saw mirrored in those lovely blue-green eyes sent him striding wordlessly towards her.

With hands not quite steady, betraying the fact that he was still labouring under deep emotional strain, he took a hold of her upper arms and stared down at her intently, his dark eyes searching, devouring each lovely feature in turn. 'Do you mean that, my sweet Sarah? Do—do you mean you really care for me?'

She managed to raise one arm, and stroked his cheek with gentle fingers. 'Didn't you know? Didn't you even suspect?' she murmured before his mouth came down to cover hers in a kiss so full of loving tenderness that had there been any doubts left in her mind of the depth of his feelings for her they would have been instantly swept away.

'I felt sure you liked me,' he murmured, burying his face in her soft curls. 'But I never dared to hope that. . .'

'That I could ever have been foolish enough to fall in love with such an arrogant, overbearing creature,' she couldn't resist teasing. 'Yes, it quite amazes me, I can tell you. But I recall my dear mother telling me years ago that women are not always sensible when it comes to matters of the heart.'

There was little gentleness in him this time. Moulding her body to his so that she was frighteningly aware of every hard sinewy muscle in that powerful frame, he captured her mouth with a possessive hunger that left her lips slightly swollen, her senses reeling and her mind in little doubt of his very ardent desire for her.

'I think we had better sit down,' he suggested, rather breathless himself from the passionate exchange. 'I managed to contain myself last night, but much more of this. . .well, I cannot promise to continue behaving like a gentleman. I'm only flesh and blood when all's said and done.'

She laughed at his rueful expression as he drew her down beside him on the sofa, and looked down at the shapely hand still retaining a gentle hold on her own. 'When did you fall in love with me?' she asked shyly, resting her head against the comforting strength of his broad shoulder.

'I'm not perfectly sure, my darling.' His lips curled into a warm, reminiscent smile. 'I cannot say that I'm a believer in love at first sight, and yet. . .I knew for certain when I kissed you in the barn, remember?'

'Oh, yes. I remember,' she responded softly, smiling herself at the memory. 'I thought you had done so to punish me.'

'No, not to punish you, Sarah. I was merely trying to show you how dangerous it was to be alone with a man. And all I succeeded in doing was proving to myself that I had fallen in love for the first time in my life.' He dropped a kiss into her hair, and then, placing his hands on her shoulders, held her away from him so that he could look down at her enchantingly lovely face. 'And, of course, I was not best pleased over your obvious regard for the young Captain?'

She found this rather surprising confession extremely gratifying, but didn't hesitate to reassure him. 'I certainly liked Captain Carter, but I was never in the least danger of losing my heart to him. And he is certainly far from ready to form a lasting attachment. That is most definitely for the future.' She frowned suddenly as yet another memory returned. 'But you won't forget to write to him, will you, sir? You promised you would.'

'No, I shan't forget. And my name is Marcus, by the way.' He pulled her back into the crook of his arm. 'Now, when will you marry me, you abominable girl?'

'Whenever you like, Marcus,' she replied, finding his name came quite easily to her lips.

'Do you want to be married in London, or somewhere quiet?'

'I think I should prefer a quiet wedding.'

'And so should I, my darling. I'll leave for the capital in a day or two. I promised Stubbs I'd take that wretched necklace to Bow Street. Whilst I'm in London I'll obtain a special licence, and then we can be married as soon afterwards as you like.'

'Tomorrow wouldn't be too soon for me,' she responded and was rewarded for her good sense with a further demonstration of his masculine passion.

'Nor me, my love.' His mouth remained hovering above her sweetly parted lips, but before he could experience the considerable pleasure of kissing her again, the door opened.

'Good God!' He bestowed one of those famed, heavy

scowls upon the intruder. 'You've barely given us time to get acquainted.'

The Dowager, completely unmoved as always by her grandson's black looks, focused her attention on Sarah, noting the flushed cheeks and brightly sparkling eyes, not to mention the decidedly swollen lips. 'By the look of your future wife, I should say I've been away decidedly too long already!' She turned to her butler, still hovering by the door. 'Clegg, bring up a bottle of champagne from the cellar. I do believe we have something worth celebrating!'

'We do, indeed,' Marcus concurred, quickly setting aside his resentment at the interruption.

'And Sarah and I will need to put our heads together and work out the wedding arrangements.' The Dowager resumed her seat by the fire, looking a picture of blissful contentment. 'Have you decided where in London you intend holding the ceremony?'

'We've decided on a quiet wedding,' her grandson informed her.

She looked mildly disappointed at this, but brightened almost at once. 'Yes, that might be best. I dare say Sarah wouldn't care for hundreds of strangers milling round her on her wedding day.' She smiled warmly at the loving couple, who seemed to be experiencing the greatest difficulty in keeping their eyes off each other. 'Will you hold the wedding at Ravenhurst?'

This drew Marcus's attention. 'No, I think we'll be married from here, if you don't object. Then, afterwards, I shall take Sarah to Ravenhurst.' He looked at his intended with that wonderful smile that had won her heart. 'Unfortunately, my love, with that Corsican upstart still reigning supreme on the continent, a honeymoon abroad is out of the question. So I suggest we spend a few quiet weeks together at Ravenhurst, and then go to London.'

This sounded perfect, but before Sarah could voice her wholehearted approval to the scheme, the door opened again and Buddle entered.

Her shrewd dark eyes took in the situation in a trice, and a suspicion of a satisfied smile hovered about her lips as she looked across at her mistress. 'There's a footman here from the big house. His lordship's compliments. . .and would you, Master Marcus and Miss Sarah care to join the family for dinner this evening?'

'No, we would not!' the Dowager snapped. 'My son only wants to ferret out what has been going on.'

'He knows already,' her grandson countered. 'I explained everything to him this morning. No matter what your opinion of your son may be, ma'am, you cannot deny that he is extremely discreet, as, too, is Aunt Henrietta.' An arresting look suddenly took possession of his features. 'Wait a moment! Isn't my aunt's estimable brother staying with them?'

'Yes, he is. And that's even more reason for not accepting,' the Dowager muttered. 'Who wants to sit down to dinner with that prosy old bore?'

'I most certainly do!' He turned to Sarah with all the excitement of a schoolboy. 'The Countess's brother is a bishop. I can obtain a special licence from him. We will be married tomorrow!'

'What!' The Dowager looked across at her grandson as though he had taken leave of his senses. 'You must be mad! We cannot possibly arrange everything in so short a time. Surely you want all the family and your friends to be present?'

'No, not particularly,' he responded with brutal honesty. 'Of course I shall invite the Earl and Countess. But we can hold a big gathering to celebrate our marriage when we're in London.'

'Shabby!' The Dowager beat a tattoo on the carpet with her ebony stick, her usual method of informing people that she was vexed. 'And you Ravenhurst of Ravenhurst! Shabby, that's what I call it!'

'But, ma'am, it would suit me very well,' Sarah assured her and then, diplomatic to the last, added, 'And when we do go to London, you could join us there. I couldn't possibly arrange such a big party without your help. I would need you to advise me on who to invite, and to help me organise everything.'

This suggestion seemed to placate the outraged Dowager somewhat. 'Yes, yes, I think I could be of help to you, child,' she agreed, betraying more than just a little enthusiasm for the scheme; then her brows snapped together again. 'But that doesn't alter the fact that the ceremony itself would still be a paltry affair.'

She fixed her staunchly disapproving gaze on her grandson. 'And you haven't given any thought to poor Sarah,' she remarked in a last valiant attempt to make him see reason. 'She hasn't anything in the least suitable to wear for such an occasion. Though I don't suppose for a moment that it would bother you one iota if the poor girl turned up for her own wedding dressed only in her shift!'

He resisted the temptation to respond to this highly provocative suggestion, though Sarah noticed the wicked gleam that sprang into his eyes before he turned them towards Buddle, who was still standing silently by the door, waiting for a positive answer to pass on to his lordship's footman, and who had a suspicion of a wicked twinkle in her eyes, too.

'Buddle, you most admirable of creatures! I'm relying on you to come up with something suitable for my future bride to wear on her wedding day.'

'Well, sir, there's the cream silk gown and matching bonnet. If I furbish them up a bit, I think they would serve very nicely.'

'You traitorous wretch!' The Dowager waved her ebony stick threateningly. 'You dare to encourage them in this folly and. . .and I shall turn you off!'

Buddle thrust her scrawny bosom out to its farthest limits. 'Master Marcus, sir. . .I'll do it on that score alone!'

Historical Romance™

Coming next month

MARRYING FOR LOVE
Sally Blake

Amy Finch was on a voyage to Ireland to visit her
employer's nephew, Marcus Bellingham, when Lady
Bellingham contracted a fatal fever. Amy arrived in
Ireland having never met Marcus—and she had to endure
the humiliation of throwing herself onto his mercy. And he
suspected she was a gold-digger! But surely he knew her
better than that from the intimate letters she'd used to
write to him on his aunt's behalf...

Then Marcus and Amy discovered the terms of his aunt's
will. They had to marry within six months or neither of
them would receive a penny! But when they agreed was it
yes to money—or yes to love?

THE BARON'S BRIDE
Joanna Makepeace

Gisela of Brinkhurst had never thought about marriage,
and enjoyed life managing her father's keep. Her dear
friend Kenrick of Arcote might ask for her hand, but
there was no rush. Not until the king placed his man, Sir
Alain de Treville, in Allestone Castle to protect the area
from increasingly daring marauders. Within a heartbeat
life changed—Brinkhurst was attacked, Kenrick killed
and Sir Walter severely injured. When Alain asked for
Gisela, Sir Walter had no hesitation in accepting, for who
else was better placed to guard his daughter? Gisela was
given no choice—that didn't mean she had to like it!

WINTER WARMERS

How would you like to win a year's supply of Mills & Boon® books? Well you can and they're FREE! Simply complete the competition below and send it to us by 30th June 1998. The first five correct entries picked after the closing date will each win a year's subscription to the Mills & Boon series of their choice. What could be easier?

THERMAL SOCKS	RAINCOAT	RADIATOR
TIGHTS	WOOLY HAT	CARDIGAN
BLANKET	SCARF	LOG FIRE
WELLINGTONS	GLOVES	JUMPER

T	H	E	R	M	A	L	S	O	C	K	S
I	Q	S	R	E	P	M	U	J	I	N	O
G	A	S	T	I	S	N	O	I	O	E	E
H	T	G	R	A	D	I	A	T	O	R	L
T	A	C	A	R	D	I	G	A	N	A	T
S	H	F	G	O	L	N	Q	S	W	I	E
J	Y	H	J	K	I	Y	R	C	A	N	K
H	L	F	N	L	W	E	T	A	N	C	N
B	O	V	L	O	G	F	I	R	E	O	A
D	O	E	A	D	F	G	J	F	K	A	L
C	W	A	E	G	L	O	V	E	S	T	B

C7L

Please turn over for details of how to enter ➪

HOW TO ENTER

There is a list of twelve items overleaf all of which are used to keep you warm and dry when it's cold and wet. Each of these items, is hidden somewhere in the grid for you to find. They may appear forwards, backwards or diagonally. As you find each one, draw a line through it. When you have found all twelve, don't forget to fill in the coupon below, pop this page into an envelope and post it today—you don't even need a stamp! Hurry competition ends 30th June 1998.

Mills & Boon Winter Warmers Competition
FREEPOST CN81, Croydon, Surrey, CR9 3WZ

EIRE readers send competition to PO Box 4546, Dublin 24.

Please tick the series you would like to receive
if you are one of the lucky winners

Presents™ ❏ Enchanted™ ❏ Medical Romance™ ❏
Historical Romance™ ❏ Temptation® ❏

Are you a Reader Service™ Subscriber?   Yes ❏   No ❏

Mrs/Ms/Miss/Mr.........................Initials ....
(BLOCK CAPITALS PLEASE)

Surname ....

Address ....

....

....Postcode ....

(I am over 18 years of age)   C7L

mps
MAILING
PREFERENCE
SERVICE